GODSONS
Counting Sunsets

by

Paul Gait

Grosvenor House
Publishing Limited

All rights reserved
Copyright © Paul Gait, 2011

Paul Gait is hereby identified as author of this
work in accordance with Section 77 of the Copyright, Designs
and Patents Act 1988

The book cover picture is copyright to Paul Gait

This book is published by
Grosvenor House Publishing Ltd
28-30 High Street, Guildford, Surrey, GU1 3EL.
www.grosvenorhousepublishing.co.uk

This book is sold subject to the conditions that it shall not, by way of
trade or otherwise, be lent, resold, hired out or otherwise circulated
without the author's or publisher's prior consent in any form of binding or
cover other than that in which it is published and
without a similar condition including this condition being imposed
on the subsequent purchaser.

A CIP record for this book
is available from the British Library

ISBN 978-1-908596-70-3

This novel is entirely a work of fiction. The names, characters
and incidents portrayed in it are the work of the author's
imagination. Any resemblance to actual persons, living
or dead, events or localities is entirely coincidental.

Paul Gait asserts the moral right to be identified
as the author of this work.

Dedication

The big 'C' affects so many people in many ways, people become patients; families become unwilling spectators; doctors become miracle workers; nurses become 'heroes'. This story is dedicated to this myriad group of people,

Especially to my friend Stuart who has survived the ravages of cancer; to the memory of friends, Brian and Peter who sadly succumbed to their illnesses

This dedication also extends to their wives Jacky, Stella and Ann, and to their families, who stood by and supported Stuart, Brian and Peter during all the dark days of their illnesses. For they too have shown incredible strength of character, often frustrated at being unable to do more than sit, wait and worry.

It is also dedicated to the army of their carers, often forgotten 'heroes' of these serious illnesses; who should also be applauded for their selfless dedication and kindness whilst helping others at their most vulnerable

It would be remiss of me not to also mention my own Godchildren: Sarah, Mathew, Paul, Thomas and Jessica. To whom, just like the character in this book, I have also been an absent Godfather.

Paul Gait
November 2011

Thanks

To my wife, Helen, for allowing me to spend countless hours developing this story.

To my family (especially to my Grand daughters' Rose, Amy and Molly) and friends for their support and encouragement,

To Janet for spending many hours copy editing my manuscript.

PART ONE

The Nightmare

Chapter One

Monday September 1st

Angrily he floored the accelerator and felt the immediate response from the Porsche as the 'G' forces pushed him back into his seat, its tyres screaming at the hot tarmac; a banshee wail echoing off the rocky outcrops of the winding mountain road. The bends were coming faster and faster as he sawed at the wheel, steering the sleek car around the switchbacks of the D63 to Monaco.

He was angry that he had wrongly put his life on hold whilst undergoing the numerous treatments. In reality the last two years had been an expensive and painful waste of time. He was still going to die.

His usual self-assured confidence had evaporated; his head was in a whirl. He was frightened; frightened by the death sentence he had just been given. He knew that he was driving recklessly; it was as if the devil himself was chasing him.

But he was running away; he wanted to hurtle back through time to where he hadn't heard the words of the dreadful diagnosis.

He hoped the screaming tyres would erase the words from his mind; Like a child blocking out a parental admonishment by plunging their fingers into their ears. His irrational thinking led him to believe it could even change the dreadful medical prognosis he had just received.

The devastating message had come like a bolt from the blue. It had been a mind numbing shock. He had dared to believe that his two year nightmare was finally over, for, today, he was feeling so much better. He had even driven from his home in Monaco to Nice instead of taking the usual helicopter trip which had been his routine over the last two years, whilst undergoing the tough treatment regime.

So confident had he become, that he had even got a bottle of champagne in the car to celebrate the expected good news with Nadine. He was going to surprise her, hoping to rekindle their life together.

But the message had been blunt. The cancer had spread. The treatment options had been exhausted. It was a mind numbing shock to realise that there were no further possible solutions. After the emotional rollercoaster of remission and re-emergence, there had always been the anticipation that the next new treatment would be the right one, but nothing had worked. His hopes were finally dashed. A chill ran through his body at the realisation. It was the end of the road.

As Professor Santander gave him the devastating news, it was as if time had suddenly slowed. The Oncologist's voice had become a distant noise. He watched his lips move in slow motion, saw the shaking of the head, the sadness in his eyes, felt the reassuring hand touching his.

Today's visit would be the last time he would ever go to the specialist's clinic.

He recalled the first appointment, a few years previous, when he and Nadine had gone together. They had waited, nervously holding hands, not speaking, fearful.

He had already undergone the intrusive DRE and given a blood sample for a PSA count. His Doctor had previously done an Ultrasound check and performed a Biopsy.

Geoffery had assumed the worse when the medic referred him directly to the Oncologist.

It was at that initial meeting with the Professor that they were given the results of the biopsy, which had confirmed the dreadful diagnosis of prostate cancer.

He remembered he had picked up a brochure about the clinic and tried to absorb the detail of it's all white, super sterile consulting rooms, the air conditioning – boasting of maintaining a dust and germ free environment by a positive pressure system. Of the meticulous efforts which were made to prevent patient cross contamination, including banishing street clothes and shoes. And the regime even extended to the receptionist, who was clad in a sterile medical gown, whilst she operated a tablet computer by a touch sensitive table, with no keyboard or screen.

'Here I have vulnerable people. I need to prevent anything else impacting on their already frail health – hence the disrobing room outside my 'clean' area,' the Professor had told him. 'Not all my colleagues agree with my fastidious regime but then I owe my patients the highest level of care,' he had informed Geoffery. 'I cannot understand the barbaric level of hygiene in some English hospitals where MRSA and C Diff are killing off so many patients. It is a fundamental hygiene requirement, not rocket science,' he said, becoming animated. 'Apologies. As you can see I am quite passionate about basic hygiene.'

The Professor's outburst had given them great confidence that Geoffery would be in safe hands. They were reassured by the professional environment. So when he said they could beat this disease no matter what, they believed him. Sadly, it had been a false hope. Even worse, the treatment regime put a strain on their relationship, eventually causing Nadine to leave him.

The next hairpin bend came quicker than he was expecting. He had to use all his driving skills to power slide the car around it. Adding to the cacophony, the squealing tyres kicked stones from the very edge of the tarmac into a calypso tempo against the metal barrier. If he lost control here, it would be only these thin corrugated metal sheets that would save him from crashing down the steep mountainside, and certain death

Bizarrely, he thought this must have been the way that the lovely Princess Grace had died all those years before, along this very same serpentine road.

Perhaps that's what he should do; just lose control of the car; at least it would be over quickly.

In addition to the tears of frustration that blurred his vision, the mountain road was also cloaked in mist, a usual hazard for travellers at this time of the day. Suddenly through the white blanket he saw a large yellow shape emerging. A school bus was lumbering up the pass, its bulk straddling the road at the next hairpin, blocking his route.

Instinctively he hit the brake hard, the automatic cadence braking immediately beating a hectic rhythm against the sole of his foot. The car fishtailed as he fought to maintain control. Tyres screaming on the threshold of adherence; His death wish was going to come true; he was going to die after all.

The front of the bus was coming faster, getting nearer and nearer. He was running out of space. Above him the coach driver was wide eyed as he 'sawed' frantically at the steering wheel. Black smoke billowed out from the exhaust of the struggling bus.

The Porsche had slowed to 60mph as it squeezed past the front of the coach. He caught a glimpse of the children screaming as they watched him millimetres from the coach bodywork.

In a fraction of a second that it took for the car to traverse the length of the coach a small gap had opened and the Carrera slithered through, squeezed between the Armco metal barrier and the rear corner of the coach.

Immediately Geoffery came off the brake and planted his foot on the accelerator and power slid the car around the hairpin, away from the jagged mountain wall. He had made it, just.

Over the pounding of his adrenalin filled heart and squealing tyres he heard the coach driver lean on his horn to express his anger at the near miss.

The incident made him rethink his ideas about ending his life in his car.

Chapter Two

Back in his penthouse flat he poured himself a stiff whisky to relieve the stress of the morning. His hands were still shaky as he tipped ice into the exquisitely cut lead crystal glass. As he sipped the 25 year old single malt whisky he felt a glow course through his body. Eventually, after a second drink and feeling slightly calmer he pulled out the specialist's report and scanned it minutely, wanting to find something to contradict what he had been told, hoping against hope that he had misheard or misunderstood what the Oncologist had told him.

But the report confirmed the terrible message that Geoffery had been given. His hands shook as he read and reread the words.

'The increased level of calcium in the bloodstream is confirmed. Bone metastases has been identified in several sites. Any form of treatment is unlikely to be successful. Life expectancy: 3 to 6 months."

'Jesus,' he said, clutching on to the table to steady himself. 'Three to six months!

He slumped into an armchair his mind whirling, thinking of all the treatments he'd undergone; countless hours cocooned in the claustrophobic confines of CT and MRI scanners; undertaking innumerable sessions of chemotherapy. He remembered the first time he heard the frightening shrill of the 'Chemo' alarms alerting nursing staff to replace empty bags of the powerful concoctions. Then he had to be tattooed with 'crosshairs' to ensure the radio therapy was delivered consistently in the right place. The repetitive nature of the treatment had depressed him, knowing that it would all have to be repeated again and again until the tumour had been defeated. He had allowed himself to go through all that, for NOTHING.'

He was distraught. Fearful for what lay ahead in the last few months of his life; he had always believed that he could beat this thing. Think positive he had told himself. That's what had kept him going, but now what!

The seemingly endless treatment regime hadn't worked.

'I've paid all this money to so called experts for nothing. Engaging the best Oncology consultants and agreeing to undertake radical leading edge treatments was a gamble that hadn't come off. They'd all let him down.

He was devastated by the thought that he was going to die. He was going to die before his three score years and ten. It was so unfair.

He had worked so hard to achieve his millionaire lifestyle but now he was never going to enjoy the full fruits of his endeavours. He had steeled himself so many times over the last two years listening to negative reports on his deteriorating health, but always there had been a slender chance of hope, but not now. There were no more options. They had run out. It was all over.

In a daze he moved out on to the penthouse balcony and gazed across the exclusive skyline of Monte Carlo to

Monaco bay, his tears misting the view of his yacht bobbing at anchor in the gentle azure blue Mediterranean. Rocky fingers of the majestic Alps dipping into the sea, as if testing it for the correct temperature for its rich clientele. He had always felt at home here. The backdrop of the dominant mountain, Mont Agel, reminded him of the gentle rolling hills of his birthplace in England, the Cotswold Hills. There, the ever present escarpment gave him a sense of security; like an ever-vigilant mother, always there, holding him tight to her earthly bosom.

He fondly recalled the many evenings that he and Nadine had been together on the balcony, watching magnificent sunsets. Standing behind her, he would enfold her soft body in his arms, Nadine placing her tiny hands on his as they stood without speaking, gazing at the kaleidoscope of colours from the setting sun. The Mediterranean sky, Mother Nature's canvas, painted in a symphony of reds, oranges, golds and yellows.

Now the sunsets in his life were numbered. There was a limit on how many he would ever see. Perhaps he ought to count them; an abacus of his remaining lifespan.

He thumped the metal railing in frustration. 'Damn it,' he said, 'I've wasted enough time hoping for a miracle. It's time to move on while I can. I've had my life on hold for long enough.'

He strode back into the elegant, luxurious lounge that Nadine had designed for him. Her extravagance had created a room fit for a King. She had furnished it from the most expensive shops in Fifth Avenue New York, Avenue Montaigne in Paris and La Rinascente in Milan.

'I shall have a farewell party to end all farewell parties,' he said, feeling the most positive he had for a long time. 'I shall attend my own wake. No point being the richest man in the graveyard. It will be one of the most lavish parties ever seen in Monaco.'

He'd make sure they would talk about his farewell party long after he had gone….well at least until the next party obliterated their memory of his existence,' he thought cynically.

Immediately he had second thoughts; doubts flooded his mind. Could he summon up the energy to party? He became tired so quickly these days doing even the simplest of tasks. So what would be the point if he wasn't even there?

Perhaps he would invite his consultant and persuade him to prescribe a stimulant or something so that he could party as he used to, at least for a few hours.

'Yes he would do it,' he decided.

It would be two fingers to the great reaper, defiance in the face of his impending death. After all, people would expect this of him. He had been known for throwing a party at the slightest excuse, especially when Nadine was with him.

It seemed right to celebrate all the successes he had achieved, while he could.

It was during this planning stage that he would miss her the most. She was always so good at organising this sort of thing, had all the right contacts, knew who to invite and who was out of favour.

He missed her so much, his heart ached at the very thought that she was no longer part of his life. The void she'd left had intensified the pain of his illness.

She had left him, soon after he'd started the chemotherapy, nearly two years before.

She tried hard to come to terms with his condition, but she became distant.

Their lovemaking had ceased. She said she didn't want to catch it...stupid, lovely, wonderful Nadine.

She apologised endlessly about how she couldn't get her head around it.

She told him of her fears, recognised her irrational feelings, but couldn't come to terms with the ugliness of his illness or the effects of the treatment; the hair loss; the lethargy; the sickness; the steroid bloating.

His body had changed dramatically. No longer an athletic 6 footer, 13 stone with a thick mop of black hair. The hours, regularly working out at the exclusive gym had been negated by the treatment regime. He had become pale and gaunt, had lost 3 stone and all his hair.

So he couldn't blame her for leaving him. She was a beautiful butterfly. Sick people had no place in her perfect world.

He soon found that even some of his long term friends couldn't cope with the thought of him being eaten away by this cancer.

It had taken him a long time to become one of the 'in-crowd' but now they didn't want to be around him anymore. He was no longer the person they once knew.

Initially they had been very supportive, concerned, and sympathetic but as the effects of the seemingly endless series of treatments changed him, they became less understanding, less tolerant.

Every time he had a setback, the number of concerned callers dropped until nobody appeared to show any interest anymore. He had become a pariah. Sympathy fatigue had set in; to all intents and purposes he had already disappeared off the 'scene' and out of their shallow minds.

A spasm of pain broke into his deliberations, reminding him of his condition; his fragility. The exertions of his manic dash down the mountain road had caught up with him.

He walked slowly into his bedroom where he kept his medication. He quickly jammed two painkillers in his mouth and slumped down on the bed.

The stylish bedroom that Nadine had designed still smelt of her. For although it was almost two years since she had been there, he kept a bottle of her favourite perfume on the dressing table and would spray it around occasionally just to maintain her presence in the room.

He tortured himself again with the memories of her. Reliving the passionate nights they spent together. Imagining kissing her soft voluptuous lips, her long neck, stroking her soft gentle peach like skin. Running his fingers through her shoulder length auburn hair, he recalled how it sheened, like a halo, in the Mediterranean sun. He imagined her little button nose and her beautiful eyes that would light up with her wonderful smile.

He reached for the photograph of her that he kept on his bedside cabinet. It was his comforter when things got bad.

He hugged it against his chest and closed his eyes waiting for the medication to work.

It was much kissed and cursed. The silver frame twisted and dented from many occasions where he had thrown it across the room whilst raging about the injustice of his illness and the pain of losing her.

Always the same question. 'Why had she left him when he needed her most?' Her softness would help to block out the worst of the gnawing pain. Her mere presence lifted his spirits during even the blackest days of his depression.

His fingers walked to the electronic panel and stroked the buttons that made the bed move, gyrate, caress and massage his aching body.

His eyes became heavy as the gentle motion of the bed and painkillers sent him off to sleep.

Then he was running, running through the fog, running away.

He could hear heavy wings beating rhythmically, getting louder getting faster. The angel of death was hunting him down, getting closer.

He was running through a graveyard dodging around memorial stones, statues and stone crosses that suddenly appeared out of the swirling mist.

He could hear his heavy footsteps, the rasping of his own breath.

He was getting away from the beating wings when suddenly his foot struck something, he tripped and fell.

He put his hands down to brace himself from the fall but there was no ground, nothing under him.

Instead he fell in slow motion, twisting and turning in the air.

He fell for what seemed an eternity until he gently hit the bottom.

Up above he could see light coming from the top of the pit.

A figure appeared at its edge, in its hand a large golden spade.

The figure started shovelling dirt into the hole.

The dirt fell in slow motion until it eventually fell on him, anointing his head, covering his shoulders.

He was shouting out 'please stop.' but the figure kept throwing more and more dirt down on him, ignoring his pleas.

Soon the soil was up to his chest. It was constricting his breathing.

Then he saw the face for the first time. He recognised the smile.

'Nadine, Nadine, please stop,' he pleaded, 'please stop.' but she kept shovelling more and more dirt. He was going to be buried alive.

He felt the texture of the mud on his face, smelt her perfume and then Nadine's face disappeared from the edge and in her place the dark Angel looked down at him, its red demonic eyes piercing his soul and its evil laugh filling his head to bursting point.

Then as he desperately fought to free himself... he awoke. He was sweating profusely, panting, his mouth dry.

The dream was always the same. But the Angel of death was getting closer.

He lay there for a few minutes listening to his hammering heart. Was he still alive?

As a test he lifted the photograph to his lips and was relieved to feel the coldness of its frame. He gently kissed the smiling face.

'Oh Nadine, please help me get through this,' he pleaded.

With the prognosis of his illness, the uncertainty of his life expectancy had been quantified, he had a yardstick in which he could cram all the things on his 'bucket list', before he slipped his mortal coil.

As he lay there considering his mortality, he decided that after the party, things would change. He had an irrational desire to leave the trappings of his lavish millionaire lifestyle, a primal instinct to go back to his roots in the Cotswold's.

He was going home to die.

Chapter Three

Friday September 12th – Sunset count 12

The party idea turned out to be a great distraction; it had given him something positive to concentrate on as he coped with the negative aspect of winding down his life and business affairs.

It was a lavish affair, held at the exclusive Hotel du Mediterranean, overlooking the famous Monaco harbour. A large and opulent flotilla of magnificent yachts, moored inside the inner harbour walls of Port Hercule, supplementing the accommodation for many of his guests.

Security at the hotel was extremely tight because of the many multi-millionaires that made up the guest list. All guests were issued with biometric identity swipe cards which were cross checked several times by the huge security team. The card being fed into an electronic reader ensuring faces and bio details matched database records. As well as the ever present personal body guards, a specialist anti kidnap team from the Corps des Sapeurs-Pompiers, Monaco's finest, were also in attendance.

Originally he was going to theme his party on a mock funeral, a dry run of the real thing, as he felt sure none of those at the party would attend his actual funeral.

Although he partially got his own way, when he insisted in being fitted into a white fur lined coffin and having it dramatically carried on to the stage. He had also ensured that they enacted his fantasy of having eight long legged models, wearing Basques and black silk stockings, as his pallbearers.

However, his party organisers persuaded him to go for a party themed on the Rocky Horror show instead. No expense was spared.

A theatrical company had designed and built the set which was complemented by a professional lighting rig and theatrical sound studio. A live band supported a cast of professional actors and dancers who performed key parts of the show to a very appreciative audience.

Everybody got into the spirit of the party and had come in authentic costumes, wearing realistic makeup.

Nadine had come alone, looking as stunning as ever. He realised that he loved her as much now as he always had. However the brief hug she gave him was a gentle 'sisterly' embrace, only a kiss on the cheek with no lingering eye contact.

He was distraught at the realisation that this encounter was confirmation, of what he already knew in his heart, it was finally over. Reconciliation was never going to happen.

Although Geoffery was pleased that she still wore the exclusive perfume, that he had commissioned for her all those many years ago, from the 'House of Jules'. The wonderful aroma rekindled memories of the intimate times they had shared together.

But time had done little to protect him from the hurtful reminder that she was no longer part of his life.

However, he didn't have long to dwell on his distress for there was a long line of other guests, all waiting to talk to him, which buoyed up his spirits. As the evening progressed he was pleased to see that everyone seemed to be enjoying it.

Near midnight, however, the powerful drugs that he had taken to prop him up started losing their potency and his energy level started to decline rapidly. He felt nauseous and started sweating profusely. Realising he had reached the end of his endurance he gave the MC a pre-arranged signal to halt the proceedings.

The Master of Ceremonies, dressed as a Circus Ringmaster, resplendent in Red tail coat, top hatted and wearing shiny black leather boots, called the party to a halt with a loud crack of his bull whip. With meticulous timing the music faded and a spotlight illuminated him centre stage.

'L-a-d-i-e-s and G-e-n-t-l-e-m-e-n, would you please put your hands together for your host, M-i-s-t-e-r G-e-o-f-f-e-r-y F-o-s-t-e-r.' he intoned loudly to the 'well healed' ensemble.

The guests all did as instructed and gave Geoffery a rousing round of applause, 'whooping' with champagne fuelled jubilation as he was carried into the spotlight in his coffin; where he was placed carefully onto two strategically placed stands. Two of his scantily clad pallbearers helped him sit up and stayed close as he looked around at the assembled group.

After a few minutes absorbing the applause, most of which he knew to be forced, Geoffery put his hand up and the noise slowly subsided.

He had decided that as it was going to be the last time he would ever see them, that there was no harm in burning a few bridges with a short and pointed speech. There was no longer any need to keep up the 'airs and graces' to keep prospective business partners 'sweet'.

Already equipped with a radio microphone, he cleared his throat and addressed the audience. 'My friends and hangers on.' This brought a nervous laugh from many, some of whom looked at the floor embarrassed at identifying themselves with the label.

'Thank you for coming tonight. It's a pleasure to see you spending my money.' More nervous laughs.

'I'd like to thank my friends for their support during the long period of my illness.' Murmurings from the crowd. 'I'd like to thank you, but I can't.' More nervous laughter.

'Just joking,' he continued, allowing a few seconds of silence for those who had suffered from sympathy fatigue to feel guilty. His ill health had prevented him from being able to maintain his presence at the exclusive inner circle events, consequently he had quickly become an 'outsider'. He thought how like a pack of animals they were, turning on their own because he had shown weakness.

'As most of you know, my battle with the Big 'C' is now nearly over.' Gasps from the audience as they absorbed his blunt message. Manicured hands clutched their partner's arms. It was not the done thing to be so blunt and open about one's mortality.

'I'm told it's just a matter of time now,' he said, searching out Professor Santander in the crowd who also looked at the floor. Heads turned to see who Geoffery was looking at.

'So I've decided to go home and have a last look at the beautiful part of the English countryside, called the Cotswolds, near where I was born.

Since coming here over twenty years ago, we have seen a lot of changes and I shall miss you…'At this, his voice cracked as he realised the enormity of his words. In the darkness he could see people dabbing at their eyes.

'But I have to tell you that I have been in business discussions with the Big Man upstairs.' Nervous laughs. 'And I have secured an exclusive contract to supply security staff at the entry to the Pearly gates. So for the few of you who will be going upstairs, make sure you come with your platinum cards if you want to go on through for celestial joy. As you'd expect I've got a few other schemes that I'm working on, including a franchise on Angel Wing coiffures and celestial robe laundry franchises.

For the majority of you, I'm in business discussions with him downstairs too.' Again polite laughter.

'Anyway, enough of this doom and gloom. You came here to party didn't you?' Cheers from the crowd. 'I hope you've donated to the Cancer Charity generously. My staff will be checking that your credit cards have been used appropriately.'

Un-expectantly Nadine walked up to the stage and stood by him. Taking his hand in hers she spoke to the hushed audience about the good times that had all shared together with Geoffery; of his wonderful generosity and friendship and she wished him a tearful goodbye, leading the applause as she walked back to the dance floor very distressed.

With a lump in his throat Geoffery managed to blurt out 'Thank you for being you and goodbye.' Wild applause and wolf whistles as the music started at his cue.

Speeches over, Geoffery was helped out of his coffin and, to the amazement of the audience made his exit from the party enclosed in a small tethered 'rocket' that rose dramatically from the stage. Guided by wires it took him once around the vast hall and then behind a screen where he alighted, feeling slightly dizzy from the ride and the firework fumes which generated the simulated rocket smoke.

By choosing this method of departure, it avoided any individual goodbyes, any awkward final teary farewells, including the most hurtful one of saying good bye to Nadine. He had written her a letter which he witnessed being given to her before he left the party. She took the letter and looked around to find him, but he was hidden behind the screen. He blew her a kiss as he turned and left the building; the hurt starting again, this time in his heart. Tears ran down his cheeks as he climbed into the limousine taking him home.

Nadine opened the letter in a toilet cubicle.

'My Dearest Darling Nadine,

I couldn't leave without saying goodbye, but I know that words would fail me if I had to gaze into your beautiful eyes, hence the letter.

By the time you read it I shall have left the party and sadly will never see you again.

'Oh Geoffery,' she sobbed, her tears tumbling onto the letter.

Thank you for sharing your life with me for those three wonderful years. You made me the happiest man on the planet. Your magic touch turned this rough diamond into something refined and presentable.

It was your thoughtful insistence that I sought medical attention for my 'problem'. Had I ignored it, perhaps I wouldn't even have had the last two years, although without you by my side it has been a very lonely and miserable time.

For the pain of losing you was worse than any pain of my disease. I know you tried to come to terms with my illness. To win you back was the goal I used throughout the many hours of my dreadful treatments. But now it seems I have lost on two counts, your love and my life.

I hope you have found somebody who will love you and treat you like the Goddess you are. I will always love you.

Goodbye my sweet, perhaps we'll meet again in heaven.

Love Geoff

Nadine wailed uncontrollably, brokenhearted in her distress. The agony of her guilt at leaving him when he needed her most, resurfaced again. She had tortured herself so many times about it before. There was no escaping from what her heart was telling her. She had loved him so deeply, but for that awful disease she would have been at his side forever.

Chapter Four

Sunday September 14th – Sunset count 14

A few days later he boarded his chartered jet, a luxurious eight seater Hawker 800XP, at the Aeroport Nice Cote d'Azur. As he waited for the pre-flight checks to be completed, he gazed across the shimmering tarmac, lost in thought. The party had been a great success. For in between telephone calls finalising all his business arrangements, he had received numerous compliments from the partygoers who rang to say how much they'd enjoyed it. Few made any mention about the future. He was happy that the party comprehensively punctuated a farewell to his privileged life in Monaco.

He thought about all those things he would be leaving behind, those things he would miss; his daily walk along the Quai d'Albert admiring the sleek fleet of expensive yachts at their moorings. There was always somebody trying to outdo the others with a more exotic vessel. He'd miss his morning session in the sunshine with his newspaper drinking an espresso outside the Rascasse Café, famous for its Formula One association. As many of the racing drivers used Monaco as a tax haven, it was not unusual to pass a famous *pedestrian* Motor Racing driver whilst out shopping. The Cruise liners haemorrhaging thousands of tourists ashore had cheapened the exclusive nature of the City he thought, but the tourist dollar was always welcome in a city obsessed with money.

He would miss the excitement of securing an important business deal, the buzz from important and a seemingly never ending series of phone calls, the business lunches, the sporting hospitality boxes and the Grand Prix circus.

In contrast he wouldn't miss the treatment regime; the cannulas with the painful attempts to spear a chemotherapy hardened rubbery vein; The radio therapy hot spots, the MRI scans; the awful tasting dye he had to drink so that they could track it as it coursed through his system, or the concoctions that they injected which made all his body warm from the inside. He could now empathise with women on the 'change of life'.

He resigned himself to accepting that the treatment phase was over. Now it would just be palliative care which, hopefully, would maintain the quality, not the length of his life. At least he would have his dignity back; but sadly not the exotic lifestyle that he had worked so hard to achieve. He promised himself there would be no time spent on self-pity. What did he used to say to some of his complaining customers when he was a builder? 'Life's a shit and then you die.' Well the last few years might have been; but the pre-cancer days had been a mind blowing life of wonderful decadence.

The sudden bang of the fuselage door closing made him jump; for the slamming of that door signified his multimillionaire lifestyle had come to an end and the start of the final chapter of his life.

Chapter Five

He flew into a grey overcast London aboard the charter plane and was whisked through to the Business arrivals lounge on a passenger buggy. In the celebrity parking area his brand new car, a luxurious Mercedes Benz CL63 AMG coupe, the two door S class version, was waiting for him. He had pre-ordered the car having decided to spoil himself, possibly his final indulgence.

He got an immense, almost carnal, pleasure from owning a new car. The sheer joy of being the first to possess it and to have the primary stewardship of a piece of technological art excited him. Whatever it was, the scent of a new car appealed to his primal senses. Although the party and winding up activities had taken a lot from his frail body, seeing the new car lifted his spirits.

After his luggage was loaded into the boot of the car, he drove his new toy west along the busy M4. He revelled in testing the cars performance in the outside lane, ignoring the 70 mph speed limit. He had decided that a driving ban was the least of his worries. Pleased with the performance of the Merc he was surprised how soon the 'Sat Nav' was instructing him to leave the motorway at Junction 18. Passing the brown tourist signs for Bath Spa and Westonbirt Arboretum, he steered the car up the slip road leaving the motorway and turned onto the A46 heading towards Stroud. En route, he made a few diversions along narrow lanes to undertake a slow meandering trip through many of the small ancient and beautiful Cotswold villages. Chocolate box pictures of honeycombed cottages sprang to life in front of him as he traversed the narrow winding roads.

He planned to keep sightseeing for as long as his health allowed him until eventually booking into the hospice where he had reserved a bed. His ambitious tour started in Tetbury – with its ancient 17th century Market House, local shoppers often rubbing shoulders with members of the Royal family who lived nearby. Then on to Cirencester - a major town in Roman times; Bibury with its Trout farms, the ancient 'Lockup' in the small Cotswold town of Northleach; Finally his trip took him to Bourton on the Water, which he found 'heaving' with sightseers; children splashing happily in the shallow River Windrush, while some tourists were picnicking on its banks; others were queuing for Bird Land or the exquisite miniature village.

Thankful to call a halt to his travels, he booked into a luxury country house hotel just on the outskirts of Bourton, his tiredness lifted briefly as he surveyed the historical architecture of the former manor house set in wonderfully manicured gardens. After a brief rest he showered and went down for an evening meal in the five star restaurant. After the meal of locally bred venison he wandered around the grounds, breathing in the autumn air, although tired, he felt relaxed and at home.

The following morning, having had a leisurely full English breakfast, he moved on to the ancient market town of Stow on the Wold set on top of a hill aside of the ancient major arterial Roman road called the 'Fosse

Way'; then on to Chipping Norton, boasting of being at the heart of an area of outstanding natural beauty; His tour included the north Cotswold principal market town of Moreton in the Marsh, home of many celebrities; it's High Street still populated by Eighteenth Century Inns; His itinerary included the old wool merchants town of Chipping Campden with it's 400 year old annual Dover's Hill Olympick games, a must on any Cotswold tour and then on to Broadway with its large and impressive folly tower sitting on the edge of the escarpment skyline, a prominent feature, watching over the village.

On the second night of his tour, he had decided to stay at the ancient 16th Century Paragon Arms Hotel at Broadway; however, by the time he booked in he was completely exhausted by his over ambitious schedule. The nostalgic overindulgence visiting so many beautiful villages had taken its toll on his frail body.

He had decided to forgo the visit to the restaurant and made his way to the wonderfully ancient bedroom, tastefully decorated in an appropriate period style.

He slowly undressed and lay down on the ancient four poster bed, the painkillers he had been taking all day to keep him going, quickly sending him off into a deep sleep.

Chapter Six

Tuesday September 16th – Sunset count 16

'Geoffery, Geoffery. Can you hear me Geoffery?'

It was the Dark Angel. He had caught up with him. He could feel the fierce claws on his shoulder shaking him.

'Geoffery, Geoffery,' the voice continued, insistently.

'If I keep still, keep my eyes closed, he'll think I'm already dead and he'll go away,' thought Geoffery irrationally.

But the pressure on his shoulder continued and he could feel the hot breath on his cheek. The voice was hypnotic, demanding, and persuasive. He fought the voice filling his mind, frightened by the prospect of staring into the face of evil.

But as hard as he tried, his eyelids fluttered. He had lost. He was going to have to open his eyes.

'That's it, just open your eyes for me.' The voice became softer, coaxing.

He had given in to the sirens call. The Dark Angel was going to win, was going to pluck out his eyes, steal his soul.

'Geoffery, can you hear me? My name is Robert. I'm a paramedic. Don't worry. It looks like you've had a bit of a deep sleep, that's all. It's nothing to worry about.'

A face swam into Geoffery's vision. Its eyes were not red and piercing as he expected. It was not the face of the Dark Angel.

'What, where am I?' Geoffery croaked, his mouth dry.

'You're in your bedroom at the Paragon Arms. Can you remember?'

'Paragon Arms?' Geoffery repeated slowly, his mind trying to make sense of the words.

'Looks like you needed to catch up on a bit of sleep. Are you on any medication at the moment?'

'Medication! Medication?' Geoffery fought the mist in his mind. 'Yes, um over there, in my jacket,' he whispered.

As Geoffery's level of consciousness improved he could see that there were two green uniformed people in the room. Behind them a concerned looking man in a suit whom he recognized as the receptionist who had booked him in the previous evening, alongside him a pale faced woman chewing her finger nails.

The man calling himself Robert was sitting on the bed, his hand warm on Geoffery's thin wrist as he measured his pulse. The other green uniform dug into Geoffery's jacket pocket.

'I'm on painkillers. I have bone cancer' Geoffery volunteered. 'I have a place reserved at Dorothy and Tom's hospice in Hampton Leck. I was hoping not to have to use it just yet.'

'OK, no problem,' said Robert casually as if he had this sort of conversation every day.'

'Well you gave the maid quite a shock,' said the other Green uniform studying the label on the bottle that he'd retrieved from Geoffery's pocket.

'How do you feel now Geoffery?' Robert asked, looking deep into Geoffery's eyes.

'Not sure at the moment,' Geoffery replied trying to summon his thoughts.

'OK, we'll give you a couple of minutes to catch your breath,' Robert said joining his companion.

The two Paramedics went into a discussion while Geoffery came to terms with this set back in his plans. He had hoped to spend at least a week sightseeing before going into the hospice.

'OK Geoffery, here are the options,' Robert explained. 'We either take you to our hospital in Evesham or we help you make arrangements to go straight to the hospice.'

'My car is…'

'I don't think it would be wise for you to drive there,' Robert replied quickly.

'Your car will be perfectly safe here until you can arrange to have it collected.' volunteered a very relieved Receptionist.

'My recommendation would be to go straight to Dorothy and Tom. They'll be able to give you everything you need to help you.'

'Yes, you're probably right,' agreed Geoffery. 'I think I over did it a bit, I probably just need some rest, that's all.'

'OK, so how do we get you there is the next challenge?' The other Green uniform said.

'Why can't you?' Geoffery said puzzled.

'We wouldn't be able to take you because we're a fast response unit. You'd have to wait for control to do some jiggling of available patient ambulances,' added Robert.

'But that's crazy,' Geoffery exploded. 'Surely, as you're here…'

'Sorry, our hands are tied.'

'I've read about the chaos in the National Health Service but always thought this was just media hype.'

'Sorry,' said Robert, 'but the rules are the rules. Your alternative is a taxi or private ambulance.'

'Yeah, there is no shortage of those Private Ambulances around here these days. The NHS supplements the normal fleet with them very often,' the other Paramedic said bitterly.

'And their crews are better paid too.' Robert added. 'It costs the NHS a fortune, but it comes from a different budget,' he added cynically. 'So they tell us it doesn't count.'

'But it's all NHS money at the end of the day,' the other exclaimed.

'I've no problems paying for one. It's just that I'm disappointed that the UK has come to this. It's not the marvellous, free for all, National Health system that I used to boast about in Monaco,' said Geoffery disillusioned.

Chapter Seven

Wednesday September 17th – Sunset count 17

The private ambulance passed Nurse Andy Spider as it drove up the long tree lined driveway through the beautifully manicured hospice grounds.

Andy saw it arrive, but his thoughts were elsewhere as he made his way to prepare the room for its new occupant.

He'd had an emotional morning attending yet another funeral of one of his patients. Although only 37, Andy had already seen a lot of people go through the hospice and he had built up a coping mechanism to help him deal with the emotion of losing a patient. The bereaved family had been very grateful for his professional 'friendship' during their period of involvement with the hospice. Sound bites of their gratitude played in his mind.

'Thank you for making his last few days so peaceful and dignified,' the man's widow had told him sincerely.

'We're all so grateful for you looking after Mum as well as Dad during his last few days,' the deceased man's son had said.

'I don't know where you get your strength from to do this job,' his daughter had said through her tears. 'You deserve a medal. You've obviously got a heaven sent gift.'

'Heaven sent! Perhaps she was right,' he thought. For it was the indifferent treatment that his dear Mother had received, during her last few days in hospital, that had set him on the course to be a nurse. He remembered how gracious she had been, in spite of the severe pain she was suffering. She stopped the family 'bothering' the nurses to give her pain relief because, they were busy dealing with others, who, she said, needed them more than her. He had so desperately wanted to help her, to stop her pain; 'Mum, what can I do to help you?' he had pleaded, holding her painfully thin hand.

'Son, she said, 'there are some things you can't change – but just remember, YOU CAN change some things.' At the time, he didn't understand what she meant. But when he started nursing the 'penny dropped' – he couldn't stop people dying from incurable diseases but he could give them compassion and dignity in their final days. He had used this adage to 'add value' to his nursing throughout his career.

He was only ten when she died but he knew then where his future lay. He had joined St John Ambulance and he had been nursing since leaving school. The most rewarding period of his nursing career, he felt, had been during the last ten years working at the hospice.

Andy enjoyed his job there. He was a people person. He had a great bedside manner which enabled him to deal in a detached but sympathetic manner with patients who, in their last days, needed special care. Family and friends also received sensitive understanding during the course of their relatives stay.

As a counter to the sometimes draining emotions of his work he threw all his energies into his young family and a Scout Troop that he ran in a deprived area of Gloucester. It was thinking about the programme for the Scouts future meetings that replaced his thoughts about the morning's funeral.

He was finishing his meticulous sterilisation work in the room when the door opened and a procession of people entered.

A woman dressed in a smart business suit led the way followed by a patient in a wheelchair pushed by a paramedic from a private care company.

'Hello Ann. Sorry, I think you've got the wrong room'. Andy said, looking at the patient in the wheelchair.

'Andy this is Mr Foster,' said Ann Place. 'He will be your new patient'.

'My new patient?' repeated a puzzled Andy. 'Are you sure? I was expecting somebody else.'

'There's been a change of plan. Mr Foster has had to take up his option sooner than expected. So Mr Jones won't be coming in just yet.'

Andy switched his gaze from Ann to Geoffery. 'Good morning,' He said stretching out his hand.

Geoffery almost missed Andy's proffered hand, as he was taking in his surroundings.

'Hello,' Geoffery said, shaking the others hand.

'I'm Andy Spider, I gather I shall be your, umm, nurse for the duration of your stay,' he said, casting a side glance at Ann.

'Andy will look after you, but if there's anything that you want, please let me know,' she added.

Andy was clearly perturbed at Geoffery's arrival. 'I wonder if I could have a word with you?' he said and indicated to the woman that he wanted to speak to her outside.

'If you'll excuse us, I shall be back with you in a second,' Andy said, leading Ann towards the door.

'I'm on my way too' said the private ambulance driver, side-stepping the pair.

The woman followed Andy out, flashing a comforting smile at Geoffery as she closed the door.

Alone in the room Geoffery took in his new surroundings.

This was not quite the opulence he had become used to. The room was even smaller than his guest's bathroom in his penthouse in Monaco.

The walls were painted a light sky blue and murals of fluffy white clouds covered the entire ceiling.

The centre of the room was dominated by a high hospital bed, it's white tubular side panels folded down ready to corral him if necessary and prevent him falling out on to the scrubbed vinyl flooring.

Like the bed in his penthouse, it too had an electronic panel to ripple the mattress and lift the head and feet sections.

The clean starched white sheets were folded back ready to cocoon him, its next incumbent.

Over the bed, a collection of medical paraphernalia festooned the wall; gauges, pipes and oxygen mask.

Nearby, an emergency buzzer hung from the wall panel, its lead hanging like a limp snake, a bulbous pear shaped button affixed to its end.

A lounge chair and small table sat in the corner of the room making up the rest of the furniture.

Net curtains covered the large sash windows providing a small element of privacy into the ground floor room.

Beyond the net he could see a well-tended garden, stocked with plants and shrubs, chalky Cotswold stones randomly positioned along the rolling banks.

He had chosen this hospice for his palliative care because it was close to his original family home and he had a nostalgic memory of working here as a young builder after he'd left school.

He reached into his small briefcase and pulled out the twisted and dented silver frame. 'Here you are Nadine,' he said to the smiling face, as he put the picture on to the bedside table, 'this is our new home. At least for a short time anyway.'

Chapter Eight

He decided to explore the grounds later. It would be interesting to see if the building work he had done those many years ago was still standing.

'In any case,' he thought, 'if it's not, the warranty is long gone.'

'Strange,' he thought,' how his life had gone full circle. Here he was. Fate had brought him back to his roots. The cruel irony brought a smile to his thin face.

As a young workman he felt chilled by the thought of being so close to the people who were seeing out their last few days, imagining that he could pick up their infection for dying.

He had imagined that the patients must feel like being in the condemned cell on death row, waiting for the sands of time to run out. Perhaps he had become infected after all; for here he was, a ticket holder in God's waiting room, with an uncertain time to wait.

'So this is where it will end,' he thought. There were no tears this time. He had finally got to grips with staring his own mortality in the face.

He had even accepted that there would be no miracle cure.

At least he was home and at peace with himself. No need to put on any pretences anymore. Being in familiar territory had given Geoffery an unexpected boost to his morale. Although physically tired from the accumulation of activities he had been undertaking; the farewell party, the winding up activities in Monaco, and his tiring drive through the Cotswolds, he felt surprisingly energised by his surroundings.

Raised voices in the corridor outside broke into Geoffery's thoughts. He strained to hear the now heated conversation.

'I'm sorry but Mr Foster has taken certain commercial steps which will ensure that the ongoing funding of the hospice will be considerably eased,' the Administrator explained finally.

'Tell that to the Jones family. Their problem is today, not tomorrow. They need help now.'

'I'm sorry Andy. I have to juggle many balls, and I'm afraid at the moment the Hospice has been thrown a lifeline. I'd be negligent if I let this opportunity slip away.'

'So, anybody with money can leapfrog the list and buy themselves into the Hospice?' the Nurse said angrily. 'What about Mr Jones and his family. They had been promised that bed.'

'Yes, and as soon as another bed becomes available we will bring him in,' the Administrator replied calmly. 'But in the meantime he will continue to receive treatment by our Hospice at Home service.'

'Mrs Jones is at the end of her tether,' Andy shouted. 'She was hoping for the respite, I promised them!'

'Then you were out of order in raising their hopes. You know how circumstances can change quickly.'

'Yes, but they are desperate,' he implored.

'There's nothing further to say on the matter.'

The Administrator turned on her heel and headed back to her office.

Andy took a deep breath and composed himself before re-entering the room..

'Apologies for leaving you. How was your journey to us this morning?' Andy asked, trying to sound calm but was obviously still tense from the argument.

'I came by Private ambulance from Broadway. But I expect you disapprove of that don't you?' Geoffery replied curtly.

Andy ignored the comment, fighting to regain his usual placid bedside manner. 'Well if you want to have a rest before I take you on a guided tour, I'll pop back later.'

'Yes, perhaps that might see us both in a better mood.'

'I'm sorry?' Andy asked puzzled.

'I overheard your conversation.'

'Yes. Well I'm sorry, but as you gathered, I was led to believe Mr Jones was going to be my patient, I was surprised that's all. I can assure you that I will give you my full professional attention.'

'That is in spite of my money?'

'Yes, well not everybody has the means to buy their way into good health care.'

'You see, I find your attitude strange. People normally bend over backwards to ingratiate themselves to me,' Geoffery said staring at Andy.

'It doesn't mean anything to me if you're rich or poor. As a Nurse I treat everybody the same,' Andy said standing his ground.

'Well at least that's reassuring to hear.'

'You see, I know the Jones family, and I know the trauma that they have been going through watching Mr Jones's health deteriorate, seeing the increasing strain on the family.'

'You mean he's in the last throws. What do your brochures call it, 'End of Life care?'

'We try to avoid indelicate language, but yes it won't be long now.'

'So I guess his wife is having a hard time of it?'

'Yes, it's all too easy to forget the pain and frustration that the relatives are experiencing, while we are so focused on treating the patient.'

'Well you don't have to worry about that in my case, I have no family left, oh except a nephew, but I don't even know where he is.'

'Oh!'

'Yes, well all my friends are in Monaco, I doubt they will make the trip to visit me. Anyway, I've had my wake with them. I've said my goodbyes,' Geoffery said unemotionally. 'My father used to say; Son, you've either got money or friends. You don't have both. How right he was.'

'I'm sorry about earlier, but I was concerned about Mrs Jones that's all,' Andy continued apologetically. 'They live in a council house. It isn't suitable for the type of home care that Mr Jones needs. And as an older couple it's doubly difficult.'

'That's very noble of you, but I'm afraid I have to look after number one.'

'Yes of course you do.'

'Well I'll let you settle in and I'll pop back later, Andy said. 'In the meantime if you want anything please telephone reception. Alternatively if you have a medical emergency please press the panic button for immediate assistance. The doctor will be along later to establish your medication needs.'

Andy left the room still angry that his careful plans for the Jones family had been overridden by monetary and not sympathetic considerations.

After putting his few clothes into the wardrobe Geoffery wandered slowly into the garden and went to find the place where he had worked all those many years ago.

He was pleased to see that the pergola he had built was still there and blended in well by Mother Nature.

He sat on a bench and allowed himself a moment of reflective indulgence.

He recalled the patient that used to watch him build it. What was his name? Jimmy, that was it, Jimmy. As soon as Geoffery arrived and put his tools down, the old fellow was there.

Jimmy liked to talk. He had a broad 'Glawster' accent. The 'West Country' brogue was soft and gentle on the ear. Londoners often incorrectly labelled Gloucestrians as coming from Cornwall. Geoffery noticed that since he had been back in England his erudite business-speak had all but disappeared. He now spoke again as a Cheltonian. It was an unconscious reaction to being home. As if he needed to fit in, to ingratiate himself with his old tribe.

Jimmy used to tell him about his life. How he had been invalided out of the RAF because a plane had rolled over his foot.

In spite of receiving a serious injury, poor Jimmy got laughter not sympathy when he told the story, because everybody could imagine him hopping around holding his foot and the mental picture it conjured up made it funny. Geoffery had laughed as well he recalled.

Then the old man relayed his moments of fame in Amateur Dramatics, treading the boards, wearing the makeup, dressing up. He hoped to make the big time but never made it beyond the local village halls.

How eventually he became a Union Convener for the mighty print Union. His chapter, he used to call it, was very militant. He confronted the Management many times on behalf of his 'Brothers.' He used to tell Geoffery that doing something for his 'brother' worker, was a very important part of his life, looking after his less able brethren.

It all sounded too much like communism to Geoffery.

The old fellow was also a Scout Leader or something or other in the Scouts as well.

The dib dob brigade was not for Geoffery. He had joined in ridiculing the kids from his council estate who joined. Woggles and neckerchiefs were not for him; although he was envious when they told him of all the exciting things they got up to, canoeing, climbing and camping.

How different Geoffery's life had been. He had used all his energies on making his own fortune, not wasting his efforts on helping the masses. Look after number one was his motto and that's what earned him his millions, by just looking after number one.

CHAPTER NINE

Thursday September 18th – Sunset count 18

'Andy, did you send Mrs Jones some flowers?' Ann asked looking up from her report.

'No, why would I send her flowers when I don't even send them to my own wife.'

'Well I know you're a bit of a softie. So if you didn't, I wonder who did. She's just called to say thank us for sending her a beautiful bouquet. She seems to think they came from here. It had a card attached apologising for the delay in finding a bed.'

'I bet I know where they've come from. Perhaps he's got a conscience after all.'

'Who do you mean?'

'Mr Geoffery Foster, your benefactor, the man who arrived yesterday.'

'Yes that's a point. I'd imagine in his healthier days he would have been quite an attentive suitor. Yes, quite a catch!' she said giggling nervously.

'Ha, just like I said. He thinks that money solves everything.'

'It might not solve everything, but it certainly goes a long way to making life easier though doesn't it?'

'Does he really think it makes up for the extra angst he caused her?'

'Listen Andy, it was not his fault. He didn't know about our internal arrangements. Come on, this isn't like you to bear a grudge.'

'Yeah sorry, it's just that I was made to look a fool.'

'I appreciate you wanted to help the Jones family but you were out of order promising something which was beyond your control.'

'Anyway I must go. I promised to take him around the gardens today,' Andy said curtailing the dressing down.

Andy entered the day room. His sensitivities smarting from being told off for being sympathetic to a family in need.

'Do you still want to go around the gardens Mr Foster?' He said stiffly.

'I went on a brief excursion myself yesterday, but yes please,' Geoffery said putting his paper down.

'I assume it was you that sent those flowers to Mrs Jones?'

'Yes. You pricked my conscience after what you said.'

'Well apparently it made her day to think somebody was thinking of her,' said Andy. 'She thought the Hospice had sent them.'

'You know, I haven't sent flowers to a lady for a long time,' Geoffery said, thinking back to the regular bouquet orders he used to send Nadine.

'You can walk around the gardens but the grounds are quite big so you might like to use a wheelchair.'

'Yes sounds like a good idea,' Geoffery said moving into the wheelchair. 'I was even more relieved to learn that a bed will be coming available earlier than expected for Mr Jones.'

'I'm sorry if we got off to a bad start. It was just...' Andy said awkwardly.

'No need to apologise. You were right, I should have waited my turn. I could have booked into the hotel for a few more days.'

As they moved from the day room into the garden Andy pulled a blanket over Geoffery's shoulders.

'I love seeing Mother Nature's autumn finery. There's a certain magic to it. The reds, the golds, the browns,' Andy said, breathing in the season's fragrances.

'Yes I've missed the English autumns. The gardens are beautiful at this time of year aren't they?' said Geoffery taking in the scenery. 'I guess it's a big drain on resources to maintain the gardens like this.'

'No, you'd be surprised. Like many things associated with the hospice it's all done voluntarily.'

'Really? Well they do a magnificent job,' Geoffery said surveying the well-stocked rock garden. 'Volunteers you say? I'm afraid you wouldn't have caught me volunteering.'

'Oh, why not? Surely part of belonging in a community is all about helping each other, caring for one another,' Andy said, helping Geoffery on to one of the many donated garden benches.

'Thanks,' said Geoffery sitting down.

'Unfortunately we live in a world where a lot of people expect something for nothing. There is an attitude that seems to be prevalent in today's society where many believe that the state owes them a living, not that they have to go out and earn it; It's always somebody else's problem. People don't take responsibility for themselves and their kids,' Andy continued passionately.

'Look after number one, that's how I made my money,' Geoffery said seriously 'Getting off my backside and seizing the opportunities.'

'What did you used to do?' Andy quizzed.

'I started off around here in the building trade when I was a teenager. My old man was a builder so I cottoned on quickly how to make money work. I bought an old place and did it up, I sold that, invested the money into a bigger one and then sold that. The next one I did up I converted into a block of flats. Of course there were lots of students around here in those days, so no shortage of takers. I just kept investing the money. Money grows money.'

'So I've heard. I've never had enough to invest in the first place,' Andy volunteered.

'Started a property business, looking after other peoples buy for rent stuff. I had to do my own so it seemed a logical extension of that,' Geoffery continued relating his path to his millions.

'So how come you went abroad?'

'Got into the tyre business. India and China were emerging. They'd improved the quality of the stuff they were producing, beyond the joke stage and were churning out saleable merchandise that I could sell over here for a good margin. Picked up the world distribution rights and the spondulies started rolling in.'

'Wow.'

'The Arabs were also a good contact; lots of oil money to spend. I started investing in Jewels, diamonds mainly, as a hedge against the fluctuating currencies and the ups and downs of gold. The rest is history, once you've got it, you invest wisely and it just keeps growing.'

'I'm afraid my savings in the building society aren't going to make me rich.'

'No but with your family responsibilities, it's probably the wisest thing to do with your money'.

'Too much month left at the end of my pay packet that's for sure,' Andy said patting his pocket resignedly.

Chapter Ten

Friday September 19th – Sunset count 19

Geoffery checked the time on his Rolex Yachtmaster watch as Andy entered.

'Late this morning Andy?' he said, removing his reading glasses and laying the Times on the bed.

'Yes sorry. My car broke down on the way here. It stopped suddenly, belching clouds of smoke. I think its terminal.'

'Oh dear, do they have a hospice for cars?' Geoffery joked.

'In my case I think it's the knacker's yard. It couldn't happen at a worse time. We've got little Molly's christening on Sunday. Oh well, we'll have to get a taxi that's all.'

'You could always use my car.'

'Your car! Oh I couldn't!' Andy said, surprised at the offer.

'Well the offer's there if you want it,' Geoffery repeated.

'As much as I'd like to, we are not allowed to accept gifts from patients. Besides, I'd be scared to death to drive a fast car like that. What is it, a Mercedes?'

'It's a Mercedes CL63 AMG. I decided to treat myself to a sporty little coupe. It's a parting gift to me to say goodbye to this life.'

'Well that's an interesting way of looking at it at least.'

'There is a way around this gift restriction thing though,' Geoffery suggested thoughtfully.

'How?'

'You're allowed to take me out aren't you?'

'Well yes, but....'

'So, you take me out on the day of the christening and use my car to get you there.'

'I couldn't,' Andy said not convincingly. He felt awkward after their earlier angst, but it would solve a big organizational headache, and save money he couldn't afford to spend on a taxi.

'The down side is you have to put up with me for the day, invite me to the Christening.'

'Well that wouldn't be a down side. That would be an honour. But I'm not sure?'

'Don't look a gift horse in the mouth. Remember what I said about seizing opportunities?'

'Well, it certainly would help. Are you sure?'

'Yes perfectly.'

'I'd need to run it past Helen, my wife, but it sounds great. Although there is one thing you should consider and you might want to change your mind. I won't blame you if you withdraw your kind offer.'

'Which is?'

'We're ...the family...we've got a few rough diamonds coming. They're OK but they tend to call a spade an 'Effing shovel'.

'Andy, don't forget, I was a Cheltenham council house kid myself. I haven't always had money. That will be OK. No problem.'

'Thank you, thank you very much,' Andy said beaming at this sudden change of luck.

CHAPTER ELEVEN

Sunday September 21st – Sunset count 21

Geoffery Foster sat slumped in the passenger seat as Andy drove the white CL63 tentatively down the long sweeping drive of the former Country Mansion. Although Geoffery was not feeling a hundred percent, he was grateful for the change of scenery.

The car made its way slowly through the avenue of trees flanking the road, almost stopping as it went over each tarmac hump, the traffic calming 'sleeping policeman'.

'You don't need to slow down that much to hurdle those speed bumps. The Mercedes has great suspension,' Geoffery instructed.

'Well. OK, but I'm conscious that I'm driving somebody else's very expensive car, I'd hate to damage it. You'd be surprised at the number of broken exhausts we get along this bit of road. Besides, I have to think of the comfort of my passenger, don't I? We don't want that pain pump line to come out now do we?' Andy replied.

'No I suppose not,' Geoffery said, unconsciously putting his hand to the box, secured to his waist, which was intravenously delivering a preset rate of morphine.

'Thank you for loaning me your car,' Andy said gratefully. 'Are you sure you're OK?

'Yes,' said Geoffery unconvincingly.

Andy looked across at the grey face of the man sitting beside him and wondered about the merit of continuing.

'It needed to be driven,' said Geoffery. ''She's a thoroughbred; needs to be exercised.'

'I don't know what we'd have done without your kind generosity,' Andy admitted.

The car nosed its way through the ornamental gateposts and joined the traffic on the busy lane and headed towards Gloucester.

'Where did you say the windscreen wiper switch was?' asked Andy, randomly flicking switches on the stalk of the steering column.

'It's automatic,' said Geoffery watching the rain streaking up the windscreen. 'I hope this clears up soon, otherwise it'll spoil your day.'

'Weather forecast was good though. Lets hope it's just a passing storm,' Andy said, feeling very smug as pedestrians stopped and stared as the car passed them. 'What a car,' he said, running his hand lovingly over the steering wheel. 'I'd never be able to afford something like this.'

'Pennies and pounds' Geoffery said remembering another one his father's pieces of sagely advice. 'Look after the pennies and the pounds will follow.'

'Sorry, what did you say?' asked a puzzled Andy.

Unaware that he had actually spoken his thoughts, Geoffery, however, repeated it. 'Something you might like to consider,' Geoffery counselled. 'Look after the pennies, invest them, and the pounds will follow.'

'Unfortunately there are too many other family demands on my pay packet to be able to do anything like that,' Andy admitted.

As the Mercedes entered the former council estate, groups of women stopped their gossiping and stared.

The car was out of place. Only drug dealers drove posh cars like that on to the estate.

Geoffery started to feel uneasy about the area into which they had driven. Although he had been a council house kid many years before, the nostalgia of his own childhood, growing up on a council estate, no longer matched what he was seeing. For after leaving the estate in his late teens, he had been leading a 'sheltered life' away from the cramped estate where everybody knew everybody else's business. The pampered lifestyle he had led in Monaco had robbed him of his tough council kid veneer. He knew that entering places like this, in this sort of car, was asking for trouble.

As they meandered deeper into the estate he felt more and more uncomfortable. It made him think he was entering a ghetto. He was expecting any minute to run into a barricade, or to be car jacked and be dragged out of his beautiful car and beaten up.

Andy looked across at Geoffery, his growing anxiety evident by his frightened mannerisms.

'Don't worry,' he said. 'It's not as bad as the papers make out. It's safe I can assure you.'

Geoffery didn't feel reassured by the Nurse's words.

Surely this was the very environment he'd read about in the English newspapers where feral youths dressed in hoods roamed the streets and mugged people for their mobile phones. Even worse, they beat people to death for just looking at them.

Surely these were the same dull dwellings where the occupants abused themselves and their families and who spawned children who would go on to perpetuate the abuse.

This was the very environment where young girls got themselves pregnant just to get a council house.

Pregnancy gave them some element of self-esteem. Probably for the first time in their life they became 'special' and were recognised by society as being a person, a grown up, a mother, not just another worthless teenager.

Sadly, many had never experienced a proper childhood before they themselves became an inadequate mother.

Birth control was seldom used because with baby came a priority house and appropriate social benefits, sometimes with the boyfriend in tow, who then moved in rent free.

Yes, they would all know how to milk the benefit system. With the exception of Andy and his family this was probably an estate full of spongers, leeches on society. Geoffery surmised.

His apprehension increased even further as they drove deeper into the estate. A gang of hoodies on BMX bikes blocked the road, forcing them to stop briefly. The group was showing off to each other, doing kerb side acrobatics.

His anxiety worsened when he saw in his wing mirror that the group had stopped their antics and started to follow the car. Standing up on their pedals, they made a comical sight. With no gears they were pedalling extremely fast. The cadence of their legs would not have looked out of place in a silent keystone Kops movie.

The hoodies were shadowing the car.

'Have you seen those yobs Andy?' Geoffery said hoarsely.

'Yes, they're nothing to worry about,' replied Andy calmly.

'I hope you're right.'

But the car slowing down was not what Geoffery was expecting.

'Right, here we are, won't be a moment,' Andy said, parking the Mercedes outside one of the council houses.

'Do you want me to sit in the back?' Geoffery asked, hoping to keep Andy's company for a little longer.

'No Geoffery, you're better there. Don't want the little one knocking your pain pump if you're sitting in the back. Are you still OK?'

'Yes fine, thanks,' Geoffery lied, not mentioning his anxiety about the group of hoodies.

'Right I'll be back in a minute,' Andy said, getting out of the car. 'Helen should be ready.'

'Don't worry about me; you sort your family out'. Geoffery reassured him hoping he wouldn't be long.

As Andy disappeared into the house Geoffery studied the area. It was not dissimilar to his own childhood home.

The former council houses, built in the 1950s, lay in regimented uniformity with privet hedges bordering the tarmac pavement.

Post war building priorities were only focused on quick construction; architectural merit was not one of the parameters used in developing the early fifties housing stock.

Several in the row of semidetached properties showed signs of DIY, probably part of a tenant purchase scheme, he mused.

Other shabby properties interspersed with the neat ones showed the mix of people on the estate. Perhaps his initial judgment was wrong. Perhaps they weren't all lethargic spongers.

Andy's house was one of the shabby ones, much in need of a bit of TLC; clearly he wasn't much into house and garden maintenance. Whereas his adjoining neighbour was obviously quite meticulous, his privet hedge showed elements of topiary as it arched over his carefully painted black metal garden gate.

Chapter Twelve

Geoffery's heart sank as he spotted the Gang of hoodies coming around the corner and cycling up towards the car.

His hand immediately flew to engage the central locking which gave a reassuring clunk as all doors locked in turn.

The group had stopped several yards away from the car and seemed to be planning something. After a brief discussion one of their number detached himself from the others and came towards the car and started circling it on his bike.

The yob stared menacingly down through the tunnel of his hood like some modern day grim reaper, his features hidden.

Geoffery wondered when a brick would materialise and come through the window. He realised he was sweating; his mouth dry.

In his younger, healthier days he would have been out the car and seeing off the 'little shit'. He would have been able to cope with any agro that could have developed. But now, with only the energy of a baby, he felt vulnerable, threatened.

Geoffery was unsure what to do. Should he sound the horn to warn the nurse that the Hoodie Gang was outside?

If he sounded the horn it would attract their attention to him.

His mind struggled to resolve the dilemma; the morphine was clogging his thought processing.

As he was trying to think of a strategy, the one who had been cycling around the car dropped his bike and went to Andy's house. He pushed open the small metal gate sending it crashing against the moth eaten privet hedge and slouched his way down the concrete slab path. He leant on the bell push screwed to the paint chipped door frame.

The others stood smirking by the gate.

If only Geoffery had the telephone number of the house, he could warn Andy not to open the door. Through the fog in his mind he remembered that Andy had given him his mobile number. Why hadn't he thought about it earlier? 'Stupid man' he chided himself.

The youth at the door took his finger off the bell push and thrust his hand deep into his pocket. Something shiny appeared. Was it a flick knife?

Geoffery's trembling hands dug into his own pocket and pulled out his mobile, quickly flicking the Motorola open.

'Contacts...contacts' he instructed himself. 'Where's the number?'

Too late! As he highlighted Andy's number the door opened and the Nurse stood on the threshold and gazed down at the face of the Hoodie.

The young man raised his arm towards the Nurse's face.

'Oh my no,' thought Geoffery, he's going to slash his face.

Andy raised his arm in response, apparently trying to block the blow, their hands touched and parted.

The Hoodie's arm went forward again into Andy's midriff this time in a thrusting motion which stopped suddenly as if it had struck something solid.

Geoffery decided to call the Police.

As he glanced at the two on the doorstep, he expected to see the Nurse collapsing, screaming, and falling into a pool of blood. Today of all days this should not be happening. It was going to be a celebration of a new life. The child would never know her kind father.

The Nurse bowed forward and stepped down from the doorstep, obviously hurt.

Geoffery punched in the first nine, but couldn't bear to take his eyes off the events unfolding on the doorstep.

The Nurse grabbed hold of the youths shoulder for support as he appeared to fall forward.

Geoffery keyed in the second nine.

The two were now in a full embrace.

'What was going on?' Geoffery wondered. 'Was he just thrusting the knife deeper, twisting it to cause maximum internal damage?'

The Nurse appeared to be smiling. Was this the final grimace before death?

The police, Geoffery reminded himself. The last nine and the green phone symbol, don't forget the green phone.

Geoffery glanced up again. Now Andy had let go of the youth and was standing and appeared to be laughing. Was this how stabbed people died?

Perhaps he should take a photograph of the Gang and the perpetrator so the police could trace them. Why hadn't he thought of that before? 'Stupid, stupid, old fool,' he berated himself.

His thumb came off hovering over the green phone and back onto the options button, quickly scrolling through to find the picture option.

'Quickly' he urged himself. The Hoodies will soon be leaving now they had done their terrible deed. Perhaps they would turn their attention to him as he had witnessed it all.

His panicking hands struggled with the buttons. He forced himself not to look up until he found the capture option.

In his peripheral vision he was aware of movement coming towards him; still he worked on the phone.

Chapter Thirteen

'Got it,' he said to himself, finding the option. As he brought the phone up to take the photograph, the face of the youth from the doorstep was just yards away and heading directly towards him.

Geoffery pressed the button and heard the reassuring sound of the photograph being taken.

As he pressed the button again to capture another image, Geoffery was taken by surprise. For instead of the rest of the Gang heading in his direction it was the smiling face of the Nurse. But the youth had his hand behind Andy's back, was he there at knife point?

Geoffery's confusion about what he had thought he had witnessed had caused his heart to race, blood coursing through his ears. He could see Andy speaking; perhaps he was going to persuade Geoffery to unlock the car, so it would be undamaged, pristine for its new owner.

Geoffery sought the option to dial again. Nine, nine... but something was wrong with what he was seeing.

The nurse was saying something and gesticulating. He was still smiling.

'Mr Foster, Mr Foster,' he was saying.

There was no blood on the Nurse's white shirt. Down the tunnel of his hooded top, the youth too was smiling. Was this a trick?

'I'd like to introduce you to...

'Introduce! Introduce? Victims don't introduce people who have just stabbed them.' Geoffery's mind struggled to understand the situation. Nevertheless he lowered the window a fraction.

'It's OK, he won't bite. This is my friend Ben. He and his mates thought I'd won the lottery when they saw me driving your car,' Andy advised.

'Ben! Ben!' Geoffery struggled to remember. 'Ben, yes the nurse had told him of this Ben while he was helping him dress the other day. Something about....'

'He's one of my Scouts. Do you mind if he sits in your car for a second?'

Scouts, of course! So he hadn't been witness to a vicious attack after all. 'I thought he was attacking you,' admitted Geoffery.

'Attacking me?'

'Yes.'

'Nothing sinister, just a high five and a special Scout handshake, that's all.'

Now it was obvious. He had let his imagination run away with him. His negative thoughts against all young people and Hoodies made an innocent greeting into a murderous attack. He felt foolish at the realisation of it.

Geoffery flicked the central locking off as Ben stretched for the door handle. 'Step in young man. Please sit here in the driving seat.'

Ben wasted no time and slid into the luxurious Black Passion leather seat.

'Wow, this is some car.'

'Now don't get touching anything,' the Nurse instructed.

Almost instantaneously Geoffery heard the sound of BMX bikes dropping onto the pavement as the rest of the Gang ran towards the car.

'Can we sit in the back Mister?' asked one spotty faced youth standing by the passenger door.

'Is that OK Geoffery?' asked the Nurse.

'Yes that's fine, be my guest,' a relieved Geoffery replied.

'I ain't going to sit in there,' another one of the Gang said,' I don't want to catch it.'

'Don't be daft, cancer isn't catching is it Mr Foster?' Ben said, admonishing the speaker.

Clearly, Andy had told Ben and the others about Geoffery's condition.

'Ugh, has he got cancer? I ain't going in there either,' muttered another. 'You never know.'

Geoffery was taken aback by the indelicate comments of Ben's mates. His emotions were all over the place; frightened at coming on to the estate, terrified at what he thought was a murder, relieved when he realised he had misread the situation and now being slapped in the face with some kid's ignorant view of his condition. He didn't need reminding of his mortality.

Ignorance breeds bias, he reflected, not missing the irony of his own misjudgment of young people and Hoodies.

'Don't mind him Mr Foster,' the youth by his side reassured him. 'He's a bit of a pillock, don't know nothing'.

'He doesn't know anything,' Geoffery unconsciously corrected.

'That's right,' Ben riposted, 'thick as shit'.

The Nurse cleared his throat loudly in admonishment.

'Sorry, meant to say thick as S, H, one T,' Ben continued, almost in the same breath. 'My Gran died of cancer last year and I ain't caught it. This is a nice motor. Merc CL63 Coupe; Seven speed box; 525 Brake Horse; 0 to 62 in 4.6 seconds.'

'You seem to know a lot about Cars.'

'Yeah we have car maintenance courses down at the hut and well everybody round here is always doing up cars.'

'Come on then Ben, I've got a christening to go to. Say thanks to Mr Foster,' said Andy.

'Thanks mate. I'll have one like that one day,' Ben said, quickly sliding out of the car as requested.

'I bet you will,' Geoffery thought, 'but will you be the owner?' He quickly chided himself for his bias. 'OK' he said. 'It's nice to meet you.'

As the group around the car dispersed, Geoffery could hear Ben vilifying the spotty youth and as a result there was some pushing and shoving. He just hoped they weren't going to get into a fight, his nerves were already at breaking point.

Andy's wife came towards the car, 'Andy we're already running late, I thought for one moment you were going to hold a Scout meeting out here.'

'Helen, this is Mr Foster, Geoffery, this is my wife Helen.'

Helen put her hand through the open window almost curtseying as she did so.

'Oh I'm sorry Mr Foster, didn't mean to expose you to a 'domestic',' she said apologetically. 'Pleased to meet you.'

'Likewise, I'm sure,' said Geoffery, noting the frilly white blouse terminated by chubby hands and a crude red nail varnish job. A single plain gold ring on her wedding finger, the only adornment. So different from the Dior bedecked, jewel laden ladies of his former life.

'Come around this side love,' the Nurse instructed. 'It's only got two doors and I don't want Geoffery leaping in and out of his own car.'

'That would be the day. I'm afraid my leaping days are over, but there's still life in the old dog yet,' Geoffery added.

Ben's wife was preceded into the car by a pretty four year old girl in a full length floral party dress and shiny black patent leather shoes, a big white bow crowning a head of long blond hair that cascaded over her shoulders.

As she climbed in, she stopped and proffered her little hand, 'Hello Mr Foster. Thank you for lending us your car. It's my little sisters Christen-ning today and it's very important for baby Jesus to see my sister. Her name is Molly. Do you like my dress Mr Foster? It's my special party dress.' She said without pausing for breath.

'Come on darling, you'll have plenty of time to talk to Mr Foster later on, now move over and let Mummy get in with Molly,' she said patiently to the little one.

'Andy, hold Molly while I get in. Oh and we'll need the baby seat for Amy. Thanks for loaning us your car Mr Foster.'

'Please, it's my pleasure. It's the least I can do for you on such an important day like today. Besides your husband is a lovely man and does much more for all of us than he needs to. I'm just pleased to be able to help and get away from the hospice to see the outside world again for a few hours.'

'Here you are love.' Andy passed the child's seat to his wife and climbed in. 'And the fresh air will do you good too, Geoffery. Right everybody got their belts on? OK we're off then.'

Ben and the gang were still on the pavement as Andy pressed the starter button and the car purred into life.

'Give them something to cheer at,' Geoffery instructed, 'leave them with a squeal of tyres.'

'Are you sure? They're your tyres.'

'Don't worry about that, I doubt I shall be buying anymore tyres anyway.'

'Positive thinking Geoffery, come on,' chided Andy.

Andy duly floored the accelerator and shot off down the road to the obvious delight of the Hoodies leaving a line of rubber behind him.

'Andy, don't forget you've got a precious cargo on board,' Helen reminded him concerned. 'And you've already got three points on your licence.'

Andy slowed down as instructed.

Geoffery was less on edge as they drove back through the estate, feeling slightly foolish at his earlier concerns.

Chapter Fourteen

Geoffery was now feeling a bit more relaxed having met some Hoodies, 'face to hood' so to speak.

'Those kids!' Geoffery said, relieved.

'Not what you expected?' quizzed the Nurse as he steered the coupe out of the area.

'Not exactly, no,' Geoffery replied. 'To be honest, I wasn't sure what to expect'.

'They're not at all the demonic characters that the newspapers like to make them out to be. That's not to say they don't have a few antisocial habits. But when you understand the family environment that some grow up in, you can understand why a few have rough edges.'

'That Ben seems to have his head screwed on the right way.'

'He's tough too, but then he needs to be.'

'Come from a single parent family?'

'Yes. He lives with his Mother. But don't get me wrong. Not all single Mum's are bad, but her passion for drink, drugs and men has made Ben's life hell.'

'Poor Sod!' Geoffery said, suddenly feeling sorry for a kid he'd only just met.

'During one of my days off, I got a call from the school. They know I run the local Scout Troop. Ben had been sent to the Headmaster's office for fighting and being insolent to his teacher. Apparently he was in a right state. They were going to send for the police at one stage and exclusion would have been automatic.'

'But they rang you, why not his Mother?' Geoffery asked puzzled.

'The school is aware of his Mother's problems and knew that I had spent a lot of time trying to sort Ben out when he first joined the Scouts.'

'What did you do?'

'I went to the school and had a private session with Ben. I mainly listened to him off load. But it took sometime before I got to the bottom of it. Apparently on this particular occasion his Mother had come home in the early hours out of her mind on drugs or drink with a new boyfriend. The new boyfriend ripped his trousers on Ben's bike, which Ben kept in the hallway. Boyfriend got mad and kicked Ben out of his own house at three o'clock in the morning.'

'That must have been terrifying,' Geoffery said, imagining the fear Ben must have experienced. 'So Ben was wandering the streets at three o'clock in the morning, He must have been scared witless. The man wants shooting. Where was his mother in all this?' Geoffery asked.

'Probably didn't even know anything about it. Ben normally gets himself to school in the mornings anyway,' interjected Helen.

'So you can understand why Ben was a bit 'tetchy' that morning?' Andy added.

'What happened?'

'Well the school was very good about it when I explained the circumstances; they said they'd give him another chance.'

'Did you report it to Social Services?'

'Ben made me promise that I wouldn't involve them, if he told me the full story. He's fiercely loyal to his mother. So I went round to see her and we had a long chat.'

'Was she sober?' Geoffery asked.

'When she's on planet earth she can be quite sensible,' Andy said calmly.

'Where was the boyfriend in all this?'

'Oh he'd got what he wanted and was long gone. I arranged for Ben to spend some time with his Grandad while she sorted herself out.'

'I can't understand how people get themselves into these situations,' Geoffery said 'Clearly doesn't understand her parental responsibilities.'

'Sadly, it's the age old story. Got pregnant when she was still at school, missed out on teen life while she's bringing the kid up and now she is trying to make up for lost time. Unfortunately the booze has robbed her of her self-respect and dignity,' Helen said.

'Poor kid deserves better doesn't he? What chance does he have in life with a start like this?' Geoffery said concerned.

'He's going to have to be tough if he's to avoid spending half his life in prison,' Geoffery thought, as they sped off along the main road towards the Church.

Chapter Fifteen

'Here we are then,' announced Andy as the car stopped.

They had drawn up outside an ancient Church on top of a hill. A small castellated tower sat at the left hand side of the building with an unsightly drainage pipe running down the face of it spoiling the architect's design.

The long nave, almost the same height as the tower was supported mid-way by a wide stone buttress. Two stone arched windows equidistant from the buttress made it look like a giant stone face complete with blank staring eyes.

In front of the building was an ancient graveyard with tall crumbling gravestones that stuck randomly out of the short grass at rakish angles.

The Church was completely encircled by a line of small black metal railings that segregated it from the rest of the hill.

Although only a relatively short excursion, Geoffery was feeling exhausted from his first trip out of the hospice, he felt relieved that the journey was at last over.

As soon as the nurse opened the car door it had become the centre of attraction from a small group of people dressed in their 'Sunday best' waiting by the railings.

'Wow Andy, where did you nick this one from?' asked one of the group, admiring the Mercedes, his gold earring shining in the autumn morning sunshine.

'Where's your motor?'

'It's a long story'. Andy said.

'Won the lottery Andy?' another asked.

'Nice isn't it. It belongs to a friend of mine. I'll introduce you to him in a minute.'

'Yes please. If he trusts you with this fantastic Merc, he must be worth touching up for a few quid,' the gold earring wearer said, stroking the paintwork.

Ignoring the comment, Andy lifted the driver's seat forward and took the baby from his wife.

'Sorry,' said Geoffery suddenly aware of what was happening. 'Let me get out and that would make it easier for all of you.'

'No, that's OK Geoffery. I can slide out from the other side,' said Helen moving from behind Geoffery. 'It's not a problem.'

'Just as well, the christening would probably be over by the time I got myself up from here,' he said cheerfully, starting to feel excited about the event.

'I'll just get the family inside the church and I'll come back for you Geoffery. Is that OK?' Andy said, helping Helen out of the car with his free hand.

'Yes no problem, I'll just soak up this lovely scenery.'

Geoffery opened the car door and slowly struggled out, as the excited group of family and friends made their way through the black metal gate and along the steep winding path that led through the ancient graveyard up to the church.

Geoffery leant his exhausted body on the car door and gazed around.

'I guess they built the Church here because it's closer to God,' he mused.

As he savored the cool autumnal air, a flash of something caught the corner of his eye. He strained to peer through the morning mist that swirled like ectoplasm around the gravestones.

Then he heard the sound of digging. He felt a chill in the pit of his stomach as he recalled his nightmares.

Behind a green gauze the gravedigger was at work, or was it his imagination playing tricks. 'Did gravediggers work on a Sunday?' he wondered.

The sun glinted off a spade as it deposited more dirt on to a growing pile.

'Of course they do,' he chided himself. 'Don't let your imagination run away with you. Anyway, he would be calling on the services of the gravedigger himself, soon,' he thought dispassionately, almost as though he was thinking about somebody else, not his own demise. He had decided on an interment rather than a cremation and the permanence of a carved headstone rather than a plaque to mark his final resting place.

'Still, he'd had a good life. He couldn't complain. It was better than Andy or his wife was ever likely to experience, unless they won the lottery,' he mused.

'I suppose it's a nice place up here for friends and family to come and visit to remember their loved ones,' he decided.

Although now his ties with the Monaco set had been cut, he wondered who would be visiting his mound of soil anyway.

Chapter Sixteen

The little group of family and friends meandered through the graveyard along the narrow pathway to the ancient building.

At the head of the group the Nurse proudly carried baby Molly. He beamed at her little face framed by an old fashioned lacy bonnet, a tiny bundle cocooned in a long off-white satin christening robe that enveloped her small frame and cascaded over his arms. Helen's family heirloom worn by generations was stored with great reverence after each ceremony to be used in perpetuity, continuing the family tradition.

'It's a pity Geoffery didn't want to be one of Molly's Godparents,' Helen observed, adjusting the oversized bonnet that had slewed over Molly's eyes.

'Well I did offer.'

'What did he say?'

'He was already an absent Godfather and in debt to his own Godsons.'

'What does he mean by that?' she asked, puzzled.

'I don't know, but I assume he's already a Godparent. He also said he doubted he'd even be around to see Molly's first birthday. So he declined.'

'That's a pity isn't it? But is that right about his life expectancy though?'

'Probably, the prognosis isn't too good.'

'Poor Geoffery!'

'Well, while he's still here, let's help him enjoy whatever life he's got left.'

'I don't understand why he isn't living it up in some posh clinic considering he's a millionaire. I mean what's he doing at your place?'

'He'd obviously heard about me and my amazing care skills,' Andy quipped.

'Nothing like blowing your own trumpet is there?' Helen responded quickly.

'He's a local boy, said he wanted to come home and see his birthplace again before he died.'

As they arrived at the ancient oak door a grey haired man in clerical gowns was waiting for them.

'Hello Vicar,' Andy said.

'Good morning Mr Spider. Ah, this must be little Molly. She looks lovely, don't you darling?' the Vicar said bending to address the baby. 'Do you know the order of service Mr Spider?'

'Yes, I assume it's the same as when you christened Amy.'

'Oh. I thought I recognised the Christening shawl. Where is she?'

'She's with her uncle and little cousin Rose,' Helen said, beaming with pride.

'Love, if you'd like to take Molly, I'll go and get Geoffery,' Andy said, handing the baby to Helen.

He turned back and walked quickly down the path towards the car park and the waiting Geoffery.

'You sure you'll be able to push him up the slope by yourself?' Helen called as he made his way down the steep path.

'No problem. I'm wheelchair pusher first class. It's part of my job. Remember?'

Halfway down the path Andy could see that Geoffery had already got himself out of the car and was struggling to get through the kissing gate.

'Geoffery,' he muttered under his breath, 'that's probably not a good idea.'

Andy broke into a jog.

As he got to within six feet of the struggling invalid, Geoffery's legs went from under him.

Geoffery managed to hold on to the gate long enough for Andy to catch him.

'Gotchya' said a breathless Andy. 'Why didn't you wait? I said I'd be back.'

'I didn't want to be a burden on your special day. You've got family and friends to look after. You don't want to be fussing around with me.'

'Now listen,' Andy slipped into a Franglais accent and joked, 'I s-h-a-l-l t-e-l-l you dis only wunce. You are part of my family for the day and I want you to relax and enjoy it. Now hang on here please while I get the wheelchair.'

'OK, I'm sorry...'

'No problem.'

Andy walked the few paces back to the car and deftly removed the wheelchair out of the Mercedes.

Making sure the car was locked, he made his way back to Geoffery and within a few minutes they were weaving their way through the gravestones that flanked the path.

'There we go. See. No time at all.'

'Lovely old place isn't it? Geoffery said feeling a bit light headed after his exertions. 'I was reading the brief history of it while I was waiting. It's Norman 12th century and the font is supposed to be 14th Century.'

'Just imagine the generations of children who started their spiritual lives here and my little girl is going to be one of them,' Andy beamed.

'Quite something isn't it, being part of history,' replied Geoffery trying to concentrate.

'It's supposed to have been built within an old Iron Age camp, in which case we're talking seriously ancient.'

'I've never been one for historical things, but this is fantastic isn't it?'

'They've got an illuminated Cross on the top of the tower that can be seen from miles around. Villagers say it's like a homing beacon when they return to the village after being away. Local legend has it that the fence was put around the churchyard to stop the dead from escaping out of the graveyard,' Andy relayed.

Coupled with the beautiful surrounding in which the ancient church stood and Andy's infectious excitement, Geoffery couldn't help but feel excited too.

'Look at that view across to the Cotswolds. Isn't that fantastic? You can see the edge of the escarpment snaking around the Severn plain for miles. The woods! The quarries! The hills! Magic!' Andy continued excitedly.

Geoffery was having difficulty hearing, Andy's voice sounding as if it was coming through a tunnel.

'The Cotswolds was one of my reasons for coming home,' Geoffery said thickly.

'You OK?' The nurse's instinct kicking in at the change in his patient's response.

'Yes, fine' said Geoffery unconvincingly, 'don't worry about me, you've got a little girl to introduce to Jesus, isn't that what Amy was saying?'

'Yes, bless her.'

Andy was scanning the graveyard as they made their way. 'You know there are some strange headstones here; somebody must have had some money. Look at that grotesque Angel.'

As Geoffery turned his head to look at the statue he felt drunk, his head swam, and his eyes didn't want to focus. The statue danced in front of him.

'I must fight this,' he thought, 'I don't want to mess up their day.' Geoffery felt strange, his emotions all over the place. He felt happy and sad at the same time.

'Phew, this is a bit of a push up here,' Andy said breathing heavily. 'No wonder they built another Church at the bottom of the hill. Imagine walking up here with a coffin in the olden days. I wonder how many pall bearers had heart attacks en route?' Andy remarked lightly.

'There was something about that on the board down there,' Geoffery said slowly, feeling queasy. 'Apparently they had stopping places where they could put the coffin down and have a drink.'

Geoffery felt the nausea rising. 'Oh no, I'm not going to be sick,' he told himself.

'Here we are. That made me sweat a bit,' Andy said, panting as they entered through the low doorway. 'I'll help you out of your chair and then I need to go and join the family.'

'That's fine, please don't bother about me,' Geoffery replied earnestly hoping Andy hadn't spotted that he too was sweating profusely.

The ceremony got underway as Andy joined the group around the ancient 14th century font.

Geoffery stood up unsteadily. He held on to the pew in front to steady himself. The ceremony seemed to be taking an eternity. He couldn't take it in, couldn't concentrate. His knuckles were white with the effort to stay upright as he fought to remain conscious, his eyelids fluttering.

Distantly he heard the vicar say.

'As Molly's parents and godparents, you have the prime responsibility for guiding and helping her in her early years. This is a demanding task for which you will need the help and grace of God. Therefore let us now pray for grace in guiding this child in the way of faith'.

Geoffery had heard that charge three times before when he too had stood at a font holding babies. His Godsons.

'What had he done to help and guide them? Nothing! In reality, he had almost forgotten his commitment by the time he'd left the church grounds. It was, after all, just a ceremony and didn't mean anything anyway. Did it?' He fought the noise in his head to try to remember their names.

'The first one must have been…'he forced himself to think, 'must have been… Rupert, his nephew. Yes, that's right. Funny little chap.' He had lost touch with his crazy sister and her in laws almost immediately after the Christening. That was until he had moved to Monaco and then the begging letters began. He didn't go to her funeral, even though she was the last member of his family. A business meeting or something had got in the way. Still he'd sent a wreath.

Then there was Tim. Tim his former lover's child. Lovely Kay. Kay had married that numbskull, George. How he regretted losing her. There was something different about Tim; he couldn't remember what Kay had said.

And finally there was James. That was it. James was the son of his best friends Silvano and Cecilia. He was orphaned when their plane crashed over the Pyrenees. Geoffery had tried to help, but the family fortune was what had really helped James. At the age of eight he was a millionaire, so he probably wouldn't need any help anyway.

Geoffery felt himself wavering; he tightened his grip.

Where were his Godsons now? What had they made of their lives without his 'help and guidance?' They were probably alright. Perhaps he should find out. Yes, perhaps that's what he'd do, look them up.

He needed air. He was so hot. 'Must concentrate,' he chided himself, 'think of something. Surely it must be nearly over soon,' he reasoned.

Faraway the voice of the Vicar broke into his fevered mind. Lights danced in his failing vision as the Vicar lit a candle from the altar for Molly.

'God has delivered us from the dominion of darkness and has given us a place with the saints in light.

You have received the light of Christ; walk in this light all the days of your life'.

The poignancy of the last few words was not missed by Geoffery as he lost his battle to remain conscious and slumped noisily to the floor.

Chapter Seventeen

The Vicar spotted the sudden movement and rushed the final words of the ceremony.

Andy turned round at the sudden noise to see that Geoffery was no longer where he'd left him. He broke away from the group and sprinted to the unconscious figure lying on the flagstones almost underneath one of the pews.

'*Shine as a light in the world to the glory of God the Father,*' the vicar concluded

Andy's finger expertly targeted the pulse point on Geoffery's neck. Relieved to feel a pulse, he could feel Geoffery's heart was racing.

The congregation stood and gazed at Andy and Geoffery, concerned. The christening forgotten momentarily.

'Perhaps, you'd like to make your way out and let us sort this little matter,' directed the Vicar.

'OK everybody, he's just fainted, nothing to worry about,' Andy announced, as the group filed past gazing at the prostrate figure.

Helen arrived by Andy's side with Amy.

'Is he deaded Daddy?' asked the little girl innocently.

'No darling, he's just fainted and bumped his head, that's all. He'll be OK in a minute.'

'Why have you put his feet on those pillows instead of his head? Has his feet gone to sleep?' she asked puzzled.

'No darling,' he reassured her, suppressing a smile. 'It's to help him get better.'

'Come on darling, we'll see if they're taking photos of Molly outside shall we?' Helen said, steering the little girl out of the Church.

As they went, Helen turned to Andy and mouthed 'Is he really alright?'

Andy nodded affirmatively.

'Do you want some water for him?' asked the Vicar nervously as he joined Andy. 'I've only got consecrated water though.'

'Right now he could do with all the help he can get, and if it's going to give him a bit of spiritual assistance lets go for it.'

Geoffery's nightmare returned. He was chasing footsteps through the graveyard. This time grotesque statues materialised out of the mist. The angel that he had seen when they came through the ancient graveyard sprang to life. Its eyes red! Liquid pools of magma! Mesmeric! They were boring into his soul.

The gravedigger he had seen earlier climbed from behind the green gauze. It was Nadine.

Three cherubic looking babies holding hands blocked his way. Their angelic voices were demonically distorted, booming in his head and filling his mind.

'Godfather help us, help us, help us,' they pleaded.

He tried unsuccessfully to side step them, the babies flew at him, attacking him, clinging to his legs. One jumped on to his back, arms tight around his neck, throttling him. He couldn't breathe.

All the time their voices were filling his head, pleading for help.

He couldn't run. He started falling and falling and...

As the Vicar returned with a glass of water Geoffery was thrashing around.

'Geoffery can you hear me? It's OK Geoffery, you're OK. Take your time,' Andy said reassuringly.

Geoffery seemed to respond. His limbs stopped flailing.

'You dozed off during the service. The Vicar wants to have words with you about disturbing his ceremony, isn't that right Vicar?' Andy added lightly.

'Where, where am I?' Geoffery asked thickly. 'Who are you? Get away, get away from me.'

Through his distorted vision Andy's face took the shape of a fearful gargoyle.

'It's OK Geoffery, it's me Andy. You just fainted that's all. Just give yourself a few minutes and you'll be fine.'

'OK, OK, I'll help you, I'll help you,' Geoffery continued, addressing the babies in his dream.

'You sure you don't want me to call an ambulance?' said the Vicar reaching for his mobile.

'No he'll be OK.'

'But he's so white and look at that bump on his forehead. You don't think he's got brain damage do you?' asked the concerned cleric.

Geoffery was still fighting to regain consciousness, all the while muttering incoherently.

'He ought to be regaining consciousness by now,' said Andy starting to feel concerned.

Andy's hand accidentally brushed Geoffery's coat aside as he bent over him exposing the small box attached to Geoffery's belt which had clear plastic pipes disappearing under Geoffery's clothing.

'Ah, here's the problem,' he said studying the box. 'His morphine is set on high delivery. He's mildly OD'd.'

'What do you mean?' asked the other, puzzled.

'Sorry for the jargon,' said Andy, 'He's mildly overdosed. Geoffery have you had more pain?' he asked looking closely into Geoffery's white face.

'Pains? pains?' Geoffery repeated, trying to make sense of what was being asked.

'Are you sure about this ambulance? They could be here within five minutes, the ambulance station is just down the road,' asked the Vicar insistently.

'No,' said Andy standing to address the concerned cleric. 'He will be OK shortly; I've reduced the dosage down to a normal level. But if you could help me get him back into his wheelchair we'll be out of your way.'

'So long as you think he's going to be OK?'

'I can assure you, it's nothing to worry about. I have been caring professionally for Geoffery for a while now.'

'OK.'

'Geoffery, we're going to put you into your wheelchair now,' advised Andy gently touching the back of Geoffery's hand reassuringly. 'The fresh air will help clear your head.'

'I'm sorry; I'll make up for it. I didn't have time,' Geoffery muttered, still talking to the phantom children of his fevered imagination.

'What's he talking about? Are you're sure he's OK,' said the Vicar moving the kneeling cushions supporting Geoffery's feet.

'Still a bit delirious I think, but I'm perfectly sure he's OK,' Andy reassured him lifting Geoffery into the wheelchair and securing the waist and shoulder straps. 'He's a bit high at the moment. I wonder if we knocked the switch on his pain pump when I stopped him from falling down by the gate.'

Helen and a group of concerned relatives and friends were standing on the path as they emerged through the low entrance door.

'OK folks, sorry about the little drama in there. It appears that Geoffery went accidentally on a trip. He'll be OK in a minute.'

'He doesn't look it,' said Helen, concerned.

'Yes he's fine don't fuss,' said Andy tetchily. The over concern of others was starting to make Andy irritable. They were, after all, questioning his professional judgement.

'Daddy, why did Mr Foster lay down in the church?' enquired a still concerned Amy.

'It's because he is poorly darling,' replied Helen gently. 'Daddy will make him better, so don't worry.'

'I wish I could,' thought Andy. 'Yes that's right darling, don't worry,' he said gently.

Geoffery was beginning to take in his surroundings, the nightmare fading. He felt something touch his hand and struggled to open his heavy eyelids. Amy was standing by his side, her little hand resting on his.

'It's OK Mr Foster, don't worry, my Daddy will make you better,' she said standing on tiptoe hugging him. As she removed her little arms from around his neck she gave him a kiss on his hollow cheek.

Immediately, unaware of the impact her moment of compassion had made, she ran off join her friends.

However, the little girl's touch had a devastating effect on Geoffery. Somehow he stopped himself from wailing like a baby. But as the tears of self-pity flowed, he bowed his head to hide them. He hadn't been hugged for a long time. The only touching of his failing body had been by the impersonal medical inspection by a series of health professionals. Oh how he longed for Nadine to hold him as she used to, just to cuddle him to her soft perfect body,.

'Ahh isn't she a little darling,' said Helen proudly, 'Compassionate, just like her Dad'.

Andy, ever vigilant, spotted the effect on Geoffery and to save his embarrassment he pushed the wheelchair to the front of the group leading them quickly back to the car.

'Come on let's get to the pub before those sandwiches get too curly,' he said trying to brush aside the drama.

As they got closer to the car Geoffery heard Amy being asked by her five year old cousin if he was going to die?

'No of course not, my Daddy will make him better,' Amy said innocently. 'Come on let's catch Uncle John.' They dashed off; party frocks billowing, leaving Andy to help Geoffery into his car.

'Of course I'm going to die,' Geoffery thought, 'but not before I've sorted out a few things. What was that George Elliot saying? It's never too late to be what you might have been. Watch this space,' he said, positively, under his breath.

PART TWO

Quest and Challenges

Chapter Eighteen

Monday September 22nd – Sunset count 22

'It was a lovely christening yesterday, thank you for inviting me. I'm sorry about…you know, the…my…problem. I hope I didn't spoil your day,' Geoffery said awkwardly.

'It was a pleasure to have you there, and no, the church thing didn't upset anything. I'm so grateful for the loan of your car,' Andy reassured him.

'I've been thinking about things.'

'Oh?'

'I am going to get my solicitors to track down my Godsons,' Geoffery announced, as they walked slowly towards the day room.

'Really, that's good. Why do you want to find them?' quizzed Andy.

'I just thought it would be nice to find out something about them as I haven't seen them for years.'

'Sounds like a good idea,' Andy agreed.

'I suppose, if I'm honest, I've got a bit of a guilty conscience,' Geoffery confessed.

'About what?' Andy asked, puzzled.

'If I analyse it, the reasons seem pretty pathetic.'

'Why?'

'Well my business life has prevented me from fulfilling my Godparent duties. You know the *help and guidance* thing. And so I thought I'd make up for lost time. What do you think? I value your opinion.'

'Depends what that involves. I wouldn't advise that you chase around the country after them. You need to look after yourself.'

'You mean just keeping myself ticking over for a bit longer? No, sorry, I need to have something to focus on and I think this will make life here more interesting,' Geoffery said enthusiastically. 'Yesterday's incident was a timely reminder of my frailty.'

'Well, yes I understand your reasoning, but I'm just suggesting you pace yourself, that's all.'

'In the past, my life has been very business-focused and now I've got a chance, while I can, to think of people rather than making money. If I was to compare myself against you and the way you conduct your life, it reminds me of how self-centered I have been,' Geoffery confessed.

'But our lives are so very different, we're poles apart,' Andy said, flattered that anybody should envy his life.

'True, my money has bought me a lot of material things but I've never had true friendship. Whereas you've got a different perspective on life and it appears that your love of humanity attracts friends.'

'Love of humanity! I'm not sure everybody would see it that way,' laughed Andy.

'I don't think it's too late to show my Godsons, even after all these years, that I can help them do you?' Geoffery continued, his eyes gleaming with purpose. 'Perhaps ease their financial burdens.'

'Oh, is that what you mean by helping them, giving them a legacy.'

'What's wrong with that?' Geoffery stopped and looked at Andy.

'I'm sorry. I'm speaking out of turn,' Andy said quickly.

'No Andy, please carry on, I value your advice. I'm not terribly good at this benevolence thing.'

'Are you just going to buy yourself into their lives? Is that your intention?' Andy asked earnestly.

'Well I'm not that far removed from reality to know that everybody could do with a windfall, a surprise stroke of luck.'

'OK, perhaps I'm being naive, but how is this going to help you fulfill your intentions as a Godparent?'

'Well I'm sure they'll have debts, things that they want; A new house, a holiday, a boat. I'll be helping them.'

'Sorry to be blunt, but will this ease your conscience?'

'Conscience money! What's the matter with that anyway?' said Geoffery surprised that his good intentions were being questioned.

'If it makes you feel better. I'm sure your gesture will make them very happy.'

'Right that's what I'll do then,' said Geoffery ruffled.

'OK, fine.' Andy could detect Geoffery's growing tension and decided a change of topic might help.

'What did you want for your dinner today?'

'I'll have the soup and...So what else could I do?' said Geoffery seeking further clarification.

'Sorry, I shouldn't interfere. They're your Godsons.'

'Yes, yes that's right. My Godsons,' said Geoffery defiantly.

'What would you like for your main course? I understand the chicken chasseur is very nice.'

'Yes, I'll have some of that, if you say so.'

'And your sweet?'

'Rice pudding,' said Geoffery still niggled by having his good deed proposals questioned.

'Come on then Mr Humanitarian, you're the one who has been accumulating points on your Pearly Gates privilege card. Help me out here,' Geoffery pleaded.

'Sorry!' said an amazed Andy. 'I think we'd better continue this discussion at another time. You're clearly still suffering from the effects of yesterday's overdose.'

'Look, I don't even have a church loyalty card to start with,' Geoffery said, uncomfortably. 'I suppose, the bottom line is, I'm just trying to make up for things I should have done.'

'It's not unusual for people at your stage of illness to look for a way of seeking spiritual peace,' Andy added.

'You must think me a hypocrite. I expect you see a lot of your patients looking for ways to rectify past misdeeds, even turn to religion?'

'It's perfectly understandable,' Andy said sympathetically. 'But I don't think you can suddenly turn it on. It's a life style thing. At least that's the way I've always thought about it.'

'So you're saying I've left it too late?'

'No. I'm not saying that. Sorry, this is getting a bit heavy for me. I'm not a great theological thinker. I don't know whether there's a god or a heaven or hell. All I know is that it feels right to treat people with respect, to help them in whatever way I can, to help make their life enjoyable,' Andy explained passionately.

'Right then, I reckon that's what I'll do for my Godsons. Make their lives enjoyable. I can still do that, even if it is many years since I last saw them.'

'You are probably right, please ignore my scepticism.'

'I can see you're quite passionate about the people thing. Obviously, or you wouldn't be doing this job.'

'Please don't make me out to be some kind of Saint, because I'm not. I have my faults and failings just like everybody else. I do this job because I need to clothe and feed my family, not because I'm on an evangelical mission. I just happen to like doing it. If I can help improve people's quality of life in their final few days, provide them with some dignity when they are at their lowest, then that's a bonus.'

'OK, message received. I didn't mean to put you on the spot. But will you help me?'

'Help you? To do what exactly?'

'Help me to find a way to help my Godsons without just throwing money at them.'

'I'm not sure,' said Andy reluctantly.

'But you were the one who was telling me I was going to do it all wrong and now you...'

'I'm sorry but I haven't got time, I lead a pretty full life as it is, what with the kids and the Scouts and...'

'OK, I'll employ you full time then. How about 4K a month and...'

'Four thousand pounds! Andy stared at him open mouthed.

'Yes, what do you say?'

'Sorry I need to get your meal choice to the chef,' Andy said, turning on his heel and heading towards the door.

'What! Where are you going? Geoffery said surprised.' I didn't mean to insult you. Isn't it enough? OK, how about 5K and expenses?'

Andy left the room without further comment, closing the door quietly behind him.

'Now what did I say?' Geoffery was perplexed. 'Either he's a cool negotiator or I've touched a raw nerve,' he thought.

Annoyed at the rebuff, Geoffery petulantly threw his papers on the floor. 'I can't do right for doing wrong. Bollocks, why bother,' he muttered. 'Who does he think he is anyway, throwing my generosity in my face?' Geoffery continued, rattled at Andy's apparent rudeness. 'I'll find a way to make him change his mind. There are many ways to skin a cat,' Geoffery said, reaching for his mobile.

Chapter Nineteen

Andy opened his front door and lifted his bicycle into the hallway; he was hot and sweaty from his ride home.

'Evening, love,' Helen called from the kitchen. 'Tea will be ready in about another thirty minutes. Sorry it's delayed, only I met Sarah in town and we had a good old gossip.'

'I'm hungry now, can we get some chips?' Andy asked, unbuckling his helmet and putting it on the coat hook.

'No I'm doing us a proper meal. You need to watch your weight,' Helen instructed.

'This bloody cycling will do that for me. I'm knackered and that traffic,' Andy replied irritably.

'How was your day?' Helen asked, putting a saucepan onto the cooker.

'It was OK,' Andy said unconvincingly.

'Oh dear, what's upset you?'

'Oh, nothing!'

'Well it doesn't sound like nothing. Have you lost a patient?

'No.'

'So what's brought this on?'

'Nothing!'

'Come on, we've been married long enough now for me to know when there's something up. What is it?'

'Stop interrogating me, will you? I'm going to have a shower,' Andy called, as he ran upstairs.

'Oh dear, we are in a mood. I wonder what's brought this hissy fit on,' Helen mused as she continued with the meal preparation.

Andy joined Helen later at the meal table after his shower.

'So, are you going to tell me what's up or are we going to have a Mr Grumpy all evening?'

'Nothing, I'm just tired that's all,' said Andy sitting down at the table picking up his cutlery.

'While you're in a bad mood, you might be interested in the bill from the garage,' Helen advised. 'The car is going to cost £1500 It needs a new engine; something to do with a broken cam belt and bent valves.'

'Oh great, that's all I need.'

'Oh and I see the stair carpet is starting to wear through. That will have a hole in it soon and it will be dangerous, so we'll need to change that too.'

'Where the hell are we going to get money like that from?' Andy said, slamming his cutlery down.

'It's not my fault. I wasn't driving the car when it broke. I'll just have to get a job in the evenings that's all, if we're ever going to replace the car,' replied Helen.

Andy stood up and started to move away from the table.

'Now where are you going?'

'It's Scout night.'

'You've got time to eat your tea. Now sit down. You're not being a good example to Amy. More importantly, you tell me what's wrong. You can't expose those kids to your miserable face. Now what is it?' she demanded.

Andy sat down heavily at the table.

'Mr Foster has offered me a job.'

'And you're upset that a millionaire has offered you a job! That's brilliant. What is it?'

'Oh he wants me to help him do something for his Godsons.'

'His Godsons?'

'Yes.'

'Such as?'

'He doesn't know. That's why he wants me to help.'

'Why you? He could afford to buy anybody's services.'

'I don't know. He says I'm more in touch with people than he is.'

'Well, he's not wrong there. That's a nice compliment. You should be pleased that he recognises it.'

'Yeah but if I accepted it, I'd have to give up my job at the hospice. Who would look after Mr Jones and Mrs Smith?' asked Andy plaintively.

'That's not your worry. That's up to the hospice to replace you,' said Helen forcibly.

'But I'm a nurse. I don't know anything else'.

'So, in your deliberations you've obviously thought about the financial implications as well.' said Helen, wanting to know more. 'What sort of salary is he talking about?'

'That's another thing; these people think that by throwing money around they can solve everything.'

'Well it would certainly help our problem.'

'I've got principles,' Andy replied, looking at his wife hoping to see some understanding in her eyes.

'You've got bills too and a family to feed. How much was he going to pay you?

'Fifty to Sixty thousand pounds a year.'

'Fifty to Sixty thousand pounds a year,' Helen echoed incredibly. 'What the hell are you doing turning that down? You should be ripping the cheque out of his hands.'

'Look, I love my job. But look at his life expectancy. Well what happens when he dies? My place at the hospice would be filled and there's so much unemployment. I can't take the risk,' Andy pointed out.

'What are you always telling the kids at Scouts? Life is full of opportunities, seize the day. Isn't that what you say?' Helen reminded him.

'Yeah, but this is different.'

'Yes it's a chance in a lifetime, an opportunity to get us out of debt, improve our life, for the kids, for us.'

'I'm not sure.'

'Andy, wake up. You can't lose this chance. You didn't have any problems using his car for the christening, did you?'

'Ah, but that was different.'

'How was it? You were using his wealth then.'

'But I was going to take him out anyway.'

'Now you're splitting hairs, justifying your actions, We benefited from his money.'

'Look we shouldn't even be discussing it. I'm not going to do it and that's final.' Andy said firmly. 'Now I need to go. The kids will be causing chaos outside the hut. You know what the neighbours are like.'

Chapter Twenty

Tuesday September 23rd – Sunset count 23

Geoffery's employment offer and their mounting bills gave Andy a disturbed night. He couldn't stop his hectic brain from constantly running through Helen's accusations of failing his family or the possibilities if he accepted the offer. Was he right to stand by his principles? After tossing and turning for several hours, finally, at three am, his tired mind gave into merciful sleep.

It seemed like barely seconds that he had been asleep when a continuous ringing woke him up with a start. Someone was ringing their door bell, followed by frantic hammering on the door.

'What the?' he muttered through sleep dried lips.

The noise woke Helen too. They both sat bolt upright in bed.

'Whoever is that likely to be at this time of night?' she quizzed.

'Don't know,' shouted Andy, running downstairs pulling on a dressing gown.

'Be careful Andy.'

Helen followed him to the top of the stairs apprehensive of what he would reveal behind the door.

As Andy opened it he was confronted by Ben who was clearly distraught. He was breathing heavily, his face dirty and sweaty. 'Ben, what the…'

'Andy, Andy, quick. It's the hut,' he shouted urgently.

'What about it?' Andy asked perplexed.

'The hut's on fire, come quick,' he urged.

'Oh no! Have you called the fire service?'

'Yes, they're on their way. But I think it's too late. All our stuff's gone. I tried to put it out but…'

Ben turned on his heel closely followed by Andy and they ran towards the hut.

As they got closer Andy could see the flames reflected off the column of smoke. Behind him he heard the distinctive sound of the heavy Fire Engine making its way through the estate.

A group of neighbours were standing around helplessly watching the terrapin building being devoured by the flames.

'I told him it would end like this on this estate,' Andy heard them say as he ran through the small group.

'I'm sorry,' Ben said looking at the flames. 'I did try to put it out. But it spread so fast.'

'So long as you're alright, that's the important thing,' Andy said, putting a comforting hand on Ben's shoulder. 'You were obviously sleeping in there tonight then?'

'Yeah, but I didn't start it,' Ben said defensively.

'I'm not suggesting that you did,' Andy replied quickly. 'I'm just glad you're safe that's all. Whoever did this wants stringing up.'

'I didn't see anyone.'

'Did you cook anything tonight for your tea?'

'No.'

'Problems at home again then?'

'Yeah. Mum's still knocking around with the same bloke that kicked me out when he ripped his trousers on my bike. So I don't even hang around these days.'

'I'm sorry to hear that, but what are you going to do tonight now? What about your Grandad?'

'No, he's not very well. Oh shit, now what am I going to do?'

'You'd better come home with me tonight and sleep on the settee and we'll sort something out in the morning.'

Andy and Ben were the last to leave the smoldering twisted skeleton of the hut. All his hard work turned into ashes. Years of work gone up in smoke. Andy was gutted.

'Now what would he do for future Scout Troop meetings. Just another worry to add on top of everything else,' he thought tiredly.

Chapter Twenty One

Wednesday September 24th – Sunset count 24

Andy brought Geoffery's breakfast in the following day looking very depressed.

'Morning Andy, you look a bit glum this morning, not like you. If you're still feeling upset about yesterday, I'm sorry. We won't mention it again.'

'Morning,' Andy said putting the breakfast tray down. 'No. It's not that. We had a bit of a fire at the Scout Hut last night.'

'What a campfire?'

'No, I'm afraid the hut burnt down.'

'Oh I'm sorry to hear that,' replied Geoffery sympathetically. 'Much damage?'

'Totally destroyed I'm afraid, along with some car engines the kids were working on.'

'Insurance job then is it?' Geoffery explored.

'No I'm afraid that the 50p subs we charge the kids wouldn't cover the cost of getting insurance. The hut was a site hut, left behind by some builders when they were renovating the estate. I managed to scrounge it off them.'

'Oh dear, what are you going to do then?' asked Geoffery, trying to sound concerned.

'Don't know. The trouble is, the kids won't have anywhere to go and they'll be up to mischief in no time.'

'Can I help?' asked Geoffery.

'Do you know anybody in the building trade that might have an old hut we could scrounge?'

'Sorry, I've got no local contacts around here anymore.'

'Yes, of course not. No, well never mind. I'm sure something will turn up,' Andy said with false optimism.

'How about I donate something to your Scouts instead?' said Geoffery.

'That would be very helpful, but...'

'But I know, you shouldn't even be considering it. Well you're the one wondering what the kids will get up to.'

'Yes I know but....'

'But nothing, I am prepared to make a donation to help out.'

'That's very generous of you. It's likely to cost several hundreds of pounds to find a replacement.'

'Well how much do you need?'

'Well actually there's not much in the bank account if I'm honest.'

'Perhaps we should start with a new hut then,' Geoffery proposed.

'A new hut! Well that would be nice, but fundraising is not my thing and the kids' parents aren't very supportive either, so it will take forever to raise the money for a new hut.'

'Who said anything about having to raise funds?'

'You don't mean you would...'

'Buy it? Yes of course.'

'No, I couldn't possibly accept.'

'Why not, it's for your young people isn't it?'

'Yes but...'

'Don't look a gift horse in the mouth.'

'Well, are you sure?'

'I wouldn't have offered if I hadn't meant it,' confirmed Geoffery.

'Well, yes please. That's more than I could have expected in my wildest dreams.' Andy beamed.

'So, you can forget about fundraising and continue to focus on doing things directly with the kids.' Geoffery reiterated, feeling smug.

'Thank you so much. That's brilliant.' Andy felt like hugging his benefactor, but thought better of it.

'You'll have to tell me the size and type of building you want etc. and I'll arrange to get it delivered. When do you want it?'

'Well I suppose the sooner the better.'

'How about two to three weeks, is that soon enough?'

'That would be wonderful if you could make it happen that quickly,' Andy said happily.

'I'll see what I can do.'

'Thanks, I'll make sure the site is cleared. The kids will be over the moon when they hear, thanks so much,' Andy said, overjoyed.

'Umm, have you thought any more about my offer for helping me find my Godsons?' Geoffery asked, immediately seeking to capitalize on Andy's euphoria and knowing that he would want to repay the other's kindness.

'Yes, Helen and I have talked it through.'

'And?' Geoffery quizzed.

'Please hear me out before you say anything. I know you've been very kind about the hut and well, I'm a nurse. I care for people. I don't have any administration skills that I believe can help you. I'd be taking your money under false pretences if I agreed to help you.'

'There you go again putting yourself down. You'd be my full time nurse but you'd also be giving me some guidance that's all,' explained Geoffery.

'Well would you consider an alternative suggestion?'

'OK, what is it?' said Geoffery curiously.

'That I work for you part time,' Andy said hesitantly, feeling ill at ease, hoping that he hadn't jeopardised Geoffery's generous offer for a new Scout Hut.

'Part Time, Mmm, would that work though?' Geoffery said mulling over the suggestion.

'Yes, so I carry on working here and...'

'I'm not sure. As you can appreciate, with the time I've got left, there's a bit of urgency required,' interrupted Geoffery.

'That's another of my concerns,' added Andy.

'Of course I understand that, but I'd make sure you and the family would be well looked after... When I've gone.'

'No, I've decided,' Andy continued firmly. 'I will help you on a part time basis or not at all. That way it won't interfere with my care of other patients either.'

'You're a principled individual aren't you? However, I respect you for that,' Geoffery said, conceding. 'OK, it's a deal then. You help me and I'll help you.'

'The cat was well and truly skinned,' Geoffery thought smugly. He knew he would get his own way eventually. He usually did.

Chapter Twenty Two

Friday September 26th – Sunset count 26

A few days later there was a flurry of activity with a series of Couriers bringing parcels and letters to Geoffery. His spirits were high as he called Andy into his room for a meeting.

'I've got the details of all three Godsons now,' said Geoffery excitedly, laying three large folders on his bed. 'It includes photographs, details of their domestic arrangements, current occupation etc. although only one of them is in employment.'

'How did you get all this stuff so quickly?' asked an incredulous Andy, gazing at the array of documents.

'My solicitors employ several Private Investigators. They do all the leg work, mostly former Policemen. They still have contacts within the force. You'd be surprised what big brother already knows about us.'

'Oh I see,' said Andy, looking at the pile of folders spreading across the sheets.

'So where do you think we should start?' asked Geoffery buoyed with a new sense of purpose.

'Don't you think it would be a good idea to actually meet them in person?' Andy suggested.

'Really, what for? I'm not sure I have the time or energy,' Geoffery said.

'Sorry, but I would have thought talking to them face to face would be the first step, otherwise how will you know how you can help them, if indeed they need help.'

'Well, judging by these reports, they all need help, I can assure you.'

'So how do you intend to help them?'

'Well there's only one who has some element of financial stability. The others definitely could do with an injection of finance.'

'So you're going to buy yourself into their life after all.'

'If that's what I need to do, yes. I don't have time to do anything clever, to sow seeds and wait for them to germinate. I want to see quick results and if by injecting money into their lives it will give some instant improvements, then that's the obvious answer.'

'OK, it's your money.'

'And that's what I'll do,' Geoffery said forcefully.

'Why don't you arrange to meet with them first?' Andy persisted.

'I still don't think it's necessary, I have all the facts here. How will that help?'

'Well you can't suddenly walk into their life after all these years. You're a virtual stranger to them,' said an incredulous Andy.

'Mmm, well perhaps you're right,' said Geoffery reluctantly. 'See, that's why I need your help. You understand people.'

Andy picked up a photograph from one of the folders. The picture was of a 'down and out' sitting on a park bench. The man had obviously spotted the photographer and was giving an angry Vee sign to the camera. His eyes were red rimmed and blood shot. He had long greasy hair, a long and matted beard and was wearing a filthy overcoat over what appeared to be filthy grey baggy jogging bottoms. On the pavement surrounding the bench were several empty cider bottles.

'This one is probably the worse shock for me,' admitted Geoffery, taking the photograph from Andy and staring at it. 'This was the lad who was a millionaire at eight. His parents, my friends, were killed in a plane crash. His name is James Charles. Like a lot of their friends I was there for him when his parents died but my life got in the way and I lost touch with him. I tried to help in the early days and we talked on the phone once after he'd left school about a business deal about fire damaged stock...nothing else,' Geoffery confessed, slumping back into his chair.

'Well, if he is your Godson, he certainly could do with your help. Bit of a sorry state isn't he?'

'The last time I saw him, his little eyes were red from crying for his parents and now look at him. He's obviously become a wino.'

'Are you sure it's him?'

'Yes, sadly that's him alright. They found him by his Police records by all accounts.'

Andy selected another photograph from a second folder and studied it for a moment.

'Well, he looks frightened to death. Whatever is going on here?'

'This is Rupert Screen, my nephew. He's an IT man, so he at least is doing well for himself,' advised Geoffery.

'And the woman? Is that his wife?' asked Andy.

'The sour faced one? Yes, she looks like she's giving him a right roasting doesn't it? Face like the backside of a bus,' added Geoffery. 'Obviously has a poor choice in women.'

The third photograph was of a fat man being pushed along in a wheelchair by a slight, grey haired woman.

'This is Tim Springfield, another one whom I could have helped by the look of it. Apparently underneath those trousers are two artificial legs,' explained Geoffery quietly.

'And who is the harassed woman pushing him?'

'That's a lady I know very well. The lovely Kay; she and I used to be...close. I still have a soft spot for her. Although, she's aged beyond her years.'

'So that's the three of them. My Godsons,' he said, looking at Andy. 'I wonder if their lives would have been any different if I'd been around as they grew up. I guess we'll never know.'

'No point fretting over what might have been. Put your energies into what you can still do for them,' Andy counselled.

'So, what do you think we should do then, if you're not keen on me just sending them a cheque?'

'I still think you need to meet them all.'

'OK, all together or individually?' Geoffery asked, looking to Andy for an option.

'Do they know of each other's existence? '

'Not that I'm aware of.'

'I'm still not clear of your intentions though,' Andy said, hoping to get a clearer idea of his role in Geoffery's plans.

'Neither am I,' admitted Geoffery.

'You don't make life easy do you? OK, then I suggest you see each one individually and take if from there,' advised Andy. 'Which one would you like to see first?'

'Let's track James down and get him off the streets. At least the other two have got a fixed abode,' proposed Geoffery.

'OK, where is he?

'London.'

'Do you think you'll be fit enough to travel that far?' quizzed Andy concerned.

'Yes I think so.'

'Mmm I'm not so sure. I notice you appear to get exhausted very quickly these days.'

'I'll be OK,' Geoffery said unconvincingly.

'Well, I suppose we could get a private ambulance so you could at least rest on the journey there,' Andy suggested.

'On the other hand I could always get the Investigators to bring him here,' Geoffery proposed.

'Do you think he'd get in a car with strangers, and allow himself to be driven a hundred miles, to see somebody he hasn't seen for years or probably can't even remember?'

'No probably not,' Geoffery agreed, accepting Andy's point.

'Would it be helpful if I went to London and spoke to him first, perhaps persuade him to come here. What do you think?' Andy suggested.

As if to reinforce the fragility of Geoffery's worsening health he deposited his breakfast into a sick tray that Andy deftly materialised and positioned under Geoffery's chin.

'I guess that answers that,' Andy said. 'I'll get you another anti sickness tablet,' he said purposefully and left the room.

Chapter Twenty Three

Tuesday September 30th – Sunset count 30

Andy met the former policeman at the prearranged rendezvous at the exit of the Russell Square underground car park.

The investigator was portly, several stone overweight, like a lot of policemen who had spent too many hours on surveillance and not enough in the gym. The 'number one' haircut made Steve look menacing, like a night club bouncer.

'You must be Andy,' said the investigator, stretching out a hand.

'Yes, pleased to meet you,' Andy said, shaking the proffered huge hand, feeling a little unnerved as Steve looked him straight in the eye as if doing an instant character assessment.

'I spotted the Mercedes as soon as you turned in. Nice motor. How was your journey?'

'This rush hour traffic is awful,' said Andy glad to be out of the mayhem. 'They all drive like maniacs around here. No politeness on the road'.

The thought of driving in London had petrified Andy. He had wanted to travel by train but a drivers' strike had thwarted his plans. Geoffery's impatient frustration and worsening condition had got Andy to reluctantly agree to take Geoffery's car. The assistance of the car's sat nav finally persuaded Andy to give it a go.

'You soon get used to it. You've just got to go for it round here, not like driving in the sticks is it? No tractors here boy,' he said, in a mock country yokel accent.

Andy ignored the inference.

The doorway where they stood reeked of stale urine. 'In my trade I have to deal with a lot of unsavoury smells, but this is gross. Can we move somewhere else?' Andy said, already walking away.

'Just one of the many drunks piss houses I'm afraid. They stagger out of the pubs, urinate here and get into their cars and drive home. I'm surprised there aren't many more deaths on the road the way they abuse themselves.'

'Talking about people abusing themselves, where do we find James?' said Andy cutting to the chase.

'Well normally at this time of day he's just tucking into his next bottle of White Diamond. Depends on how much he's managed to beg or whether he's been to A & E for stitching up.'

'Stitching?' asked Andy puzzled.

'Yes either fallen over blind drunk or been beaten up by somebody.'

'Not much of a life is it?' said Andy thinking this was a world apart from his own home comforts.

'It's the only one he knows.'

'How did you find him? London is massive?'

'I've still got my contacts in the Met. Police. Once you know the way they are, it's all pretty predictable. They normally keep to their own territory.'

'Oh!'

'It's down this way.'

They set off down Southampton Row avoiding the line of hemorrhaging black plastic rubbish bags that stained the cracked, uneven paving stones.

Although it was just a short walk from the car park, Andy already felt uncomfortable, threatened in these unfamiliar surroundings. Having the former policeman with him at least helped.

'How do you put up with the noise of all this traffic?' he said, shouting over the constant roar. 'The streets are filthy, choked by people, constant traffic noise, and smelly exhaust fumes. Why would anybody in their right mind want to live here instead of the countryside?'

'You just get used to it,' the other replied. 'It's got a buzz to it, difficult to explain really.'

'Tell you what though, I'm dying for a coffee,' Andy said, hoping to get some respite from the noisy environment. 'Do you know anywhere around here?'

'Here, look. It's not quite Starbucks but it does a reasonable brew and the cakes are pretty tasty too.'

Steve led them into a dingy looking café. Andy hesitated on the threshold as he took in the shabby interior. The place looked like a breeding ground for Salmonella.

Every alarm bell of his professional hygiene standards screamed danger. Nevertheless he still followed Steve in.

'How do you like your coffee?'

'Black please.'

The service was quick, but served by a sour faced woman who had obviously eaten too many of her own cakes. They found a small table in the back of the coffee shop. Uncleared cups littered the stained, chipped plastic table top. Pushing them aside, the Private Investigator took out some photographs from his lightweight jacket and handed them to Andy.

'Here's your man,' he said. 'James Charles, known locally as the '*Lord.*' cos he talks posh.'

'Lord Jim of the park bench, eh!' Andy said reflectively, thumbing through the photos. 'He looks a sight doesn't he?'

'If you don't mind me asking, what's this all about?' asked the former Policeman gazing over his coffee cup.

'Mr Foster has asked me to talk to James to see if he will come back to Cheltenham and meet him. He'd like to help him. Get him off the streets.'

'Pardon me for being sceptical but thirty five years in the police force tells there's more to this than that. People don't suddenly want to make contact with a 'down and out' for no good reason, just to offer help,' said Steve suspiciously.

'It's difficult to explain,' said Andy, feeling uncomfortable at that questioning.

'Go on, I'm all ears,' said Steve sitting up.

Andy explained as best as he could about Geoffery's crisis of conscience to the attentive investigator.

'Oh well, anytime he wants to give me any help or guidance, he's more than welcome,' Steve said astonished. 'That's a new one on me.'

'Do you think you can take me to him now please?' Andy said, putting his empty cup down, keen to leave the scruffy cafe. 'I'll pay,' he said as they got to the counter, 'I'm on expenses,' he said excitedly.

Emerging back into the noisy London street, Andy wondered how he'd let Geoffery talk him in to doing this. Perhaps kidnapping James by a streetwise Steve might have been a better answer after all.

'We'll start in his usual haunt and wander around from there,' suggested the Investigator.

Chapter Twenty Four

As the two made their way down Southampton Row, Andy was keen to make small talk to distract him from the shabby surroundings and mismatch of grubby looking shop fronts.

'How did you actually find where he was?'

'Former colleagues, still in the force with access to the Police National Computer system, tracked him down from his criminal records. He'd used his real name and gave his dwellings as the park just around the corner from here.'

'I suppose he had nothing to hide.'

As they approached a set of traffic lights Andy could see the small tree lined park. Across the other side of the road, on the same bench that he recognised from the first picture he had seen, sat the same dishevelled character.

'Right, there's your man,' Steve said, pointing across the park to James. Unless you want me to stay, I've got stuff to do.'

'To be honest, I could do with a moral prop,' Andy said, embarrassed at displaying his fears.

'Yeah, OK, um, no problem. I'll hang around here then and keep an eye on you. He'll run a mile if he sees me otherwise.'

'OK thanks.'

Andy made his way across the surprisingly litter free park until he stood in front of James.

'Excuse me, are you James Charles?' he asked hesitantly.

'And pray, what's it to do with you, if I am?' the clipped voice responded.

Although already aware of Lord Jim's nickname, Andy found difficulty in associating the posh voice with the scruffy character who spoke.

'Who are you? Another one of those Celebrity on the streets TV researchers? Looking for some mug to make a fool of on your TV programme?'

Before Andy could respond, the other continued, his words slightly slurred.

'Well if you are, you can bugger off. We've had your sorts around here before. You make a load of promises to improve our living conditions; do your filming, bugger off and forget us and your promises.'

'Well no I'm...' Andy tried to say.

'Oh of course you'll be a social services do-gooder then,' James interrupted. 'Who's your minder?'

'Look I've come from Cheltenham...'

'Ah Cheltenham, sweet gentle Cheltenham. I once played cricket for the school eleven at Cheltenham College when I was a fourth former.'

'Geoffery Foster has sent me to find you,' Andy said, finally getting a word in edgeways.

'Geoffery Foster! Geoffery Foster!' James said, trying to recall the name. 'Now where do I know that name from? Oh, of course. Geoffery,' he said, digging deep into his fuddled memory. 'How is he? Still on the Monaco circuit?'

'No. Unfortunately he is no longer in Monaco; he is in a hospice near Cheltenham. But he would like to see you and possibly help you before he...While he can.'

'Wants to help me? Why after all these years would he want to help me?' James said incredulously. 'In a hospice you say. Poor old chap, but that's life isn't it? Ha, that's life,' he repeated, smiling at his inadvertent 'black' witticism. 'Bit of a mixed metaphor there eh, what?'

'Yes I'm afraid he's seriously ill and...'

'Seriously ill, bad luck that. But I've had my share of death too.'

'Yes, I know.'

'How do you know? Are you, some sort of investigator?'

'No I'm Geoffery's nurse from the hospice. He asked me to help him find you.'

'So now you've found me, you can go back to Cheltenham and tell him mission accomplished.'

'He has asked me to take you back to see him, because he can't travel very far.'

'Come back with you? Whatever for? I have a nice park bench here and lots of real friends, street friends. Forget it. Sorry, we have nothing in common anymore, not that we were that close anyway.'

'Look, this isn't the best place to discuss this. Why don't we go for a coffee?'

'Come for a coffee!' James said, savouring the idea. 'Umm, well that's a grand idea but no cafe' will let me in looking and smelling like this,' he added realistically.

'OK I'll tell you what. I'll go and get some 'take aways' and I'll be back shortly,' Andy said, trying to think of another way of establishing an empathetic relationship with Lord Jim. 'What do you like?'

'I recall I used to drink the finest Columbian coffee. But a couple of bottles of White Diamond would be better.'

'Black Coffee it is then,' Andy said, ignoring the request for more alcohol.

'Couldn't spare us a couple quid could you? Only I'm a bit short at the moment.'

Andy found some small change in his pocket and gave it to James and headed back to the waiting Steve.

'Is everything alright? Is he going to come back with you?'

'No I don't think so. I'm not sure Geoffery would want him in his car smelling like that anyway. I'm just off to get a couple of coffees. Do you want one?'

'No I'll clear off unless you want me to hang around anymore?'

'I think he'll be OK. Seems like a nice bloke underneath that layer of filth.'

After apathetic service from a local fast food shop that failed to match the concept of the name, Andy returned to the bench, with two cardboard cups of coffee, to find the bench empty. James had gone.

'Oh blast! Now where's he gone,' Andy said under his breath scanning the park.

Hoping that James would return Andy found a part on the bench that didn't bear any suspicious stains and sat down to drink his coffee thinking about what to do next.

'Well I've found him, talked to him, what more can I do?' he thought. 'Perhaps I ought to call Geoffery and report in.'

Just as he reached into his pocket for his mobile, James reappeared with a bottle of white diamond to his lips.

'You were too slow. A man could die of thirst by the time you got your act together,' he said, slurping the cider.

'I was just thinking I'd lost you. Here's your coffee if you still want it. I'm afraid it's not your Columbian though,' Andy said, giving James the carton.

Downing the last dregs from his bottle, James dropped it noisily on the ground and reached for the proffered carton of coffee. As he did so, his stained coat rode up his arm to reveal a series of nasty weeping sores.

'How did you get these?' Andy said studying the open wounds. 'They need treatment.'

'What? Oh these. They're nothing,' he said, dismissing Andy's concern. 'The yobs think its good sport to set fire to our cardboard houses and give us a good kicking as we emerge,' James said indifferently, as if he was talking about the weather.

'Look I'm a trained nurse. I'll fix these for you, but I need to go and get some stuff. Are you still going to be here when I get back?'

'Yes of course. If I've got my own Florence Nightingale, why waste time waiting in A & E. It gives me more drinking time.'

'But before I go, will you speak to Geoffery on my mobile?'

'If I must. What do I have to do?'

'I'll call him and then I'll hand the phone over, OK.'

'Go on then!'

Andy rang Geoffery's number and was answered almost immediately.

'Geoffery, I'm with James now. Yes he's OK. He won't come back with me though. Perhaps you'd like to talk to him? OK. I'll hand you over.'

At the other end Geoffery steeled himself to speak to his Godson for the first time in decades.

After explaining what James needed to do, Andy handed the phone over, making a mental note to sterilize it before he used it again himself.

'Hello James, how are you?' Geoffery said full of apprehension.

'Hello Geoffery, long time no speak Old boy,' James replied loudly. 'I'm OK, but I gather you're on your way out.'

Geoffery was taken aback by the bluntness of his words.

'I'm in a hospice yes but...'

'Your man here thinks I drink too much. He reckons I've given myself a death sentence, but I gather you're already ahead of me on that one.'

Geoffery ignored the observation on his mortality. 'Look James, I gather you're down on your luck and I'd like to help you.'

'A tanker full of white Diamond will do, so I don't have to go dry. That will do for a start.'

'You know that won't help you. I was thinking of something more practical. How about a roof over your head?'

'What, a hostel? No thank you, they're full of down and outs. They'd cut your throat soon as look at you.'

'Perhaps something that would help you 'dry out? Get you off the streets and into a clinic.'

'Dry out? Why would I want to dry out? As your man here has found out, my world's a shit place; it's the booze that keeps me sane,' James said dismissively.

'But surely anything would be better than the dangers of living on the street!' 'Dangers! Dangers! You can't tell me anything about dangers!' James became animated as he shouted down the phone. 'Your so called 'normal' world is fraught with them. Let's see now; there's the pain of rejection, the agony of desertion, the hurt of two timing deception.'

'James, I know...' Geoffery said trying to interject calmly.

James carried on getting angrier and louder, flecks of spittle spraying onto his matted beard. '...The hateful lies, the dagger of mistrust he thrust deep into my heart. The pain was unbearable. It was as if I was being dissected alive. On my street there are no beautiful creatures here anymore; No delicate emotional butterflies. No chance of broken hearts ever again. My antidote to your cruel world is the inside of a bottle.'

'But James listen...' Geoffery tried again in vain to interrupt.

As quickly as he had become angry and animated, James suddenly became calm and said to an astonished Geoffery. 'I'm sorry old chap must fly, missing out on drinking time.'

James thrust the phone at Andy and quickly scuffed his way out of the park.

'James. James, your arm,' shouted Andy at the departing figure. 'I was going to dress your arm.'

'Don't worry; the booze is a good antiseptic. It cures most things,' James shouted without turning round.

Wiping the phone subconsciously on his trousers Andy spoke to Geoffery again.

'Well I'm not sure what you said but you've frightened him off. Now he's gone.'

'Perhaps he'll think about what I've said and change his mind. Get him a mobile so we can keep in touch with him.'

'But he's gone.'

'Don't worry I'll get the investigators to track him down again and give him a Pay as you go one. At least we'll be able to keep in touch.'

'I think there are a few practical issues you should consider first though, like charging the phone, getting him to switch it on…umm, and topping up the pay as you go card.'

'Please stop being so bloody negative all the time. Have you a better solution?' Geoffery said angrily.

'No, not at the moment,' Andy said, annoyed at Geoffery's outburst and switched his phone off without saying goodbye.

'Bollocks,' said Andy to himself. 'I knew this was going to be a waste of time.'

Chapter Twenty Five

Andy jogged off in in pursuit of James, determined not to let him slip away, and soon found him emerging from a shop, clutching another bottle.

'You know you're drinking yourself to death?' Andy admonished.

'You're like a bad smell, that I can't get rid of,' James said, sidestepping him.

'I mean it.'

'Oh turn it off. At least it would be better than this life, wouldn't it?'

'It's a horrible death,' Andy said, knowledgeably.

'You can't tell me anything about it,' James said, quietly. 'My friend John used to sleep on the bench next to me. He went last week. Nice bloke. It all went wrong for him when he lost his job. They call it the redundancy domino effect. He then lost the lot, his self-respect, his wife, his home and subsequently his kids. The bitch divorced him, and even took out a court order to stop him seeing his kids. He came down here looking for work to get himself sorted. But nobody would take him on. He just lost all his dignity. But the bottle helped.'

'That's tragic,' Andy sympathised.

'We shared a bottle or two. He got ill. Eventually he started bleeding from every orifice. The doctors told him that unless he stopped drinking, he would be dead within a week. As he said to me. 'What was the point of living anyway?' So he carried on. Ignored their advice and...' James recounted, wiping a tear from his grubby cheek.

'How dreadful.'

'Next I hear, he's been picked out of the gutter and didn't make it out of A & E.'

'Don't you think that could be you, if you carry on with this life style?'

'He's in a better place. Perhaps that's where I ought to be,' said James resignedly.

'You have a choice to live. You can do something with your life and improve your miserable existence,' Andy said angrily. 'The people I look after have no choice. Life has thrown them a bad deal too, but they have no opportunity to change things. They have no appeal against their death sentence. They are terminally ill. All the best efforts of the Doctors have failed to stop the inevitable,' Andy said passionately.

'Oh don't do the guilt trip on me. It won't work,' James said, dismissing Andy's comments out of hand. 'Life hasn't actually been kind to me either.'

Determined to drive his point home, Andy continued forcefully, 'how do you think the mother of little three year old Tansin feels when she looks at her child and knows the leukemia will take her before she is four?'

'Yeah, yeah. I've heard it all before,' James said, walking away from Andy.

However, determined to make his point about the sanctity of life, Andy went after him and continued recounting his tragic anecdotes. 'Then there is John, a budding fourteen year old musician who has....'

'Enough,' James shouted, stopping. 'I know all about the hurt. The dreadful pain of losing somebody you love. My parents died when I was only eight.'

'Yes I know,' Andy said, sympathetically, recalling James's background from his briefing by Geoffery.

'Do you know what it's like to want somebody just to give you a cuddle, when you've hurt yourself? Or to tell you how clever you've been when you achieve some academic success? I don't even know what it's like to feel the love of a family.'

'Surely your guardians gave you some love?'

'My guardians were distant, emotionally detached. They did the functional parental duties, made sure I was never short of money, but never gave me any love or even a simple hug.'

'That's so sad,' Andy said; thinking of how often he cuddled his own children and also spent hours reading them stories.

'When I met Sebastian at University, he showed me thoughtfulness, affection, caring and love. We were together for five wonderful years and then...'

'Yes?' Andy said, encouraging James to open up.

'He left me. Can you imagine my hurt? It was like my heart had been ripped out.'

'No I can't. It must have been horrible.'

'His new lover gave him HIV. His gentle heart couldn't stand the treatment regime.'

'What happened?'

'He moved back home with me when his new lover threw him out. I found him dead in the bedroom when I returned from getting his medication.'

'I'm so sorry. It must have been horrendous for you?'

'That was the start of how I ended up here.'

'What about all your other friends?'

'Yeah, they helped me forget. But only while I held lavish parties with lots of booze and drugs. When the money disappeared, so did my so called 'friends'. So now you know.'

'Could Geoffery have done anything to have helped you?'

'Why would he, he never really knew me anyway.'

'On the contrary, if he had been there during your school days...'

'Come off it. He was having too good a time, making his own millions, to have bothered with a snotty nosed boarding school kid. No, he was emotionally detached from me as well.'

'Well, he wants to help you now and would like to keep in touch with you. He says I'm to buy you a Mobile phone.'

'I don't know why he's got a guilty conscience. He doesn't owe me anything,' James said forlornly.

'It's a long story. Now, let's find a phone shop and get you that mobile,' Andy said patiently. 'Come on lets go.'

Chapter Twenty Six

Geoffery had decided to take the bull by the horns and telephone Kay, the mother of his Godson, Tim Springfield. He had discovered she lived nearby in Churchup.

He listened patiently as the number rang out until finally a woman's voice answered.

'Hello, who's calling?' She said.

'Kay?'

'Yes, who's this?'

'Geoffery, Geoffery Foster.'

'Geoffery?' The line went quiet as she struggled to comprehend the name with the sound of a voice she hadn't heard for decades. 'Geoff is that really you?' she said, quietly, in surprise.

'Yes it's me Kay. Can I pop round to see you?'

'Pop round! Well, the last time I heard about you, you were in Monaco.'

'No I'm in a…a hospice near Cheltenham; It's a long story. I'll tell you later, if it's OK to come over?'

'A hospice? Oh dear!' she said, shocked. 'Well, yes, of course. Do you know where I live?'

'Yes, don't worry. I'll be there shortly, if that's convenient?'

'Yes, um, that's fine,' she said looking around, quickly assessing the tidiness of the house.

Kay was amazed to hear from Geoffery after so many years. It was a bolt from the blue. They had been so close once and then he started making money and his life had changed. Their relationship had broken down when he attracted other women to his increasing luxuriant life style. 'Bees around a honey pot,' she recalled.

As Andy had taken the Mercedes to London, Geoffery hired a taxi to take him to Kay's small house. He didn't know what sort of reception to expect, so he asked the Taxi driver to wait. It would be so strange seeing her after those years. The investigators photographs showed that she had let herself go.

After a brief journey, the taxi pulled up outside a neat semidetached, single storey house. Geoffery looked at the red bricked dwelling as the Taxi driver opened the door and helped him out. Thoughtfully he then opened the gate into Kay's property.

'Obviously looking for a big tip,' Geoffery thought cynically.

As Geoffery made his way slowly along the short tarmac path towards the front door, he noted changes that had been made to the property for disabled access. The ramp instead of steps; the large tubular steel handrails either side of the path and the grab handles bolted to the wall either side of the widened front door. Aids installed to ease Tim's daily life, he reasoned.

The door opened shortly after he had taken his thumb off the bell push. Kay stood in front of him. She didn't have the advantage of already knowing the effect of the years on Geoffery. Her face questioned the visitor. Then her eyes latched on to his and she knew. The gaunt old man in front of her was Geoffery. It was a shock.

'Geoffery,' she said, stepping forward and giving him a gentle kiss on the cheek. 'You haven't changed at all,' she lied.

'Kay, it's so good to see you,' Geoffery said, thickly. 'It must be over thirty years.'

Kay led the way into a sparsely furnished room. The furniture it did contain, was widely spaced. Tim was sitting at a games console, intent on his game.

'He was even fatter in real life than his pictures indicated,' thought Geoffery.

'Tim, this is Mr Foster,' said Kay, introducing Geoffery.

'Yeah,' grunted Tim, still focused on his game.

'Hello Tim. Pleased to meet you,' said Geoffery, going over to the hunched figure, his hand outstretched.

'Yeah,' Tim said, his eyes still riveted to the screen His fingers deftly working a multifunction controller.

Embarrassed at not getting a greeting from Tim, Geoffery dropped his attempted handshake.

'Tim, I think we'd better turn that off while Mr Foster is here, don't you?' asked Kay, gently.

'Can't. I'm in the middle of a game. I'm winning,' said Tim, engrossed.

'Mr Foster has come to see us both so come on, switch it off please,' said Kay, pleadingly.

'Now look. I've lost a life, stupid woman,' he said angrily.

Please, just for a second. It's rude to ignore guests.'

'He's your guest. Go somewhere else if you want to chat. Shit, now I've lost another life, That's your fault, you idiot.'

Kay made her way to the switch on the wall.

'Don't you dare touch that,' warned Tim vehemently.

'Well, stop playing for a while and talk to Mr Foster,' she pleaded.

'No, it's alright honest,' interjected Geoffery, surprised at Tim's rudeness.

'Now look, I've lost the game and my world standing. Thanks for nothing, you stupid bitch.'

Angry, Tim powered his wheelchair out of the room.

'Tim, come back.'

'Piss off,' he said, as he disappeared into the hallway.

'Geoffery, I'm sorry. He's not normally like that. Please sit down, you look very tired,' she said indicating the settee.

'Thanks. I will,' Geoffery said, lowering himself slowly on to the worn two seater. Kay sat next to him in a lounge chair.

'Tim's obviously not well,' said Kay, defensively.

'On the contrary,' thought Geoffery. 'This was his normal behaviour, judging by the investigator's surveillance material.'

'You shouldn't allow him to talk to you like that,' Geoffery admonished. 'That's disgraceful behaviour. You're his Mother. He should show you some respect. I might be speaking out of turn, but I think you've got a right slob there haven't you?'

'What! How dare you come back into my life and tell me what to do with my own child,' Kay countered, angrily.

'Come on, look at him,' Geoffery replied, incredulously.

'No you look at him. Where were you, when we found out he had meningitis? Where were you, when they told me they had to amputate his little legs? Where were you, when George left me because he couldn't cope with a three year old crippled son? Where were you, when Tim was being bullied and broke his heart at the hurtful names he was being called?' she demanded angrily.

'I was….'Geoffery tried to respond.

'I tell you where you were…living it up in Monaco. Screwing all the women you could get your lecherous hands on. Not giving me, or your son…I mean godson a thought,' she quickly corrected herself. 'So don't come here with your high and mighty ways, telling me I haven't brought my son up properly. I've done the best I could. I've sacrificed everything for him,' Kay continued, slumping back into her chair.

'Son? You said son!' said Geoffery, puzzled.

'What? Oh, that was my mistake. I meant Godson,' said Kay into her hands.

'Look, I know it's been tough. I'm sure you've done more than any mother should. I appreciate what you've sacrificed. But does he?' Geoffery asked, trying to placate her.

'Of course he does,' said Kay, dejectedly.

'He's obviously got a big chip on his shoulder,' Geoffery said, summarising his first impressions of Tim.

'Yes, but I'm the reason for that,' Kay said, guiltily. 'If only I'd spotted that dreadful disease earlier. Perhaps he would still have his legs. He would have had a normal life; be a different person.'

'You can't blame yourself for that,' Geoffery said, trying to placate her.

'Well I do. If I had been more…more vigilant.'

'Listen. Please,' said Geoffery, forcibly. 'The Doctors are trained to spot this sort of thing, and by the sounds of it, even they missed the early signs.'

'I am his Mother. I should have been more aware.'

'So what difference do you think it would have made, even if you had spotted it earlier?'

'He'd still have his...'

'Legs?' Geoffery said, interrupting. 'Do you really think so? Once he was unfortunate enough to get the virus, there was probably nothing that, either you or the Doctors, could have done to save them.'

'If only I'd.....' Kay whispered, distantly, her eyes filling.

'You did all you could. You saved his life. Just keep that thought in your mind.' 'Yes, but not his legs,' Kay said earnestly, looking at Geoffery. 'Not his legs.'

'You saved his life, and it looks like you've given him your own,' said Geoffery quietly.

'It was my duty,' she said emphatically.

'Duty! Duty! It was your duty to love him, and care for him. To put him into a safe environment, but then make him independent. Not to throw away your own life on a thoughtless individual who is so self-centred, that he won't even wipe his own arse.'

'That's not true he is..., does wipe....'

'You know what I mean,' Geoffery said impatiently.

'It's not that easy. He's a grown up. He's a man.'

'Exactly. So he should be acting like one.'

'I know but...'

'Kay, just take stock of things for a second. Where is your life, your independence?'

'Look, I don't know where this is leading to...' Kay said, irritably.

'It's leading to you getting your own life back.

'I have my life and I'm very....'

'Happy? Have you looked in the mirror recently?'

'What?' said Kay, shocked at the inference.

'The mirror,' repeated Geoffery. 'Your glum face. Your appearance.'

'I haven't got time to waste on putting on all that muck,' Kay said, tearfully.

'Where is that beautiful face that I once kissed? The soft silky hair that I stroked. The body that I worshipped?' Geoffery said, gently holding her hand.

'We all get old,' Kay countered, wearily. 'Look at you.'

'Old. Yes. But not dowdy,' Geoffery said harshly, trying to goad her into a self-examination.

'How dare you say things like that?' Kay said, pulling her hand away. 'You come into my house; insult me and my son…'

'I'm sorry. That was a bit cruel,' Geoffery said realising he had gone too far. 'Look, I didn't come here to upset you.'

'Well, why did you come? Is this your guilt trip before you die?' said Kay, cruelly, trying to return the hurt.

'Guilt trip! Yes I suppose it is,' Geoffery agreed. 'I'd not thought of it like that.'

'I'm sorry. I didn't mean it,' said Kay mortified at her own words. 'That was a hateful thing for me to say,' she continued apologetically, grabbing his hand, and gently sandwiching it between hers.

'No, it's alright,' he said gently. 'I have faced up to my mortality. Yes, I guess I am trying to make amends.'

'Oh, I'm sorry. I don't know what came over me,' Kay said, distraught at her insensitivity.

'Look; now about your son. If I can help you by making Tim stand on his own two feet,' Geoffery said, thoughtlessly.

'Geoffery!' chided Kay.

'I'm sorry. That was indelicate wasn't it? What I meant to say is…If I can help by getting Tim to be more independent, and consequently taking some of the strain off you. I figure I would be doing both of you a favour.'

'Why? Why would you do that? What's the point?'

'Well, you've got admit, your life isn't exactly a bunch of roses, is it?'

'No, but then my life is…'

'Don't say over. When you're staring at the scan, and the tumour is unstoppable… then you can say it's drawing to a close,' Geoffery admonished. 'You have your health. You deserve a better life. Not playing the devoted fulltime carer to an ungrateful, idle son; somebody who should be making their own way in the world.'

'I can't. It's too late.'

'No it's not. While you've got a breath in your body you can get back your self-esteem. Resurrect that fun loving, headstrong girl that I fell in love with all those years ago.'

'I don't know.'

'If you won't do it for yourself, do it for him.'

'I'll think about it,' she said, twisting her fingers nervously.

'That's my girl,' Geoffery said, feeling pleased to be helping Kay, an unexpected bonus to his visit. 'Now the other reason I'm here, and it sounds like I've arrived at the right time,' 'I plan to give your son a reason to get off his backside and prove himself.'

'OK, but, what is it?' she said, cautiously, concerned.

'I'm giving him a physical challenge. There's a big financial reward, if he completes it,' Geoffery explained, taking the letter out of his coat pocket. 'It's not going to be easy, and you'll probably have to get tough with him to ensure he trains for it.'

'That's not as simple as you make it sound,' Kay said, knowingly; already apprehensive of the anticipated uphill battle, encouraging Tim to do anything, he didn't want to do.

'When Tim emerges from his sulk, please give him this,' Geoffery said, handing Kay the sealed envelope. 'Will you do that for me? Please.'

'Yes of course,' Kay said, taking the envelope. I'm sorry about your... your problem,' she said sympathetically, looking into his eyes. 'I wish there was something I could do.'

'I'm afraid there is nothing. But thanks anyway. Now I've got my head around it, I can manage the dark thoughts. This project, doing something for my three Godsons, is helping take my mind off things,' Geoffery informed her quietly.

'I can imagine,' said Kay, gazing sadly at her former lover.

'Don't worry about any money required for his training,' he added. 'I'll see to that. If he accepts the challenge, I believe it will be good for both of you. Try and persuade him, Kay,' Geoffery said, returning her gaze.

'I'll do my best,' said Kay earnestly, wondering how she would persuade her lazy son into doing anything, other than playing games on the internet.

'Right, I'll be in touch to see how things shape up,' Geoffery said, standing. 'Later, we'll agree the next steps, hopefully, literally,' he said, giving Kay a gentle hug; which she returned.

Kay let Geoffery out through the front door, and accompanied him slowly to the waiting taxi.

As the taxi manoeuvred back into the traffic, she headed back to her front door and waved from the doorstep, unable to hold back her tears any longer.

Chapter Twenty Seven

Kay closed the front door, and leant against it heavily. It was as if she was trying to block the tidal wave of emotions, that Geoffery's visit had rekindled, from reaching her.

She thought she had steeled herself for his visit. She was going to be distant, rational and not allowing him to get to her. Instead she had been transported back to the intimate relationships of their youth. She relived his touch, his caress, the gentle lovemaking. Her mind filled with so many wonderful memories. Her heart filled with sorrow thinking about what she had missed. The visit by the spectre of her past had sent her head reeling.

However, her trip down memory lane was rudely interrupted, as Tim returned noisily into the lounge, having heard Geoffery's departure.

'What did that stupid old bastard want?' Tim demanded, belligerently.

'Tim, I won't have you using language like that, in this house,' said Kay, testing out her new no-nonsense regime.

'Well, what did he want?' Tim persisted.

'If you had stayed to listen, rather than skulking off, you'd have been part of the conversation,' she said quietly.

'So who is he?' Tim demanded, ignoring her rebuke.

'He was a close friend of mine, from years ago.'

'So, what's he doing coming round here now?'

'He wanted to see you? He's your Godfather.'

'Godfather! What like, he's in the Mob, the Mafia? He doesn't look much like Al Capone to me.'

'Don't be daft. Of course he's not.'

'So why did he want to see me?' Tim asked, curiously.

'To find out how you're getting on. Because he hasn't seen you since you were a baby.'

'Well, now he's seen me, he can sling his hook.' Tim said, picking up his game controller.

'He's, he's been away for a long time, so he's making contact with all his Godsons,' Kay added.

'Why?'

'I don't know. Perhaps he wants to make up for lost time.'

'So, what's he going to do now he's back? Give me some back dated pocket money?' Tim said cynically.

'He wants to offer you a…' Kay had difficulty vocalising Geoffery's plans for Tim. 'A challenge,' she said, feeling uncomfortable.

'A what? A challenge! What is he, some sort of game show host or something?' Tim said in disbelief.

'It's all here, in this letter,' she said, looking at the envelope, apprehensive of its contents.

'Well, come on, give it to me then,' he demanded, holding out his hand.

Kay handed him the envelope, and watched nervously as he immediately ripped it open.

'He tells me there are financial inducements,' she continued, watching her impatient son unfolding the paper, he'd removed from the envelope.

'What, so he'll give me money if I take on one of his challenges?'

'Yes. That's what he said.'

'How much?'

'I don't know. Part of his estate, I suppose!'

'What sort of estate? A country estate with a mansion and stuff?'

'No. It means all his worldly possessions. He will bequeath to you in his will.'

'What! Has he got to die first?' Tim said, disappointedly. 'That could be another thirty years.'

'No. He's terminally ill. Months, is all he's got,' she said sadly.

'That's alright then. Come on, you can guess how much it's likely to be,' he persisted excitedly.

'He's a multi-millionaire. I suppose it's likely to be several millions,' she guessed.

'Millions! Wow, I'll be rich,' he said, already dreaming of spending his inheritance.

'It would certainly pay off our debts,' Kay said, joining him dreaming about spending his expected legacy.

'Your debts. This is my money,' he said selfishly.

'Tim, I can't believe you said that. They are debts I've accrued to help you,' Kay said angrily. 'After all I've done for you. You should be ashamed of yourself.'

'Yaddy yah!' he said, disrespectfully. 'So what's the challenge? What have I got to do?'

'Just read the letter and you'll find out,' Kay said, exasperated at his procrastination.

Tim read the letter eagerly, as Kay looked on concerned.

Dear Tim,

I appreciate that you don't know me or anything about me, but I am fully aware of the challenges you must have had to undergo throughout your life due to your physical problems. However, I believe you have a lot of potential and the possibilities of a wonderful life ahead of you, if only you seize the opportunity. I am therefore setting you a challenge which, I believe, will be the making of you. If you accept the challenge and successfully walk to the top of Snowdon, Scafell Pike AND Ben Nevis (in a manner similar to the three peaks challenge) you will become a major beneficiary from my will. If you fail to accept the challenge or fail the task; my will is written in such a way to exclude you from benefitting from my estate.

I hope you consider this, life changing opportunity, seriously.

Yours Faithfully
Geoffery Foster
(Godfather)

After reading it for a few moments, Tim shouted, 'he must be bloody joking.'

'Tim!'

'He does know that I haven't got legs, does he?'

'He knows you prefer to use your wheelchair, yes,' Kay said, calmly.

'Well, the old git wants me to climb Snowdon, Scafell and Ben Nevis,' Tim told a surprised Kay.

'Let me have a look,' she said, taking the letter.

'Has he got a brain tumour? Doesn't he realise, I can't walk,' whined Tim.

'That's not true is it? You could do it, if you really set your mind to it,' she said, wondering if Geoffery really understood what he was asking Tim to undertake, after all.

'Come on, you know I can't even walk in the garden. You got my legs cut off, remember?' said Tim evilly, playing the trump card he often used to get his own way.

Although he had capitalised on her self confessed guilty conscience many times before; this dreadful accusation still cut through Kay's heart like a knife.

'That's not fair. It was the meningitis, the blood poisoning, Not me,' Kay replied anxiously, trying to recall Geoffery's advice.

'Yeah, but as you always tell me, if you'd have spotted it earlier, I'd still have my legs,' said Tim, reminding her of her own mantra of blame.

'No, that's not right. It was the disease... unpredictable,' Kay countered, pleased and surprised by her new defensive stance.

'If you'd got me to the hospital sooner,' Tim pursued, harshly.

'It wouldn't have made any difference,' Kay parried, now feeling clear about her role in his tragic illness.

'You messed my life up. It was Child cruelty,' Tim ranted, surprised that she had not already capitulated to his indictment.

'I did everything I could and have done so all your life,' she said, firmly.

'So you should. You did this to me, Tim said, slapping his shortened thigh. 'The least you could do, is to make it up to me for making my life miserable.'

'No son. You make your, our, life miserable; by continuing to blame me for your issues; instead of living with your...problem.'

'Disability. Say it! I'm a cripple because of you,' he ranted, angrily.

Tim turned his wheelchair around and stormed out of the room.

Kay started to go after him, but stopped herself. Perhaps, Geoffery was right. She had to be cruel to be kind. Her mind was in a whirl. Tim's angry response to the letter. Images of her youth, dancing before her – memories of their indiscretion at her wedding reception, over thirty seven years ago, brought back the paternity issue.

Chapter Twenty Eight

Wednesday October 1st – Sunset count 31

The day after Andy's trip to London, and Geoffery's simultaneous visit to see Kay, the pair met in Geoffery's room to update each other on their respective trips.

'I can't see any way of helping James Charles until he admits that he has a problem,' Andy counselled. 'When he recognises he is an alcoholic, then we can help him to kick the booze. Otherwise we'll get nowhere with him.'

'Yes, I understand what you're saying,' Geoffery agreed. 'But we'll just have to be persistent. I suppose the best thing to do is to keep in touch and work on him slowly. Let's give him a call now.'

'It isn't going to be easy,' Andy said, giving Geoffery the number. 'I called the mobile earlier and got no reply, although it worked OK yesterday.'

'Let's give it another try,' he said, punching the number into his own phone. After several unsuccessful attempts, somebody eventually answered it.

'James?'

'Who you want?' An eastern European voice replied.

'James Charles,' Geoffery said, taken aback by the response.

'You got wrong number. Nobody here with that name.'
'Sorry, I'll try again.'
Geoffery dialled again.
'Hello James?'
'No.'
'Did I speak to you a moment ago?'
'Yes, you got wrong number.'
'We have spoken to him on this number before.'
'Oh, you want to speak to the tramp?'
'James, Lord Jim, yes.'
'He sold me phone for couple quid. He need drink money. Said he don't need phone.'

'Damn the man,' said Geoffery hanging up. 'He's sold the phone!'

'So what are we going to do now then?' Andy asked, already guessing the answer.

'It'll need another trip to London, I'm afraid. At least this time you know where to find him.'

'Let's leave it a couple of days,' Andy said, not relishing another trip. 'Perhaps he'll have had a change of mind by then.'

Reluctantly Geoffery agreed. 'But only a couple of days,' he emphasised.

Geoffery updated Andy about his visit to see the self centred Tim, as outside a car could be heard speeding up the drive. The driver was obviously ignoring the 10mph speed signs, and hit the first speed bump, catching the exhaust, with a clatter, on landing.

'If they don't slow down, they'll ruin their suspension as well,' said Andy, interrupting the update.

Almost instantaneously they heard the sound of the car bouncing heavily over the second speed bump, and the metallic scraping as exhaust system again met tarmac.

'That'll be costly,' observed Geoffery. 'Somebody's obviously in a hurry.'

'Could be a paramedic on a call, I suppose,' said Andy. 'Although, the hospice doesn't like or encourage people dashing around at all.'

As Geoffery continued telling Andy about the reception he had got from Kay and Tim, the car could be heard scraping its way up the drive, finally coming to a squealing halt.

Shortly after, the telephone in Geoffery's room rang. Andy answered it.

Geoffery could overhear the metallic voice of the receptionist as Andy listened intently.

'No, I don't believe he is expecting anyone. Just a second, I'll ask him.'

'Are you expecting anyone?' Andy asked Geoffery.

'No,' replied Geoffery, curious about his unexpected visitor.

'There's a woman at reception, says she's got an urgent meeting with you.'

'No, I haven't arranged anything, but tell them to send her down.'

'OK, please show her down here,' relayed Andy.

Shortly after, there was a knock on the door, which immediately burst open. A middle aged woman exploded into the room, looking flushed and anxious.

'Mr Foster, Mr Geoffery Foster?' she asked, breathing heavily.

'Yes, this is Mr Foster's room,' said Andy, standing and addressing the woman.

'Geoffery, I came as soon as I received your letter,' said the woman, walking towards Geoffery and ignoring Andy. 'How are you, you poor dear?' she said, dramatically.

Geoffery looked at Andy, puzzled.

'I'm sorry. Who did you say you are?' asked Andy, blocking her way.

The woman side stepped him and dashed to Geoffery's bedside.

'Geoffery, I'm sorry to hear of your...your problem,' she said, earnestly.

'I'm sorry, but Mr Foster isn't up to visitors at the moment,' said Andy, gauging the tension she was already creating for Geoffery.

'I got your letter, and came as soon as I could,' she continued urgently.

'I'm sorry, but I don't know who you are,' said Geoffery, puzzled.

'You sent my husband a letter,' she replied, grabbing his hand sympathetically.

'Letter?' Geoffery said, bemused, pulling his hand away. He racked his brain, desperately trying to think what and to whom he had written, which created this manic visitation. Although her face was vaguely familiar, he couldn't place it.

'Here it is,' she said, taking a crumpled piece of paper out of her handbag.

'Do you want me to have a look?' Andy said to Geoffery.

'Is it the letter I sent to my nephew, Rupert?' Geoffery said suddenly recalling a possible explanation.

'Yes, that's right,' said Sue. 'Unfortunately Rupert couldn't come. He works in Bristol and so I've come instead. I'm Sue, Sue Williams - Screen. Rupert's wife,' she said, clearly upset at the reception she'd received.

'Oh, now I see,' said Geoffery. 'It's so kind of you to come. But it's Rupert I need to see.'

'Well, when I read you were in a hospice, of course I expected the worst, so I've dropped everything and dashed here,' she said, looking to get some sympathetic credit for her urgent handling of the situation.

'But the letter was addressed to your husband,' said Andy, reading it.

Dear Rupert,

This letter will probably come as a great surprise to you, as we have not seen or communicated with each other for many years. However, I would like to redress this omission and meet up with you.

Currently my health isn't too good and I am now resident in the Dorothy and Tom Hospice at Hampton Leck, Near Cheltenham, having recently left my former home in Monaco. Hence, I would like to see you as soon as possible. I can assure you that it will be to your financial benefit to meet me.

Yours Sincerely
Uncle Geoffery (Foster)

'Oh, I always open his mail,' she said. 'He has no secrets from me.'

'Not according to my information,' thought Geoffery. 'Looks like you're in for a big shock sooner or later.'

'Well, that's very kind of you to come, Sue. But it's your husband I need to see in person,' explained Geoffery.

'I can relay any message,' she said insistently.

'When do you think he will be able to meet me?' asked Geoffery, trying to calm himself from the tide of panic that she had created.

'Well, that's difficult to say, because he's working on a very urgent job down in Bristol,' she said insistently, not willing to allow her role in the drama to be downgraded, to being purely a messenger.

'But will he be back in a day or two?' interjected Andy, annoyed at being ignored.

'Well yes, but he...I'm not sure he'll be able to...he's working on an important computer project for Lemon, the mobile phone company, and doesn't come home until late. Then he's off again early in the morning,' she said evasively.

The surveillance photos had shown a different reason for his late homecoming. The work he was doing was more about relationship building than computer projects. Rupert was having an affair. Having now met the overpowering Sue, he could understand why Rupert had strayed. 'He would hate to be anywhere near the explosion, when she found out about the clandestine love affair,' thought Geoffery.

'And what about weekends?' Geoffery quizzed.

'Oh, he sometimes has to work at weekends as well, she said, cagily. But I'm sure that he'd be more than happy for me to pass the message to him. I do most everything else in his life,' she said, a hint of bitterness creeping into her voice.

'I bet you do,' thought Andy, mentally noting to keep her away from Geoffery. Sue was obviously a control freak.

'Let's see if I can contact him now,' she said, reaching for her mobile. 'And we'll arrange the meeting straightaway.'

'Perhaps you could do that later,' said Andy. Mr Foster doesn't need to be part of your domestic arrangements, said Andy, forcibly. And now if you wouldn't mind, he needs to have his rest,' he added, indicating the door.

'Oh, of course,' she said, resentfully. 'Well,' she added. 'I'm sure they do everything for you here. But it's not a nice environment is it really, with all these sick people around? You could always come and stay with us in our guest bedroom,' Sue said, trying to ingratiate herself to Geoffery.

Sue was no fool. She could see an opportunity for controlling Rupert's expected legacy. She had done her research well. Geoffery's track record to his multi-millions was well documented on the internet.

'No, I'm perfectly comfortable here, thank you, and I have all the expertise I need on hand,' said Geoffery, looking at Andy. 'Andy will show you out now. Please ask Rupert to call me, to arrange an appointment.'

Andy led Sue back to reception to ensure she left the hospice.

'I don't know whether you're aware, but we spend a lot of time creating an environment where patients can feel relaxed,' he explained. 'The hospice is a place of calmness. I would like you to bear that in mind, if you come here again,' he admonished.

'What are you inferring?' said Sue defensively.

'Nothing,' said Andy, not willing to join in any further discussion with the woman. 'I'm just simply explaining the hospice ethos, that's all.'

'You tell your people to get rid of those stupid speed bumps then. That will improve the tranquility of the place.' Angrily slamming the car door, she added, 'they're a bloody nuisance.'

Andy watched as she drove out of the hospice grounds, the damaged exhaust dragging along the road making a clanking sound, until it finally fell off as she joined the road. He could still hear the unsilenced exhaust roar, as she disappeared off towards town.

Chapter Twenty Nine

Thursday October 2nd – Sunset count 32

The following day, the meeting between Rupert and Geoffery took place at the hospice. Unsurprisingly, it was not a weekend meeting to which Sue had originally alluded. She had obviously given Rupert a 'three line whip' to take time off. Her fear of losing shares in the fortunes of a dying multi-millionaire had made sure that Rupert's, so called 'busy' schedule, was reprioritised.

Sue marched Rupert to Geoffery's room for the meeting.

'Please don't stand,' Sue directed Geoffery, as he struggled out of his chair.

Ignoring her, Geoffery stood shakily and extended his hand to the timid looking, shallow faced, individual who followed her into the room.

'Rupert, I'm so pleased to see you after all these years,' Geoffery said, enthusiastically.

'Uncle Geoffery, um likewise,' he said, awkwardly.

Rupert's gaze slipped away from Geoffery's grey face, as memories of the final visit to see his mother, Geoffery's sister, came flooding back. He still recalled the sheer panic and sense of utter loneliness that overwhelmed him when she died. It had just been the two of them. He had always depended on her to do everything for him; he was ill prepared to be alone.

'I bet you're wondering what this is all about,' said Geoffery, breaking into Rupert's thoughts. 'Please sit down,' he gestured.

'I did tell Rupert how poorly you looked, and I said we mustn't over exert you,' said Sue, feigning subservience.

'Yes quite,' said Geoffery, annoyed that she was even there, at all.

'Sue read your letter to me over the phone,' explained Rupert.

'Yes, I'm getting in touch with all my Godsons and...'

'Oh,' said Sue, taken aback by this revelation. 'How many are there? If you don't mind me asking.'

'Geoffery has three Godsons,' said Andy, coming to Geoffery's aid.

'It would be quite nice to meet the other two,' she added, her mind calculating the possible financial implications of, 'other' Godsons.'

'I don't see that it is of any relevance to you,' said Geoffery, dismissively.

'But he's the only family member, is that right?' she asked, probing for more information.

'Yes, 'but if you'd let me continue,' Geoffery said, irritated by her continual questioning.

'Sorry,' she said, her cheeks flushing at the admonishment. But pleased to hear the competition, were not family.

'Now where was I?' Geoffery said, clearly rattled by her interrogation.

'You were telling Rupert that you were meeting all your Godsons,' said Andy calmly.

'Oh yes, that's right, yes...' said Geoffery, picking up the cue.

'Sorry for interrupting,' said Sue apologetically, realising her indiscretion.

'Please, if you don't mind,' said Geoffery, frustrated at her continued prattling.

'I'm afraid, I'm going to have to ask you to leave if you continue,' said a concerned Andy. 'You must appreciate how much this meeting is taking out of Geoffery.'

'Sorry. I won't say another word,' said Sue, resenting getting a scolding from a mere Nurse.

All the while, Rupert had been sitting quietly listening. 'Clearly he knows his place,' thought Andy.

'Rupert, I haven't seen you since your Christening. How are you?' Geoffery asked finally.

'OK thanks. We struggle by, don't we Sue?' he said, looking to his wife to support his statement or to take over the conversation, as she usually did.

A hard stare from Geoffery dared her not to respond.

Rupert recalled her urgent phone call that he had received at the Team meeting. Although his phone was on meeting mode, she had called him repeatedly, until he was forced to step out of the meeting to answer it.

She had been like an excited schoolgirl. 'You've had a letter from your Uncle, Geoffery Foster. He's a millionaire. We're going to be rich,' she had gushed. 'He wants to see you immediately. I went to see him earlier. He's in a Hospice and I think he's probably going to tell you he's going to write you into his will.' Sue's excitement was bordering on hysterical. Unnervingly, he had never heard her so happy.

'He's obviously dying, so we won't have to wait long. We could be millionaires by the end of the year. Why, it's got to be just like winning the lottery. We're rich,' she screamed. 'RICH.'

As Sue continued to rant on about how she was going to spend the money, Rupert was already thinking that this would be an opportunity for him to start a new life, away from her, and set up a love nest with his mistress.

'Now, we are going to meet him tomorrow, so I don't want any excuses about having to do urgent work there. You might never have to work again.'

Rupert shuddered at the thought of spending more time in Sue's company.

She had obviously prepared Rupert for the meeting, and devised some plan on how to capitalise early, on to his possible future legacy.

For, prior to today's meeting Rupert had been lectured about saying the right things. Emphasizing to Geoffery that they had debts, and they were scraping a living.

However, unbeknown to the calculating Sue, Geoffery already knew all about their true financial position.

'Andy,' said Geoffery, looking for help to get rid of the irritating Sue. 'Did you say that the Hospice Administration wanted Mrs Screen to complete an incident form about her exhaust pipe damage?'

'Mrs Williams –Screen, if you don't mind,' she said, haughtily correcting Geoffery.

'Oh yes,' said Andy, picking up the hint and addressing Sue. 'Sorry to hear about having to replace your exhaust system. It's Hospice policy to record all such incidents. If you'd like to come with me, and fill in the appropriate paperwork, that would be very helpful.'

'Yes, but after we've finished our discussions with Mr Foster,' she said, irritated by Andy's intrusion.

'No. You go now with Andy. If you don't mind. It would be nice to reminisce with Rupert about my sister. I'm sure he will update you later,' Geoffery said, hoping to restore some sense of order.

Rupert sat impassively as Andy led Sue out of the room, although Geoffery thought he saw a brief moment of panic in his eyes.

'I'm sure they would find it really useful, if you could give some feedback about the speed bumps too,' continued Andy, ingratiatingly.

'If I must,' she said, reluctantly following Andy to the door.

'Rupert, don't forget to tell Geoffery all those things we'd discussed earlier. Remember?' she said, fixing him with a steely stare.

Rupert looked at her briefly. As if a secret had passed between them. She nodded back and smiled.

Chapter Thirty

As Sue left, so did the tension in the room. Geoffery, used to handling tough negotiations with people of strong personalities, recognised that Sue was going to cause him some angst, during his dealings with Rupert.

Rupert, too, seemed to sit back in his chair and relax. Clearly, he was intimidated by this dreadful woman.

Geoffery could now appreciate the tenor of the reports that he had been given, Rupert was 'under the thumb', the investigators had written. Geoffery wondered if this was the real truth. Was he just a henpecked husband? Or was there something more sinister in their relationship?

'Well, Rupert, it must be over thirty years since I saw you last,' Geoffery said breaking the silence.

'Yes, I suppose that's right,' said Rupert, stiffly.

'I'm sorry I couldn't get to your Mother's funeral. I know you were particularly close to her. How did things go?'

'Oh well, you know,' said Rupert, his eyes starting to fill. 'The funeral went OK; as far as funerals go. It took me some time to get over her...her death, but she left me the house and a bit of money.'

'At least you had your wife to help you get over your loss,' Geoffery said, sympathetically.

'No, I hadn't met Sue then. I was single at the time.'

Geoffery was surprised, he had obviously missed this bit of information from his reading of the report. 'So, when did you meet your ...um, wife?'

'Oh, Sue introduced herself to me at the badminton club,' Rupert said, nervously twisting his fingers. 'She was very sympathetic about Mum. When she learnt I had a house, she told me she was looking for somewhere to live. She moved in, initially as a lodger and then...you know, Rupert added, becoming embarrassed. 'We had a bit of a fling, and she suggested we got married shortly after.'

'Yes. Sue was obviously a conniving bitch even then,' thought Geoffery. 'What sort of wedding did you have?' he said, feigning interest.

'Nothing grand, just a Registry office do. Our vicar wouldn't marry us. Sue had a row with him about her being married twice before; but he wouldn't budge. And you know what's it's like with these women, if they don't get their own way!'

'Yes, indeed. But I never got married. I didn't feel the need to. There are too many lovely ladies out there, just waiting to be loved,' Geoffery crowed, unnecessarily.

'Yes, that would have been nice. But Sue came along and...' Rupert's voice trailed off.

'And the rest is history,' Geoffery completed Rupert's sentence. 'But never say never. Eh!' said Geoffery, knowingly.

'Sue had obviously become Rupert's mother substitute. For his mother, Sarah, had quite a dominant personality too,' Geoffery recalled. 'Obviously runs in the family,' he smiled, thinking about his own personality traits. 'But, clearly the dominant genes had not migrated to her painfully shy offspring, Rupert.'

'You probably realise, by now, that time is short for me.'

'Yes, I'm terribly sorry to learn about your illness. If there's anything I can do to help you. Just let me know,' Rupert said genuinely.

'That's very kind of you,' Geoffery said, warming to his nephew. 'But your wife has already offered me a room in your house, so that she could look after me.'

'Has she? Oh I didn't know,' said Rupert, surprised.

'Don't worry. I shan't be taking her up on it. I know where my bread's buttered,' he added.

'No, I imagine, you're in the best place here,' Rupert agreed.

'Now the reason I want to see you. Many years ago, when you were a baby, I became your Godfather.'

'Oh yes, I had forgotten.'

'And that's just the point,' Geoffery added. 'I have been remiss in not being around to help and offer advice to you over the years.

'That's OK, I know that you are, have been, a busy man. Mum used to follow your progress on your companies websites.

Yes well, being successful in business also requires you to quickly judge peoples characters, and I tell you what. If I had been here, I would have advised you not to have touched that Sue with a barge pole. I'm sorry if that offends you.' Geoffery said, more outspoken that he'd intended.

'No, on the contrary. I think about the same thing every day,' Rupert said, looking nervously at the door.

'Well, that piece of advice is no good now; but is there, anything else I can help you with at the moment, Rupert?'

'No, umm, well yes I, we, were thinking of extending the house,' Rupert said awkwardly. 'Umm, Sue has umm, been diagnosed with Osteoporosis, and we were shortly planning to put in a downstairs bedroom and toilet, for when she gets worse,' Rupert recited, recalling the story verbatim, that Sue had dreamt up.

'Oh, I'm sorry to hear about that. It seems you're surrounded by people in ill health,' said Geoffery, trying not to smirk. He had been expecting something like this, when he saw the pound signs flash in her eyes, during their first meeting. Clearly poor Rupert had been put up to this, by that woman. Now he understood why she didn't want to leave the meeting. For in spite of his illness, Geoffery still had a shrewd business head on him.

'Well, I'm afraid I don't have any contacts in the building trade anymore,' Geoffery said, playing the game.

'Oh, I see,' said Rupert, now perplexed. Sue had been expecting Geoffery to immediately offer to pay for it.

'I expect there are some good ones in yellow pages,' said Geoffery, playfully.

'Yes, of course,' said Rupert, trying to think of another tack; fearful of the consequences of failure.

'The, um, finance side of things, um,' said Rupert, now shifting uncomfortably in his chair; embarrassed to ask for a handout, for Sue's mythical project.

'I believe the Banks and Building Societies are well funded at the moment,' Geoffery said, enjoying teasing him. 'So you should have no problem getting a second mortgage, especially as you can secure it against your present home.'

'Oh, that's fine, thank you,' Rupert said, squirming inside.

Rupert was now lost. He didn't want to play the stupid game anyway. All the 'what if' scenarios that Sue had rehearsed with him weren't any use now. He feared the consequences of his failure to secure an early handout from Geoffery.

'But your letter said something about financial benefit,' he recalled, hoping to save the situation.

They could hear voices approaching outside. Sue and Andy were returning.

Ignoring the question, Geoffery asked quickly, 'how can I get hold of you directly, without getting her involved?'

'Oh, um…well, here's my card,' said Rupert, fumbling into his jacket pocket. 'Call me on my mobile or text me,' he said conspiratorially, looking nervously at the door.

'That's fine, thanks. I might even get Andy to bring me down to meet you in Bristol.'

'Andy and Sue came back into the room.

'OK Geoffery? Hope we gave you enough time to chat over family matters.'

'Yes, thanks Andy. I think we made a good start at catching up, didn't we Rupert?'

Rupert nodded and looked crestfallen at the floor, not wishing to catch Sue's eyes.

'I think you've had enough excitement for the day. I suggest we call the meeting to a conclusion,' Andy said authoritatively.

'But I haven't had chance to talk to Geoffery,' said Sue, trying to sound genuinely sympathetic.

'It'll wait for another day,' said Andy, forcibly.

'We'll have another meeting shortly, OK?' said Geoffery, making a mental note, not to invite the woman to it.

'Well, I guess that will have to do,' Sue said, unable to hide her disappointment, and looking towards Rupert to see if there were any signs of a successful negotiation. Rupert avoided her gaze, and instead continued to look at the carpet, glumly.

She knew then. He had failed. Her cheeks immediately flushed with anger. What else would she have expected from this useless excuse for a man?

'OK, nice to see you both,' Geoffery said, relieved as Andy led them out.

As she drove them down the drive, the interrogation started. 'Well?' she demanded. 'How did you get on? As if I don't already know.'

'He said he had no contacts in the building trade and we could re-mortgage,' said Rupert, meekly.

'What about the will?' she demanded.

'We didn't get around to talking about it. Sorry,' he said fearfully.

'Typical. I knew I should have done it myself, rather than leaving it to you. You pathetic creature,' she said shrieking disdainfully at him.

Sue's fury suddenly erupted into uncontrollable rage, her knuckles white as she gripped the steering wheel. The engine screamed as she angrily stamped on the accelerator. The first speed bump reminded her, too late, of how expensive frustration and speed could be in replacement exhaust systems.

'Damn him and damn you too,' she screeched, launching a well-aimed blow into his groin. You useless piece of shit. Wait until I get you home.'

The punch caused Rupert to double up in agony. He gagged uncontrollably as the pain rocketed up through his abdomen.

'Don't you dare be sick in my car,' she shouted, reinforcing her command by hitting his already heavily bruised upper arm, where her previous attacks still remained, undetected.

Chapter Thirty One

Tuesday October 14th – Sunset count 44

'Well, I don't know how he did it in such a short time, but the new hut arrived, was sited, and all the services installed, in just under three weeks,' Andy explained to the District Commissioner, as he welcomed him to the opening of the new Scout Hut.

'I wish all the Scout Groups had such a friendly benefactor,' the other replied, taking in the new and well-appointed hut.

'I've asked Mr. Foster to open it. I hope you don't mind,' Andy added apologetically.

'Mind? Not at all. It's nice just to attend, rather than having to make a speech. Most of these parental audiences aren't interested anyway. They're usually here under sufferance.'

'Here he is now,' Andy said, spotting the Mercedes Benz manoeuvring into the parking area. 'If you don't mind, I'll introduce you later on,' he said, walking towards the car.

'Yes, of course. I'll go and talk to some of your young people,' the Commissioner said, heading off inside.

Geoffery had been buoyed up by the prospect of opening the new Scout Hut, so much so, that he felt strong enough to drive there.

'Hi Andy!' he said, opening the car door. 'My, look at you in your Scout Leader's uniform! Oh, I see you've got a gong too. Is that your Dib Dob badge?' he said playfully, studying the badges on Andy's shirt.

'No. That's my Medal of Merit. I'm very proud of that. It was awarded to me for setting up the Scouts in this area,' Andy said proudly.

'What's the coloured handkerchief thing around your neck called?'

'A neckerchief.'

'That's right. And it's held together with a wiggle?'

'No, it's a plaited leather woggle.'

'Well, you really look the part. It's much better than your Nurses uniform anyway.'

'I couldn't let an auspicious occasion like this pass without doing it properly,' Andy said beaming. 'How was the journey? Are you OK?'

'Took me a time to get into the car, but once I was seated, no problem. She is such a dream to drive. How have all your preparations been going?' Geoffery asked, looking around.

'Fine thanks. I've given Ben the job of welcoming everybody tonight. I'll just get him to help you into the hut. Is your wheelchair still in the boot?'

'Yes.'

As if waiting for a cue, Ben appeared by the car. Carefully removing, unfolding and manoeuvring the wheelchair to the driver's door, he invited Geoffery to sit on it. 'Here you are Geoffery, sorry,' he said, realising he was being too familiar. 'Mr Foster,' he corrected.

'No. Geoffery is fine. No need for formalities among friends.'

Andy and Ben helped Geoffery into the wheelchair and Ben wheeled him up the equal access ramp for a tour of the new hut.

'It's great! These prefabricated buildings come with so much equipment already installed,' Ben said enthusiastically, steering the wheelchair along a corridor through a doorway.

'Look! Here's the kitchen. It came fully equipped,' he enthused.

Geoffery could see a group of boys and girls all dressed in green shirts, they too were sporting the same yellow and black neckerchief that Andy and Ben wore. The group of young people was busily preparing trays of food. Shiny white china plates were being loaded with pineapple and cheese on sticks, crisps and nuts. Empty packets lay untidily in a crumpled heap on the new brown worktop. Some of the Scouts had obviously been sampling the food as it was being laid out, for they stopped chewing, cheeks bulging, looking guilty as the pair entered.

'Perhaps we shouldn't stay in there while they're preparing the nibbles,' Geoffery suggested tactfully.

'Look everybody. It's Geoffery,' Ben said, proudly, thrilled at the honour of being Geoffery's escort.

The young people stopped their preparations for a second and cheered.

Later, as Ben wheeled him into a quieter part of the building, Geoffery asked him to stop.

'Ben, I didn't get the opportunity to thank you for your thoughtfulness when we met the other day.'

'What do you mean?' asked Ben puzzled, moving around to face him.

'You know, the silly, hurtful, comment about cancer not being catching.'

'Oh that's OK. That kid's a bit of a moron anyway.'

'I hope you didn't hurt him.'

'No. I told him about my Gran, and I think he realised what a pillock he was being.'

'Oh that's good. I would have hated for anybody to have been hurt.'

'More important. How do you... you know, cope with it? Ben asked sensitively.

'Well, that's a bit of a grown up question. Sorry, I didn't mean to patronise,' he said quickly, realising his indiscretion. 'Yes I'm OK. But thanks for asking. We all have our crosses to bear Ben, don't we?' he added.

'Yeah.'

'How are things at home at the moment?'

'OK,' Ben said unconvincingly.

'I mean about your Mum?' Geoffery added.

'Oh,. You know about her?'

'Yes. Andy was telling me that you have a bit of a rough time at home.'

'Yeah, well, you just get on with it, don't you?' he said, shrugging his shoulders.

'I didn't know that Andy allowed you to sleep in the hut,' Geoffery admitted, uncomfortably.

'Yeah. But I didn't start that fire. As God is my witness. I swear.'

'No, I know you didn't,' Geoffery said knowingly.

'Well, the Police think I did. Somebody saw me running from the hut when it was on fire and thought I'd started it.'

'Well, thank heavens you escaped before it burnt down. They haven't got any evidence against you though, have they? Andy can tell them you had permission to sleep here. He'll stick up for you.'

'No. I don't want him to. I asked him not to say anything. The social services will take me into care if they know. My Mum's been warned before, about not looking after me properly.'

'Oh.'

'She can't help it. She's OK when she's sober, off the booze like. Then she's like a proper Mum. You know, she looks after me and stuff.'

'Well, I expect you know that this new hut has a small bunk room?'

'Yeah.'

'Well, I specified it, especially for you. I just hope, that you don't have to use it too often. But here's a key that I got cut for you.'

Ben looked at the key that Geoffery had pulled out from his pocket, but didn't take it.

'I don't know. What if this goes up in flames again?' Ben said, looking earnestly at Geoffery.

'I'm sure it won't. I know you won't abuse the privilege.'

'I'm not sure,' Ben said, starting to shuffle uncomfortably.

'Don't worry. I'll tell Andy I've given it to you.' Immediately Ben's response changed; clearly Andy was highly respected by the boy.

'Wow, thanks. You're a real Gent,' Ben said, taking the key and pocketing it.

' Ah! There you are,' said Andy, suddenly appearing from around the corner. 'It's time to get on with the formal stuff. What's all the secret chats about?'

'Oh, nothing really! I'll tell you later,' Geoffery said, winking at Ben. 'Come on Ben, push me to the hall.'

Andy preceded Geoffery and Ben into the main room. The room which was 25feet wide by 40feet long had been laid out with a large table in front of rows of chairs. Scouts and parents were standing around chatting as Ben positioned Geoffery's wheelchair at the front of the hall.

'OK, everybody. Quiet please!' Andy said, clapping his hands and moving to the table. 'If I could ask you all to take a seat, please.' The hubbub slowly subsided as everybody settled in to the padded banquet chairs.

'I hope you've all had the opportunity to have a look around our magnificent new Scout Hut. We'll just have a few speeches and then go for some nibbles,'

Andy said, retrieving his notes from his back pocket.

'Thanks for coming tonight. As you'll see, I'm not very good at this speech stuff. But I'd like to start by saying a big thanks to Mr Geoffery Foster for providing us with this fantastic hut; which we shall name Foster Lodge in his honour. Not only has he provided it in a record time, but he has also fully equipped it with chairs, tables, cooking pots, cups saucers, cutlery; in fact, everything that we need.

You know how much we used the other hut, and the great fun we had in it. Well, this one has got even more facilities, including a fully equipped kitchen. So now we can even teach cooking.'

Immediately there was some good humored banter from girls about the boys inability to cook anything.

Holding up his hand, Andy regained control over the noisy youngsters. 'OK folks. That will do. So without further ado, I'd like to ask Geoffery Foster to formally open the hut.'

Geoffery stood up, slowly easing himself out of his wheelchair and sat casually on the edge of the table, as Andy led the audience in a round of applause.

'Hi. Thanks for that tremendous welcome,' he said addressing the crowd. 'I have already met some of you young people, and hello to everybody else. I hope to meet you all later on. I'm pleased to be here tonight for many reasons. One of which is to thank Andy for doing such a great job as your Leader, and for giving us a reason for getting all together. As you know, Andy works really hard for you young people, so let's recognise all his hard work with a round of applause.'

The audience responded to Geoffery's request by whooping, shouting and clapping. After a few minutes, Geoffery held his hand up and the noise slowly subsided. Andy bowed his head, embarrassed by the unexpected accolade.

'Andy. That's a genuine sign of affection, that we all hold for you. The other reason for being here is to formerly open the hut, the lodge, and to turn it over to you for your use and care.'

'The hut should be really named the Andy Spider Lodge, because it was all due to his efforts that you got the replacement, and ensured it was installed so quickly. I want you young people to show all the media, by the care that you put into running this hut, that those who wear clothes with hoods on, are not all troublemakers. Will you do that for me?'

The audience responded noisily with a loud 'Yes.'

'In my day, the same media people tried to demonise the young people of my generation who wore leather jackets or mod gear. It's an easy way of categorising people. But we all know that a fashion trend does not make you a YOB. It's what you do, not how you're dressed, that is the critical factor in how you're perceived.'

The young people responded with a noisy support of Geoffery's observations.

'There will always be a small number of people who will spoil it for the rest. We see that in life generally. It is not limited to young people. Anyway, enough of my lecturing. I now declare this hut formerly opened. Please enjoy it,' Geoffery looked directly at Ben as he said. 'Treat it as your second home.'

Ben led the applause, as Andy helped Geoffery sit back into his wheelchair and said, 'Thank you Geoffery, I see we've made a convert.'

Geoffery smiled contentedly.

Andy addressed the Scouts, 'OK folks, if you'd like to bring the snacks out now, we'll start the party. But remember to keep the music down. As you know, we have close neighbours to think about,' Andy said, his words almost lost in the excited buzz.

As the evening progressed, Ben demonstrated a very accomplished break dancing routine, much to the delight of all the others, who surrounded him and gave encouraging applause.

Feeling tired from his exertions, Geoffery finally gave in to Andy's insistence that it was time for him to return to the hospice.

'Do you want me to drive you back, Geoffery?' Andy asked.

'No thanks. I can manage the short trip. Don't bother to see me off; I can see you'll be busy clearing away. I'm sure Ben could see me out. Incidentally, I've given him a key for the hut. Just in case, you know,' Geoffery said.

'Thanks. That will save me a job.'

Ben wheeled Geoffery out to his car to see two, tough looking, teenagers sitting on the bonnet.

'Get your arse off that car,' Ben shouted loudly, startling Geoffery.

The youths stared at Ben and slowly stood.

'Yeah! And what are you going to do about it, fire starter?' The nearest thug said threateningly.

Ben was at the others throat in an instant.

'You'll want to see your dentist soon,' Ben said, holding the other's coat tightly with both hands, almost throttling him. 'One more word from you and you'll need one, because your teeth will be in your stomach.'

'Ben, don't let them get to you,' Geoffery said calmly. 'Just help me in to the car and let them go. We don't want these yobs spoiling a great evening do we?'

Chapter Thirty Two

Wednesday October 15th – Sunset count 45

The knock on Geoffery's door was gentle; Kay, thoughtful as ever, didn't want to wake him, if he was asleep.

From inside, Kay heard the sound of rustling papers, closely followed by a croaky instruction to enter.

'Hello Geoffery. Is it OK for me to visit?' she said, stepping into the room.

'Yes of course Kay. This is a nice surprise,' Geoffery said swivelling his legs off the bed.

'I thought these might help to brighten up your surroundings,' she said, proffering him a bunch of delicate red purple fuchsias; their pendulous teardrop shape in contrast to the harsh, white, sterile room.

'Oh, they are lovely, thank you,' he said, taking the bouquet from her and laying them on his bedside locker. 'My, look at you though! What a change!'

'Thanks,' she said coyly, subconsciously touching her hair.

'You're starting to look like the Kay I knew,' he said smiling.

'I do feel much better for the trip to the hairdressers, that's true. But guilty.'

'Guilty! Why? Because you've done something for yourself for a change?'

'Well, I'm not used to it. I feel I should be doing things for...'

'Yourself,' Geoffery interrupted. 'This is your time. Not his.'

'Perhaps..'

'Look, I know we've already talked this to death. But you've already exceeded your maternal duties. It's now time to start letting go.'

'I can't. I've done it for so long. I feel I still owe him.'

'You owe him, nothing. But you do owe yourself a life. Independent of him. Remember Abraham Lincoln's words, 'And in the end, it's not the years in your life that count. It is the life in your years. Enjoy it while you can. I did, have done.'

'That's easier said than done.'

'No it isn't. It's time for him to let go of your apron strings.'

'He's still my baby,' she said softly.

'Ah come on. He's got to be, what, 36? He's just using you.'

'I don't know.'

'You have to stand up to him, for both of your sakes. He needs to grow up.'

'There you go again. You come back into my life for five minutes and already you're telling me what to do. I've had enough of people telling me how to live my life,' Kay replied, her cheeks flushed with anger.

'Whoa there. Remember, I'm on your side,' Geoffery pleaded.

'Anyway, you shouldn't be worrying about Tim and I. You have you own health to worry about,' she said, her voice trembling.

'I'm sorry. I don't mean to interfere. It's just that I believe you deserve a better life, and…anyway how did the challenge go down with him?'

'He thought you were mad!'

'I can understand that.'

'After he'd finished storming around the house, he eventually put his legs on and started playing with his WiiFit, but I'm not supposed to know.'

'Well, that's at least a start.'

'As to getting to the top of Ben Nevis, I think that's a step too far, If you'll pardon the pun.'

'Never say never! Don't forget, I'm happy to pay for his training or joining a Health club. In fact let me give you some money, so that he can go ahead and join one.'

'No. I couldn't possibly take your money. I have some savings set aside. I'll use that. If he wants to join one.'

'I wouldn't dream of allowing you to have to find additional expenditure to fund something that I had started off,' he said reaching into his briefcase. 'Here's a cheque for five hundred pounds. Let me know what club he joins.'

'Thank you. That's very kind of you. I will,' she said, putting the cheque in her purse. 'You know, I think you've given us both an opportunity to change. I was thinking of joining the club with him. What do you think?'

'At the risk of getting my head bitten off. I'd say do your own things. Let him get on with his own life – without you.'

'But I'd be there, to make sure he continued to train.'

'He has to do it himself; otherwise he will continue to depend on you.'

'Yes, I suppose so,' she agreed reluctantly.

'There are lots of walking clubs around; he could join one of those.'

'Perhaps, but he'll need a lot of encouragement though.'

'I appreciate that and it'll take some time, He'll have some setbacks, I'm sure.'

'At least he's trying,' she added.

'Kay, I don't know how to put this, but I'll say it anyway.'

'What? 'Kay said, intrigued.

'Something you said the other day.'

'Yes?'

'About Tim, being...being my son.'

'No, that was just a slip of the tongue,' Kay said quickly. 'I meant Godson. Don't read anything in to it.'

'But ...at your reception...we....'

'No don't. Please don't bring that up. Its best left in the past. It was a stupid mistake. We were both drunk and...'

'I know. Sorry, but the dates...'

'Forget it,' said Kay clearly getting upset. 'You're not his father. Period.'

'Right, OK, but...'

'No Geoffery. Let's change the subject shall we?' she said firmly, desperately trying to steer the conversation away. 'What about you? Did you ever marry? Have any children?'

'I couldn't find anyone who wanted me for me. They were just after my money. Except there was one special lady, who I...but that's all in the past,' he said, looking at Nadine's photograph. 'Children? Not that I'm aware of unless...'

'No. Trust me,' Kay said firmly.

'Why did George leave you?'

'I'd prefer not to rake that up again, if you don't mind.'

'I'm just curious that's all,' Geoffery said, fishing for information to supplement the reports he'd received from the Investigators.

'Because...um...He just couldn't cope with a toddler without legs.'

'I can understand that. It must have been terrible.'

'When Tim was born, he dreamt of playing football with him, and he was devastated when...after the operations. He just couldn't get his head around it.'

'So instead of staying to support his family, he took off and left you to bring up Tim by yourself. It must have been awful?'

'It was hard. The worse thing was not having anybody to turn to, a shoulder to cry on, when things got tough. It was heartbreaking seeing Tim crawling around like a baby again, but he just accepted it, and quickly adapted to having no legs. He and another toddler used to hop around and chase each other around the waiting room, by bouncing on their bottoms. It was as if they didn't have a care in the world. He was a nice little boy. But it all changed when he became a teenager, and then he became morose and sullen.'

'Sounds like any typical teenager. The trouble is, it looks like he never grew out of that phase though.'

'It was my guilt that was so hard for me to bear.'

'Guilt?'

'I live with the daily reminder of it. If only I had been....'

'Been what?'

'I failed him Geoff.'

'How do you mean?'

'Well if I'd spotted it sooner.'

'No, we've already had this discussion! Put that thought out of your mind.'

'Anyway, you're right. That's all in the past,' she said composing herself.

'That's what I want to hear. This is YOU time. Kay's time. You will be doing him a greater service, by letting him do his own thing, while you concentrate on your own interests.'

'I'll try. I really will.'

'Good girl,' he said, giving her hand a squeeze.

'Anyway, I'll go now. I don't want to tire you out,' she said thoughtfully.

'Are you sure? You don't have to. I'm enjoying your company.'

'Yes. If I hurry, I can get the bus from outside,' she said standing, giving him a peck on the cheek. 'But if you like, I'll come to see you again.'

'That would be great. Thanks for the flowers. They're lovely. Just like you.'

'I see you've still got your silver tongue,' she said smiling.

Kay left, closing the door quietly behind her.

Geoffery picked up the report that he had been reading before she arrived. It was her divorce papers. He'd just read the entry; 'reason for divorce'; Adultery. George was recorded as the 'innocent party'. The co-respondent recorded as 'unknown'. Perhaps, she had lied to him after all. According to this information he could well be Tim's father.

Chapter Thirty Three

Thursday October 16th – Sunset count 46

'Has he answered yet?' asked Geoffery, impatiently drumming his fingers on his bedside tray.

'No. It's still going to his voicemail,' replied Andy, returning his mobile to his pocket.

'Considering she was so keen to get him involved, I'm surprised he is not contactable.'

'Perhaps his phone is broken,' Andy volunteered.

'He works for a mobile phone company doesn't he? I should have thought he would have got it sorted by now. It's over a week.'

'Perhaps we've got the wrong number.'

'No. It's definitely the one on his card.'

'Should we dare ring their home number and hope she doesn't reply?'

'Worth a try isn't it?'

Geoffery opened his briefcase, and thumbed through the files until he found Rupert's.

'OK. Here we are,' he said, handing it to Andy.

'Here goes then,' Andy dialled the number, and listened. After a few moments, Geoffery could hear that someone had answered.

'Oh hello. Is that Rupert?'

'Yeth.'

'Hello. It's Andy, your Uncle's nurse. I'll just hand you over to him now.'

Geoffery took the mobile and pressed it to his ear.

'Hello Rupert. We've been trying to get you on your mobile for a week now. Is there something wrong with it?' Before he could answer, Geoffery added, 'come to think of it, why are you at home? Are you ill?'

'Yeth,' came the reply.

'Oh. That will be why then. Are you OK? You sound a bit strange.'

'I've got a broken arm! '

'How did you do that?'

'Fell down the stairth!'

'Is Sue there?'

'No.'

'Oh good. Can we come around and see you?

'Well, I'm not sure,' Rupert said reluctantly.

'I don't mean to push you, but as you realise, time is of a premium for me.'

'Well, I guess you'd better come around then,' Rupert capitulated.

'OK, we'll be there shortly.'

Andy drove Geoffery to the address in Gloucester. A very battered looking Rupert answered the door.

'Ouch! You did take a tumble didn't you? Looks like you bounced all the way down the stairs on your face. When did this happen?'

'Lathd week,' lisped Rupert, revealing a broken front tooth.

'What! After you'd been to see us?'

'Yeth.'

Rupert led the trio into the dining room and invited the others to sit down.

'We need to be quick, before Sue gets back, otherwise she'll...she'll...' said Rupert painfully; a hint of fear in his voice.

'Are you hurting?' Geoffery asked concerned.

'Yeth.'

'Did the Doctor prescribe any painkillers?' Andy asked.

'Yeth, but Sue has taken them,' Rupert said wincing.

'Why?'

'Don't know.'

'Well you can have one of mine. I've got plenty. Geoffery said, digging into his coat pocket. 'Oh, there's a couple left in this box I get from the Hospice. You can have these,' he said, giving Rupert the box.

Rupert took the box and removed a tablet from the foil and swallowed it quickly.

'Sorry Geoffery, You can't do that. You can't swop tablets around like that. They're not smarties.' Andy said firmly.

'But the guy's in pain.'

'Then he needs to get his own medication. These are strong ones, specifically prescribed for you and your condition.'

'Nonsense. They're painkillers and he's in pain.'

'I won't have anything to do with it.' Andy said walking away.

'Don't worry, nobody will know. Now Rupert, the reason we're here is.....'

'I'm concerned that she'll back shortly and will be very cross that I let you in,' he said nervously.

'OK, we'll be quick. Let's forget this nonsense about you wanting to build a 'granny flat' for Sue's

Osteoporosis, shall we?' said Geoffery, mesmerised by the bruises on Rupert's face. 'I'm here to offer you, not her, some help. You've had a few days to think about it. How can I help, apart from getting rid of your....'

Geoffery stopped, as a key turned in the lock, and the front door opened.

'Too late,' said Andy. 'The noise machine, has returned.'

'You'll have to go,' whispered a frightened Rupert. 'Please.'

'But we've only just arrived,' said Geoffery, surprised by Rupert's insistence.

'Please,' Rupert pleaded.

'Rupert, have you done the..?' Sue stopped in mid-sentence, as she entered the dining room, and saw Geoffery and Andy.

'Oh hello,' Sue said, softening her voice. 'I wondered whose car it was outside. Well, what do you think of poor Rupert? You can see he's been in the wars; fell down the stairs didn't you dear?'

'Yeth,' confirmed Rupert, turning his gaze to the carpet.

'What brings you here?' Sue continued.

'We....we a .....' Geoffery said, hoping for an inspiration to explain their presence.

'We were just passing, so thought we'd pop in and say hello,' Andy said quickly.

'Yes, but I've got an appointment back at the hospice now, so we can't stop,' said Geoffery. 'Rupert was just going to show us out. Weren't you Rupert?'

'Was I ?...Yeth, that's right, I was.'

'I'll do that dear. I know you're still a bit stiff from your fall,' said Sue forcefully.

'We don't want to bother you Sue. The walking will help his bruised muscles,' said Andy, helping Rupert to his feet.

'Umm,' said Sue suspiciously. 'When will we see you next, to continue our discussions?'

'Soon,' said Geoffery over his shoulder. 'I'll be in touch shortly.'

The three men reached the front door, leaving Sue behind.

'Call us on your mobile, when the coast is clear,' Andy whispered.

'I can't. She's got it. She's locked it away somewhere.'

'Why?' asked Geoffery, puzzled.

Rupert's response was not forthcoming, as Sue was making her way towards them.

'OK, we're off then,' said Andy quickly.

The door closed quickly behind them. Sue could be heard shouting at Rupert, as Geoffery and Andy walked to the car.

'What do you think's going on there?' Andy said.

'Don't know. But did he fall, or was he pushed?' said Geoffery, buckling his seat belt.

'I think you've found out how you can help Rupert,' Andy said, pulling the car back into the traffic.

'I think you're right,' Geoffery said. 'I shall have to think of some way to make it happen though.'

CHAPTER THIRTY FOUR

Friday October 24th – Sunset count 54

The phone in Geoffery's room rang, startling him.

'Geoffery?'

'Is that you Andy?' Geoffery asked.

'Yes. Sorry to disturb you. But I had a call from the School earlier. Ben hasn't been at any of his classes for three days. I've just been to his house and his Mother says he has run away. Apparently, she's had several phone calls from him, but he won't say where he is.

'What about the hut?' Geoffery suggested.

'No. That's the first place I looked. It doesn't appear that he's been staying there either. There's no sign of cooking or anything?' Andy added.

'Can you think of any reason for him running away?'

'He had a run-in with the law recently.'

'The police! Why? What happened?'

'The kids have this stupid game they call 'blitzing'.'

'Blitzing!'

'Yes. They ride their bikes along the pavement, behind a pedestrian, and rush past just missing them. If they get a reaction, they score maximum points.'

'What a stupid thing to do.'

'Well, following a complaint from one of the neighbours, I'd already spoken to the Scouts, including Ben, about riding on the pavement. Unfortunately, it appears, they ignored me, and consequently, Ben ran into an old man.'

'Why the hell would they do it?'

'To startle the 'victim'. The kids think it's funny..'

'Funny that is, until somebody gets hurt! So was the person badly hurt?'

'Not really. More shocked than anything. But he is in his late seventies, and the shock alone could have killed him.'

'So were the Police involved?'

'Yes. Unfortunately for Ben. They were close by when it happened, and they mounted a bit of a manhunt.'

'Bit over the top wasn't it?'

'Yes, they even had the Police helicopter up, to try and track him down.'

'What a waste of money.'

'Well eventually they got him, took him down the station and gave him a good bollocking.'

'Did they charge him?'

'No. They were waiting for the old man, to see if he wanted to press charges.'

'So in the meantime, Ben has done a runner?'

'Yes. The annoying thing is, I gather, the old man would have been happy, just to have had an apology. He's a Grandfather and knows that all kids do stupid things once in a while. He said he was young once; so he didn't bear any malice.'

'Nice to hear.'

'But inspite of his Mother's assurance, that the old man wasn't going to make a complaint, Ben still won't come back.'

'Why ever not?'

'She said Ben was ashamed, because he'd let me down,' Andy said. 'Apparently he was worried about what I'd say!'

'Blimey! I thought he was a tough nut,' Geoffery said, surprised.

'That's just an act he puts on. No, he's a very sensitive young man. Anyway, I assured her that I wasn't cross and asked her, if he rang again, to tell Ben to phone me.'

'Obviously, he hasn't rung you.'

'No. I'm afraid not.'

'Is there any way I can help?'

'I appreciate you have your own issues, dealing with your Godsons. But it would be a great help if you could, perhaps, get your Private Investigators on the case.'

'I don't think that will be a problem. I'm pleased you asked.'

'Wherever he is, I'm very concerned. There are a lot of nasty people out there.'

'OK. Do you have a photo of him?'

'No, I'm afraid not. He always made himself scarce when the cameras came out.'

'What about school photos?'

'His mother tells me, she couldn't afford them.'

'Holiday photos?'

'She seldom takes him on holiday.'

'Oh, that's a nuisance. Well, we'll just have to go with a description then.'

'Yes. Sorry.'

'Hang on a second; I've got a photo of him on my phone, haven't I?'

'Really?'

'I took it when I was in the car waiting for you. It was when you had gone into your house, to collect your family for the christening. You know, when I, mistakenly, thought Ben was murdering you.'

'Oh, then! I didn't realise you had taken a photo,' said Andy, surprised.

'Yes. Leave that with me.'

'Ben doesn't have a mobile either,' Andy said, trying to think of another angle to track him down.

'He must be one of the few kids his age who don't.'

'No. He never had any money to be able to buy one. His mother usually found any pocket money his Grandfather gave him, and she spent it on booze.'

'So if we can't track him down through his mobile records. What else is there?'

'Some of the kids were saying he's got a Facebook account, which he's been updating.'

'In that case I wonder if Rupert could help us?'

'How do you mean?'

'If he's been updating Facebook; perhaps we can track him down from that. I'll get hold of Rupert. He's an IT man. He's bound to know.'

'Thanks.'

'In the meantime, are you still planning to go to London to meet James?'

'I'd prefer to be looking for Ben, I must confess.'

'Well, until we've got a vague idea of where he is, it will be like looking for a needle in a haystack anyway.'

'Yes I know. OK. I'll make my way to London.'

Chapter Thirty Five

Saturday October 25th – Sunset count 55

Geoffery had tried calling Rupert again, but with no success on either his mobile or home phone. Still feeling frail, he decided to take a taxi to his home on the off chance that he might see him.

Arriving at the house, unannounced, was going to be particularly eventful, if Sue was in residence. But the empty drive suggested, fortunately, that she was out.

With great apprehension, however, Geoffery knocked on the door. But there was no movement to indicate that anybody was in. He knocked again and waited apprehensively. He stood back from the doorway and looked at all the windows to see if there were any curtains twitching. As there was no sign of movement, he slowly started making his way back to the taxi. Just as he got by the gate he heard a window open behind him.

Rupert was looking through a narrow opening in a small ground floor window. He beckoned to Geoffery, nervously looking around all the time.

As Geoffery got closer, he could see that the injuries to his face were worse than the previous time he had seen him.

'What's happened to you? Have you been in the wars again?' he asked, concerned.

'Please help me,' Rupert said crying. 'I can't take any more of this.'

'What the hell's going on?'

'After the last time you came, she beat me up again.'

'I thought as much,' Geoffery said.

'I'm so ashamed,' he blurted.

'You shouldn't feel ashamed. It's her that should be ashamed for doing this to you.'

'But I'm a man. I should be standing up to her, but I can't, I just can't,' he continued, woefully.

'Listen. Don't berate yourself. Thankfully, God made gentle people too,' Geoffery said sympathetically.

'I want to leave here, but I can't. Please help me,' he pleaded. 'Please help me.'

'Why can't you leave?'

'She's locked the doors and windows and taken all the phones. I'm trapped and don't know what to do,' he said starting to cry again.

'Well, the first thing we're going to do, is to get you out of there. I'll call the Police. They'll get you out.'

'No, please. Not the Police. I couldn't stand the humiliation. They'd just laugh at me. A man, beaten up by his wife. I'd be a laughing stock.'

'I'm sure there are lots of men in your situation,' Geoffery assured him. If you don't want the Police involved, I don't know what to do then. Let me think,' Geoffery said, looking around, hoping for inspiration.

'Please hurry, she might be back anytime.'

'We could smash a window, I suppose,' Geoffery said helplessly, knowing he wouldn't have the strength to do it anyway.

'No, they're double glazed. Oh no. She's here. You must go.'

'I can't leave you like this, to get another beating,' Geoffery said looking at the approaching car.

Rupert backed away from the window, as Sue steered the car into the drive. She immediately leapt out dashing across to Geoffery.

'What are you doing here?' she demanded. 'I'm afraid Rupert is indisposed. He had a dizzy turn and fell down the stairs again.'

'I would like to see him please,' Geoffery demanded.

'Well, I'm sorry. The Doctor said he was not to be disturbed.' Her tone lightened as she remembered the possible financial implications of upsetting Geoffery. 'And you, of all people, should know not to disobey Doctors orders.'

'I just want to tell him something and then I'll go,' Geoffery bluffed.

'As I said, that won't be possible.'

'It's about his inheritance. Unless I see him now, I shall be writing him out of my will.' Geoffery knew at the mention of money, Sue would open any door.

'Well in that case, I'll pop in and see if he is awake,' she said quickly, getting her keys out of her handbag.

Sue opened the two locks securing the front door, and closed it before Geoffery could follow her in.

After a few moments, the door reopened, to reveal Rupert standing on the threshold, with Sue immediately behind him.

Geoffery was taken aback by the extent of his facial injuries.

'I'd invite you in, but the place is a tip. You said you wouldn't be long either,' Sue said quickly.

'I need to speak to Rupert alone, if you don't mind,' Geoffery said, trying to get her away from him.

'Sorry. But I need to stand close to him, just in case he has another dizzy turn. We don't want you to hurt yourself again, do we Rupert?' Sue said menacingly.

All the while Rupert was gazing at the floor.

'In that case, I'll have to hang on to him myself, wont I?' he said, stepping up to the front door and taking Rupert's arm. 'It's OK. I can hold him now, thanks,' Geoffery said, staring into her glaring eyes.

Sue reluctantly let go, and backed off into the nearby kitchen. 'I'll just be here, in case you need me Rupert,' she said, the malevolence, clearly evident in her tone.

'Let's just step down here for a breath of fresh air shall we,' Geoffery said, steering Rupert onto the path.

'Don't go too far now,' Sue directed from inside.

As they walked slowly along the path, Geoffery was assessing whether they could get to the taxi before Sue would spot his intention. He knew that he wasn't strong enough to play tug of war with her. Then he spotted them. In her haste to keep her hand on to the inheritance, she had left her keys in the door. Letting go of Rupert, Geoffery rushed to the door and slammed it shut, quickly turning the key in the lock.

The response was immediate. Like an angry Rottweiler, she rushed to the door, trying to open it.

'Open this door will you! I don't know what you think you're doing, but Rupert is ill. He is self-harming,' she said, hammering on the door. 'I need to keep a close eye on him, to stop him killing himself.'

Geoffery stopped, wondering if he was doing the right thing. She had planted seeds of doubt in his mind. Was Rupert mentally ill and self-harming? Or was this another one of her deceitful stories?

Rupert was now crying, his whole frame racked with tears. He covered his ears with his hands, trying to block out the sound of her voice.

Geoffery paused only for an instant. He knew what he must do. He quickly led the pathetic Rupert, back to the taxi.

'Please, don't make me go back,' he sobbed. 'Please, don't make me go back. I can't take anymore.'

'Don't worry,' Geoffery said gently. 'You're safe now.'

'We need to get out of here quickly, or she'll be after us,' Rupert sobbed.

'No, It's OK. I've locked her in.'

'She's got a baseball bat. She'll smash her way out,' he muttered through his swollen lips.

Like a couple of arthritic old men, they moved painfully slowly to the taxi, and as if on cue, there was a loud bang and a sound of smashing glass from behind them.

'Quick, let's get out of here,' Geoffery urged the taxi driver.

As the taxi accelerated down the road, they could hear more glass being broken and Sue shouting obscenities.

'What happened? Why has she done this?' Geoffery said, studying Rupert's injured face.

'Sue found text messages to my friend on my mobile, saying I was going to leave her,' Rupert said weakly.

'Do you mean your LADY friend, Joanne?' Geoffery said, knowledgeably.

'How do you know about her?' Rupert said, surprised.

'I have my methods.'

'What am I going to do now?' he sniffled. 'I can't ever go back home.'

'What about Joanne? Does she have a house?' Geoffery asked sympathetically.

'Sue used my phone and texted her to say our relationship was all a big mistake. That it was all off, and that I wouldn't be seeing her again. Anyway, I don't want her to see looking like this,' Rupert said miserably.

Looking back, they could see that Sue had managed to escape from the house and was standing in the middle of the road, shouting.

'Oh no,' said Rupert. 'She'll be coming after us in her car.'

'No. Don't worry,' said Geoffery, still clutching Sue's keys. 'She won't.'

'I hope you're right.'

'This self-harming. She was making it up, right?' Geoffery asked cautiously.

'Yes, of course. Why would I want to hurt myself? My life is just starting to turn around. I planned to leave Sue, even before I had even heard about you, and your letter. When you said, you know, about the inheritance, I couldn't believe my luck. And now, it's fallen all around my ears.' Tears started streaming down his face, as he recalled Sue's threats to punish him if he ever left her. 'Wherever you hide, I will find you,' she had told him, during countless beatings.

'Don't worry,' Geoffery said, giving him his handkerchief. 'Let's get your injuries sorted first. Then we'll book you into a hotel, where she won't find you. When you're feeling able, then you can contact your lady friend and explain what's been going on. How does that sound?'

'Thank you,' Rupert said filling up again. 'I don't know what to say. You've helped me to get away from her. It's been a marriage from hell. Thank you so much,' he added, clutching Geoffery's thin hand and squeezing it.

'It's OK,' Geoffery said, looking away to hide a tear, running down his cheek. 'I gather that helping and guiding is what Godfathers do.'

Rupert relaxed back into the leather seat closing his eyes. Perhaps things were going to get better after all.

'But there is something I want you to do urgently,' Geoffery said, suddenly remembering the original purpose of his visit. 'Now, it's my turn to ask you for help.'

'Anything. Just name it,' Rupert said.

Chapter Thirty Six

Monday October 27th – Sunset count 57

'So you reckon he's definitely in London,' said a bemused James. 'You realise it's a bleeding big place?'

'Yes, and I think I've walked the majority of it,' Andy said edgily. 'But Geoffery has established that Ben has been posting updates to his Facebook from internet cafes in the Tottenham Court road area.'

'How's he done that?'

'His nephew is a computer expert. Something to do with IP addresses. I don't know. It's all beyond me.'

'So why don't you go there yourself?'

'I have. But the owners are a bit cagey. They don't know anything about anything.'

'What about your secret squirrel? He's got eyes in the back of his head, hasn't he?'

'He's on another case. Look, Ben's mother is worried about him.'

'Perhaps she should keep a closer eye on him then.'

'Unfortunately, for Ben, she also enjoys her booze too much.'

'She's obviously a woman after my own heart!'

Andy looked at the matted beard and flushed face in front of him and felt fearful for Ben. 'Come to think of it, you've got a lot in common with her. She's often out of her head on drink or drugs.'

'You mean, when it comes to it, she couldn't give a toss for him. I know what that feels like, being deserted by your parents.'

'Look, I'm very concerned that Ben will fall into bad company.

'Well, that's probably a certainty. There's no shortage of weirdo's here, that's for sure.'

'So will you help?'

'How?'

'Just keep your eyes open for him and let me know if you see him.'

'What's it worth? A man can get thirsty, keeping a look out.'

'If you find Ben, I'll buy you a crate of booze.'

'I could do with a bit of food now though. How's it looking for a sub?'

'What happened to the fifty quid I gave you for the hostel, that you didn't sleep in?'

'I spent it on stuff.'

'More booze?'

'Look. My pockets are empty.'

In order to prove his point, James turned his pockets inside out. Cascading crushed, discoloured cigarette ends on to the pavement. Amongst the detritus, Andy spotted sweet wrappers tied in knots.

'Don't tell me, you've been wasting your drinking money on sweets too,' Andy said sarcastically.

'Sweets!'

'There, look. You've even tied the wrappers in a knot.'

'I couldn't even tie shoe laces with hands like this,' James said, holding out his shaking, grubby hands to reinforce his point. 'I'm not interested in sweets.'

'Where did you get those from then?'

'I don't know. An ash tray somewhere, I suppose. Why?'

'No, it's too much of a coincidence.'

'What?'

'Ben ties knots in his empty sweet wrappers and crisp bags like that.'

'And so does half the population, I should think.'

'Yeah, I suppose so. But, on the off chance he was there, try and remember where you got the dog ends from, please.'

'Who knows! The Court Road is one of my regular ciggie shops. It could have been there.'

'Well, just try to think.'

'Remind me. What does this kid look like again?'

'It's a pity my battery has gone on my mobile, or I could have showed you the picture Geoffery took. Well, he's fourteen, has black curly hair, brown eyes, Olive skin and is about five feet six.'

'That describes about half the runaways in London.'

'He's got some fuzz under his nose; you know, a teenage 'tash.'

'Yeah, OK, I get the picture. Now, how about that money?' James said, holding his hand out expectantly.

'Here's a tenner. Try and get some food inside you, please,' Andy said, knowing that the request would fall on deaf ears.

'Cheers, you're a gent,' James said, already dreaming of the Sherry trickling down his throat.

'Look, I'm going back to my hotel in Russell Square,' said a tired Andy. 'I think I've walked every grotty street in London. After seeing all those 'down and outs', I just hope Ben is safe.'

Chapter Thirty Seven

James returned to his bench in the park. Around him the rush hour traffic was noisily battling to leave the choked capital. Oblivious to the commuter chaos, James carefully withdrew a large green sherry bottle out of his filthy coat pocket.

'Money for food, indeed,' he said, possessively stroking the bottle.

His turn of fortune, having Geoffery in his life, had provided him with an unexpected and much welcomed glut of booze. With the handouts from the Nurse and selling that bleeding mobile phone, it had meant that he was well provisioned, his alcoholic needs, more than satiated.

Lord Jim of the park bench was back in residence.

Startled at James's arrival, a teenager, already on the bench, stood and started to leave.

'Don't worry about me kid. As soon as I've had my night nurse, I shall be away in the land of nod. Ha! Night nurse! That's a good one,' said James, chuckling to himself at the unintended association with Andy.

Uncertain, the boy slowly sat back down, whilst keeping a wary eye on the dishevelled character.

James's continued efforts, struggling to unscrew the bottle top, was thwarted by his limited dexterity. In spite of cursing the manufacturers for over-tightening it, the errant top stubbornly refused to budge. Finally, James gave in, and asked the boy for help.

'Here kid, open this for me, will you?'

The boy stood and started to leave, unwilling to have any involvement with the drunkard.

'Hey kid, come on. Help me out here.'

'You should get off that booze Mister, it'll kill you,' said Ben, heading for the exit path.

'Don't you start. I've had enough of do-gooders telling me what to do. So piss off, if you're not going to help me,' James said continuing to struggle with the bottle.

The boy stopped in mid stride and looked back at the pathetic figure. He was struck by a pang of conscience, an empathy, an understanding of the man's need for the bottle's contents. He turned around and went back to the tramp.

'OK. Let me see if I can open it,' he said, putting out his hand. 'But you really should...'

'I know. Give it up! Save my life! I'll do it tomorrow.'

The boy took the bottle, as James continued, 'I need this, I've been traipsing around London, all day, looking for some bleedin' kid.'

The boy stopped in his attempts to undo the top. 'Why would this tramp be looking for a kid? Was he some sort of pervert?' he wondered, apprehensively.

'Come on. I haven't got all day. I'm dying for a drink.'

'Dying of drink, more likely, said the boy contemptuously. 'Just like my mother.'

'A drinking mother! Now that's a bit of a coincidence.'

'What do you mean?'

'The kid we've been looking for all day; he's got a drunkard for a mother.'

'Well, it's not mine! She's not a drunkard,' Ben said defensively. But realistically knowing, that he was right. 'She just likes to…'

'Drink!' Nothing wrong with that,' James agreed. The boy's revelation, about his mother's needs, was empathetic to his own view and dependence on alcohol.

'Precisely what I said to this bloke, Andy, that I've been with all day,' James continued.

Ben looked at the tramp startled. 'Andy! It couldn't be! Surely,' he thought.

'What does this bloke look like?' Ben asked.

'Here! Have you undone that bottle yet?' James said, unable to take his wide eyed gaze from Ben's hands, still unsuccessfully twisting the bottle.

'You know an Andy do you?' James said, salivating, in anticipation of tasting the first drops of this golden elixir.

'Yes.'

'Well, that's another coincidence, isn't it? Here, Your name's not Ben, is it?'

'What if it is?'

'Well. As I say, this bloke Andy is looking for you.'

'I don't want to see him. Where is he?' Ben said, scanning the park.

'Don't worry. He's gone to his hotel, in Russell Square.'

'I don't want to go home.'

'You look like a smart kid. Why run away from home for this shit?' James said, looking at the manic necklace of traffic chaos surrounding the park.

'It's personal.'

'OK. You don't have to tell me anything. It's nothing to do with me.'

'My mother can't get enough of this stuff,' said Ben, gazing at the still unopened bottle. 'But I can't get her to stop.'

'You're lucky. I never really knew my Mother,' said James, gazing absently at the ground.

'Why?'

'She was killed in an air crash.'

'Oh. I'm sorry,' said Ben sympathetically.

'It was a long time ago now though.'

'To be honest, my Mother's problem is... she's addicted to the stuff,' confessed Ben, twisting the bottle uncomfortably in his hands.

'My problem is, I usually can't get enough,' groaned James.

'How long have you been...addicted, then?'

'I'm not!' James said aggressively. 'I'm not. I can give it up anytime I want.'

'Only. I can't talk to my Mother about her problem. It might help if I could understand.'

'Understand! What's to understand? Drink is what gets me through the day. Anyway, what's it to you?'

'I want to help her to quit.'

'So you think by psychoanalysing me, you'll find out the reason why she drinks? Dream on kid!'

Did you want this bottle opening?' retorted Ben.

'Come on. If you can't bloody well open it, give it me back.

James slid along the bench towards Ben, the smell of his unwashed body causing Ben to subconsciously hold his nose. Ben stood and held the bottle away from James's reach.

'Don't prat around,' James said, standing, attempting to grab the bottle.

'Tell me and I'll give it you,' Ben persisted, moving further away.

'Because I can't face life if I'm sober. Is that what you wanted to hear? Now open that effing bottle.'

'Why can't you? Ben said, puzzled. How does it help?'

'Booze helps to ease the pain,' James said, sitting down, putting his head in his hands.

'Pain! What do you mean? Have you got something wrong with you?'

'No. Somebody I loved, died...'

'I'm sorry. Was that your Mother?'

'No. Somebody else. Somebody really special. It hurt so much when he went. It was as if my heart had been ripped out,' James said, becoming tearful. 'I just wanted to join him. But, I couldn't do it.'

'I'm sorry, I shouldn't have asked... I'd probably be the same if anything happened to my Mother.'

'In that case, why are you causing her more angst by running away?' James said, gaining his composure.

'I did something stupid,' Ben said, sitting back on the bench.

'So! We all do stupid things from time to time. It's not a big deal. Bottle please,' said James gesturing to be given it.

Ben ignored the request. 'I upset Andy.'

'So what's the big deal? He's nobody special. He's only a Nurse, after all.'

'He's been good to me, because of my Mum's problem. He helped sort things out, after I was slung out of my house in the middle of the night.'

'And you still love someone who would do that to you?'

'It wasn't my mother that threw me out. It was one of her boyfriends.'

'Why the hell would she let her boyfriend throw you out?'

'She was drunk, as usual. She didn't know anything about it, until the morning.'

'So why did he do it?'

'Mother came back with him from the night club, and as he came into our hall, he ripped his trousers on my bike. He pulled me out of bed. Told me to get my clothes on, and threw me out of the house.'

'In the middle of the night! Shit! Where was your mother when all this was going on?'

'She was, out of it, as usual.'

'Where did you go?'

'I wandered the streets all night…got into trouble at school the next day. But Andy sorted things with them. That was when he gave me a key for the Scout hut, so if it happened again, I'd have somewhere to go. You know, sleep in the hut.

'Perhaps I misjudged him then. Sounds like a good bloke?'

'Unfortunately, one night the hut caught fire, while I was in it.'

'Oh dear! You obviously got out OK. Was it your fault?

'No. I swear,' Ben said firmly.

'Is that why you ran away?'

'No. It was because I let Andy down by doing something… stupid, after he had already told us not to do it.'

'What did you do? Rob a bank?'

'Don't be stupid!' Ben said, annoyed at being belittled.

'Sorry kid.'

'We do stunts on our bikes; one of them is riding fast up behind somebody on the pavement and 'blitzing' them. You know, making them jump because you 'cut them up'.'

'Sounds like a pretty stupid game to me.'

'Well, this one old guy 'wobbled' as I got level with him and walked straight in front of me. I couldn't avoid him. I knocked him for six.'

'Was he badly hurt?'

'No. He was an old guy, you know, grey hair and stuff. Well, I didn't stop to see. But the police tracked me down. They even had a chopper up looking for me. Well, when they got hold of me. I got a bollocking from them and...'

'Oops. What did this Andy bloke say?'

'I don't know. I didn't see him. I guess he would be angry, as he had already given us this lecture about riding on the pavement...and well, we ignored him. It was this bloke's own fault, he got in my way.'

'But he was, on the pavement?'

'Yeah.'

'So, Who was in the wrong?'

'Yeah, alright. No need to rub it in.'

'So you felt bad about it?'

'Yeah'

'Why didn't you apologize to the old guy?'

'I don't know. I couldn't face him. Worse, I felt bad about letting Andy down.'

'So you ran away?'

'Yeah. I didn't have a choice, did I?'

'You can't run away every time you make a cockup. Sometimes you've got to stand up and admit you were wrong. Running away only makes things worse.'

'Yeah I know. Anyway, you can't say anything about it. Isn't that what you're doing, running away?'

'No, it's different for me.'

'Why is it?'

'It just is, that's all.'

'That's a typical adult response. It's different for me,' Ben mocked. 'Next you'll be saying; don't do as I do, do as I say.'

'This isn't about me. No-one is looking for me. Well, not until recently, that is,' he added thoughtfully.

'Do you mean Andy is looking for you too?'

'Well, in a way. But, he's working for a bloke called Foster.'

'What Geoffery Foster?'

'Don't tell me you know him, as well?'

'Yeah. He's a good bloke. He helped me out, too.'

'So are you going to go back with this Andy? He seems very concerned about you.'

'No, I can't.'

'Why?'

'Because I couldn't face Andy, I already told you.'

'He's not a Paedo is he?' said James suddenly.

'No he's the Scout Leader.'

'Doesn't mean anything, I've heard about things with these Scout Leaders.'

'No, it's not...he's not like that, he's got a family,' said Ben defensively.

'So did some of my teachers at Boarding school, that didn't stop them abusing us.'

'No, Andy is a great bloke, he has helped me. I told you that.'

'What about your mother? Now you're not there, to look after her.'

'I've given up trying. She keeps telling me she is going to give up drinking completely. But, she hides bottles. Thinks I don't know.'

'It's not easy to quit. When you've got a drink problem, you need help to get you off it.'

'Are you getting help?'

'No. I told you. I haven't got a problem.'

'How much do you drink in a day?'

'Not enough. Anyway what's it to do with you?'

'Mum, spends more time drinking that she does with me.' Ben said despondently.

'Sounds like we both missed out on a normal childhood,' James said. 'Whatever that is,' he added.

'I've never seen my Dad,' Ben said quietly. 'Mum says he died when I was a baby.'

'I was at boarding school, so I only saw my parents occasionally, before they died.' James added. 'Been tough for you, hasn't it? Being fatherless and having a drunk for a mother.'

'She's not a drunk. I told you. She's got a drink problem,' said Ben protectively, thinking of his Mother and how vulnerable she would be without him to nag her.

'OK kid. No offence meant.'

'I wonder if she'd be any different, if we had a normal life,' Ben said reflectively. 'Most kids at school have a Mum and Dad and they do things together; go on holidays and stuff.'

'Ah! The ideal, 2.5 children family unit. Well, we know the other side of that equation, don't we?'

'Mum's great when she's been off the booze.'

'And it's obvious, despite everything, you still love her? Well, that is my only love now,' James said pointing at the bottle.

'Why do grownups do such stupid things?' said Ben, carrying on his analysis of his mother's actions.

'Because, nobody is infallible. Especially adults.'

'But they do things which upset and hurt people. Why?'

'True, people can be selfish, and insensitive to other people's needs. But, you'll soon learn. In this world, you have to look after yourself first. You should remember that,' James said purposefully. 'Look after number one, and you won't get hurt.'

'Does that mean you have to stop loving?'

'What's love got to do with it?'

'Isn't that what makes humans, special?'

'Hell, you've got a wise head on your young shoulders.'

'Something my grandad told me, when my mother went into a special hospital. Don't hate your Mother for screwing up your childhood son. Just give her time and love,' he said. 'That's what makes us special. Love.'

'All this talk of love is making me thirsty. Come on, I need that drink. That's the only love I have, these days.'

Ben reluctantly unscrewed the top and handed the bottle over.

Lord Jim of the park bench raised the bottle to his lips and took a swig of the ruby liquid. He drank greedily, quenching his insatiable alcoholic thirst. Ben stared at the pathetic creature and shook his head in frustration.

'What's the point?' he said, standing up.

'That's better,' said James, wiping his lips with the back of his hand. His matted beard dampened by dribbled sherry. 'The world has become a better place, already.'

'Goodbye,' said Ben, walking away.

'Where are you going?' James demanded, suddenly realising that Ben was leaving.

'I've seen enough of your world, through my Mother. I'm going before you get completely stoned,' said Ben sadly. 'Back to my squat.'

'Please yourself. Should I tell that Andy, that I found you?'

'No. Mmm. Yes, OK. So that my Mum will stop worrying.'

'Trouble is, she'll worry even more, when she knows you're living in a squat. You get some right head cases in those.'

'What do you mean? Head Cases.'

'Nutters, who would knife you, as soon as look at you,' James said. Then there's the Junkies. Out of their face, most of the time. Not forgetting the Gangs, who kidnap young people, and force them into prostitution.

'Oh. Well, the people in my squat seem to be OK.'

'They're probably grooming you,' James said, elaborating his tale. 'Just be careful.'

Ben is now feeling apprehensive about returning to his squat.

'I don't even like going to hostels for the homeless. Which is why, I like sleeping in my doorway. I can please myself.' James added.

'Don't you get scared though?' Ben said intently, sitting back down on the bench.

'Scared of what?'

'Getting robbed? Being beaten up?'

'Ha! I've got nothing they'd want. Anyway, that's where the booze helps. As soon as my head hits the cardboard, I'm gone.'

'Do you...would you mind if I came with you?' Ben said hesitantly.

'Up to you kid. But I thought you'd seen enough of pissheads?'

'Yeah well,' Ben said, spooked by James's assessment of squats.

Chapter Thirty Eight

Andy's call woke Geoffery. The mission to rescue Rupert had left Geoffery feeling totally exhausted.

'You OK Geoffery? you sound tired.'

'You're right. I've got to admit, that having rescued Rupert, from the jaws of hell, it has taken it out of me.'

'So what happened?'

'Just as we suspected. The bitch has been abusing Rupert. It sounds like she's been guilty of domestic violence for a long time.'

'She was obviously very good at hiding it, then.'

'Yes. The investigators assessment that Rupert was a bit of wimp, was way off the mark. It turned out that she had been giving him a sedative, without his knowledge. He found it when he was locked in the house.'

'So where is he now?'

'I've put him in a hotel, to keep him away from her. As you can imagine, she's been trying everything to find out where he's gone, including coming here. She's threatening to go to the Police. Accusing me of kidnap.'

'What did you say?'

'I told her, on Rupert's behalf, that my lawyers were already compiling a court injunction to prevent her from contacting him.'

'It sounds like you've made better progress than I have.'

'Did you find James again?'

'Yes, and I've tramped all around London with him, looking for Ben. It has done nothing to make me like the place. There is such a contrast of the haves and have not's here.'

'It's the same in any big city, though,' Geoffery added.

'There are so many teenage run-aways here. Can you believe it? Some are only eleven or twelve. The same age as some of my Scouts. They're everywhere. In a sober moment, James was saying, that if he had the money, he'd set up a refuge just for homeless teens.'

'As much as I'd like to, unfortunately, I can't solve the problems of the world,' Geoffery added wisely.

'These kids are so vulnerable,' Andy continued, clearly shocked at the scale of the problem. 'They don't appreciate how dangerous, this running away game is that they are playing. James was telling me, he has seen the Gangs pick them up. Apparently, they ply them with drink or drugs and before the kids realise what's going on, they are forced into drug running and prostitution. That's the end of their dream and their freedom, and sometimes, sadly, their life. That's why I'm so worried about Ben.'

'Yes, I share your concern.'

'At least, finding where he was updating Facebook from was a stroke of genius, wasn't it?

'Yes it was. I hoped Rupert would be able to help. As soon as he had calmed down enough, from the 'great escape'; I got him working on the problem. He got hold of a few people at his place of work, and hey presto, they came up with the location.'

'Can they monitor Ben live? You know when he's actually doing the update?'

'No, I'm afraid not. GCHQ might be able to do that sort of thing. But these guys have got their day jobs to do as well, and only did this as a favour for Rupert.'

'Well, at least we've got an area to focus on in London. Let's just hope we find him tomorrow. I get more and more concerned as each day goes by,' Andy said anxiously.

'I'm going to have to hang up Andy. I'm not feeling too good. All this excitement has obviously got to me,' Geoffery said, barely audible.

'Push your panic button Geoffery. Get somebody to check you out. Do it now. Let me hear it. Geoffery! 'Geoffery' can you hear me?'

Chapter Thirty Nine

As the day faded into a darkening autumn evening, it started raining. And even with the 'shelter' of his alcoholic raincoat, Lord Jim decided it was time to vacate the bench and leave the park to find a dry doorway.

Ben had decided to tag along with him, after James's frightening revelations, about living in squats.

The odd couple made their way along the Tottenham Court Road, heads down against the driving rain. Ben's hoodie quickly became very wet, the rain soaking through the thin material. Ben was very cold and shivering uncontrollably.

What made his discomfort worse was the aroma that arose from his companion. For as James's filthy coat got wetter, he smelt more and more like a wet, mangy dog. The smell became overwhelming. Pedestrians parted aside at his approach and gave him a wide berth.

'Just need to nip in here,' James said, stepping into a small shop that sold a miscellany of cheap imported goods.

Ben stood self-consciously on the pavement, shoulders hunched against the rain, as James emerged with another bottle of cheap sherry.

The pair moved into the doorway of an empty shop to shelter from the rain. Faded posters of past pop concerts covered the windows. Inside, they could see that the postman had continued to deliver mail, although it was obviously not trading. Piles of letters and circulars littered the dusty concrete floor.

'Why do you need that? You've already had one?' Ben nagged. 'Perhaps the squat would have been a better choice, after all,' he thought

'I've already told you.'

'You're just like my Mother. You say one thing and...'

'Hey! You aren't my conscience, right?' said James angrily. 'Now if you don't like it, clear off, and go and hide in your squat. You talk about me facing up to things...well what about you?'

'Well, I.....' Ben started.

'So the hut burnt down! James said, interrupting, 'So what! They put up another one on the insurance, didn't they?'

'No. It wasn't insured. Mr Foster paid for a new one.'

'Oh. Mr Millionaire Foster paid for it did he? That's interesting.'

'Yes. He's a very generous man,' Ben said proudly.

'Generous and devious, is Mr Foster,' 'James muttered. 'So, of course he would.'

'What do you mean, of course he would?'

'He's after something, if I'm not mistaken,' James said, leaning heavily on the shop door.

'What? I don't know what the hell you're on about,' Ben said, confused. 'Come on, it's stopped raining. Let's get you to your cardboard box or whatever you sleep in.' Ben grabbed James's arm and started leading him down the street.

'I'm not going to Cheltenham, understood?' slurred James.

'Cheltenham! What? He's obviously lost it. This is the booze speaking,' Ben thought.

'I told that Andy, that I wasn't going back to Cheltenham. Got it?' he said, wagging his finger at Ben.

'Yes. Whatever you say,' Ben said, knowing that holding any sensible conversation with James now was going to be futile.

James suddenly stopped in the middle of the pavement and slapped his forehead with the heel of his hand. 'Bugger,' he said. 'I've just remembered. I've got to tell this Andy when I find you,' James continued, swaying unsteadily against Ben. 'Trouble is, I've just spent the phone money he gave me. Have you got any money?'

Before Ben could reply, a group of six drunken football supporters, wearing soaking wet England shirts, weaved their way along the pavement towards them.

Noisily chanting. 'Ing-galund, Ing-galund, Ing-galund.' They were spread across the whole width of the pavement, forcing other pedestrians to step into the road.

In spite of being worse for wear himself, James grabbed Ben's arm and dragged him towards the kerb, out of the way of the drunken fans.

However, as he did so, one of the staggering yobs bumped into James and knocked the bottle of sherry from his grasp. The bottle smashed loudly on the pavement, scattering glass shards everywhere. He watched mortified as his precious liquid seeped into the cracks in the pavement.

'Serves you right for getting in my way,' the yob said aggressively. The others laughed.

Full of Dutch courage and fuelled by the contents of the previous sherry bottle, James remonstrated angrily with the thug.

'You bleeding prat,' he shouted. 'That'll cost you five quid.'

'Fuck off,' said the yob, pushing James off the pavement, and sending him flying heavily into a parked car. 'You want to make something of it?'

'Hey I reckon this guys a Paedo. Did you see him trying to interfere with this kid. Let's show him what we think of Paedos shall we?'

At this inciting call, the group surrounded Ben, and the still kneeling, James.

'OK kid. We'll sort him out. Get out the way,' said the leader of the Gang, grabbing Ben's arm and pulling him out the way.

James struggled to his feet as the circle of violence closed in around him.

Ben pushed his way back through the mob, to stand in front of James.

'Don't hurt him,' Ben pleaded. 'He's not a Paedo, he's my father.'

'Your father!' The first yob said, not convinced.

'Yes I've got to take him back to the hospital. He's, uh… He's just been diagnosed as having AIDS,' Ben lied.

At the word AIDs, the group instantly moved back, as if they had received an electric shock.

'He's a fucking homo then.' The yob who had knocked the bottle out of James's hand said, vehemently.

At this, he picked up the neck of the broken bottle, and threw it at James. James attempted to duck, but the glass hit him on the side of the head, gashing an artery. Immediately, blood started pulsating from the injury site and cascaded down his face. James slumped to his knees holding his head, blood oozing between his fingers.

Meanwhile, the other yobs were looking for things to throw at the kneeling figure. Only the sound of an approaching police car, with sirens blaring, saved James from any more punishment.

The yobs quickly disappeared down a narrow street, laughing, as the Police Car sailed by, on its way to another distant emergency.

Ben immediately retrieved a handkerchief out of his pocket, and pulled James's hands out of the way, applying digital pressure to the deep cut.

'Don't move.' Just stay there,' Ben instructed James, still holding the handkerchief to the cut. 'It'll stop bleeding in a minute,' he assured him.

After a few minutes, Ben lifted the material and checked the wound. 'It looks like it's stopped. Here you hold it on now. Don't rush, but when you're ready, you can stand up.'

James staggered slowly to his feet, pressing the blood soaked handkerchief to his own head, as instructed.

'You OK?' Ben enquired, visibly shaking. 'Do you feel faint or anything?'

'That's another good thing about alcohol. You don't feel pain,' said James, studying the blood saturated handkerchief. 'I'm not sure whether being a Paedo, would have attracted a less painful beasting, than being labeled as an AIDs sufferer though.'

The assault had had a sobering effect on James.

'Sorry! It was the first thing that came to mind,' Ben said, putting his arm around James's waist, as the other swayed suddenly. Ben fought the nausea of the wet dog smell, coming from James's coat.

'I've got to give it to you kid. You've got some balls. Thanks for standing up for me. By the way, my name is James. Some people call me Lord Jim.'

'OK. Um, James.'

'Just as long as you don't start calling me. Dad. We'll get on, OK.'

'Right!' Ben said, his mouth still dry with fear.

'See kid. This is what living on the streets is like. When you're down here, you're scum. Society's kicking post.'

'What about the police?'

'Well, for a change, they came by at the right time didn't they? But they aren't interested in the likes of us, street folk. It doesn't help their crime stats.'

'I think you'll need a stitch in that,' Ben said, examining the cut. 'It's very deep, and it's cut your ear as well.'

'I don't want to spend hours down at A & E,' James said, returning the bloody hanky to his head.

'What about Andy? Where did you say he was staying?' Ben asked.

'In Russell Square. But he won't want to...in any case I thought you didn't want to see him.'

'This is different. You need somebody professional to look at that cut, and if you won't go to the hospital. Then, it's going to have to be Andy.'

'No. I'll be alright.' But, as if to undermine James's words, his legs went from under him, forcing Ben to tighten his grip around the others waist.

'Come on. Don't be a martyr. You need help.'

'Just leave me here. I shall be OK in a minute. Just need to catch my breath,' James said, leaning heavily against the boy.

'I don't think that's wise. What if those yobs come back? Come on, how far is it?'

'Not far but....'

It took them over an hour to travel the two miles to Russell square. The anaesthetic effect of the Sherry was wearing off. James was moaning, his head lolling at every step. He was obviously in pain.

'Where is Andy's hotel?'

'Over there,' he pointed. The one with the steps,' said James through gritted teeth. 'I've got one hell of a hangover.'

'Come on. Just a few more steps then,' said Ben encouragingly.

'No. I'll wait here. They won't let me in there, anyway.'

'But they'll see that you're hurt!'

'That won't matter to them. They don't like my sort upsetting their guests. I'm likely to get a kicking from their security man, to add to my injuries. Just put me on that bench.'

'Do you know his room number?' Ben asked, urgently.

'No. You'll have to ask at reception.'

Ben lowered James gently on to the bench, and ran across the square and up the chipped concrete steps. The revolving door refused to budge. A shaven headed security man lumbered to the door and unlocked the latch.

'Yes?' he demanded.

'I need to see Mr Spider,' said Ben, side stepping the overweight guard and moving towards the reception desk.

'Is he a guest here?' said the guard, following Ben closely to the desk.

'Yes, but I don't know his room number.'

With the room number grudgingly given by a foreign sounding receptionist, Ben ran up the creaking staircase. It's former grandiose glory now long gone. The threadbare stair carpet, stained and dirty. Ben ran along the corridors looking out for the room numbers on faded finger posts. Eventually, he found it, knocking loudly on the door. Over the sound of his hammering heart, Ben heard movement from within the room. After few minutes, the door opened cautiously. A face appeared. Much to Ben's delight. It was Andy.

'Ben! Ben! Come on in. Are you OK? How did you find me? How did you know I was here?' Andy gushed.

'It's James. He's hurt. He needs your help.'

'James!' Andy said, frowning. 'James who?' I don't think I know…'

'Yes you do. He's the tramp. The one you've been talking to, about me.'

'Oh Lord Jim! James of course. So he found you then?' Andy said, 'the penny at last dropping.'

'Yes. But you need to come quick. He's in a bad way. Some yobs hurt him……'

'Just a second,' Andy said, alarmed at the news. 'I'll just get some street clothes on.'

Andy changed quickly, grabbing his small first aid kit and followed Ben outside. The security guard lowered his paper briefly, as the two dashed past.

James was slumped on his side, on the bench. Kneeling down in front of him, Andy could smell the familiar, alcoholic breath.

'Well, he's alive. What did you say happened?' asked Andy, gently moving James's head to get a better look at the still weeping cut.

'Some yobs threw a bottle, and cut him. It was bleeding very badly. Like a fountain. I did my first aid on him. I remembered to apply digital pressure to staunch the flow, just like you taught us.'

'It looks like your quick action probably saved his life. The cut appears to have severed the temporal artery.'

'Can you do something for him? Is he going to be alright?' asked Ben concerned.

'Yes, don't worry. Judging by his breath, he's just sleeping the booze off. But he'll have a sore head in the morning. Give me a hand to carry him to my room. It will be easier to treat the cut where we've got some better light.'

'What about the security guard? James said he wouldn't let him in.'

'One thing I've learnt in London, is money greases palms,' said Andy, lifting James's semi-conscious figure. 'You did well to get him here,' Andy added, to a very relieved Ben.

Chapter Forty

Tuesday October 28th – Sunset count 58

It had cost Andy fifty pounds, to bribe each of the suspicious Hotel employees to turn a blind eye, allowing him to take the ungainly James back to his room.

Ben was sitting, slumped in an armchair as Andy finished dressing James's wound. 'Ben, I'd book you a room of your own for the night,' he said, looking at the dozing teenager, 'but I'm frightened that you'd run off again.'

'No. I'm done running,' Ben said tiredly. 'London isn't the place I thought it was going to be.'

'We're both on the same square there, Ben.'

'Why do people make it out to be such a great place then?'

'It's OK if you've got money. Otherwise it's tough,' Andy added.

'It's a shit hole,' Ben said, continuing his negative assessment of the capital. 'Smelly and noisy.'

'Talking about smelly and noisy. I doubt either of us will get any sleep, with James snoring his head off on my bed.'

'No,' Ben agreed, looking at the sleeping figure.

'How did he find you?' Andy asked.

'We ended up on the same park bench. He told me that he had been with somebody who was looking for me. I thought it might be you, so I was going to go back to my squat.'

'Why didn't you?'

'He scared me off, talking about nutters that sometimes go into these squats.'

'I'm glad you didn't. But why didn't you ring me?'

'I was going to but...I didn't know what to say.'

'But we've known each other for a long time. I'm not an ogre am I?'

'No, it's just that I feel... I let you down.'

'Why?'

'Because you've been so kind to me and... well...that old bloke...' he said awkwardly.

'At the risk of sounding like a school teacher, I did tell you what would happen.'

'Yeah I know, and I feel bad about it. But it was only a bit of fun.'

'For you, maybe. But not for the old man. He could have fractured his skull...'

'Yes I know, and I'm sorry,' Ben said, eyes filling up. 'I wanted to apologise, but I didn't know what to say,' he added, wiping his tears with the palm of his hand.

'I know saying sorry is difficult, sometimes. But we all make mistakes Ben, and we have to face up to the consequences of our actions. You're fortunate the gentleman doesn't want to press charges. All you need to do, is say sorry to him and the matter will be over and done with.'

'OK,' Ben said forlornly.

'So, are you going to come back with me tomorrow, um later ?' Andy corrected, looking at his watch.

'Yes. If that's OK with you?'

'Sure it is. But I'm not sure about James,' he said looking at the dishevelled figure.

'I might be able to persuade him to come back with us,' Ben said. 'We were getting on OK. Those yobs frightened me when they attacked him. I thought they were going to kill him!'

'And they probably thought it was a bit of fun too,' Andy added.

'Yeah. OK. Point taken,' Ben conceded.

Chapter Forty One

Wednesday October 29th – Sunset count 59

'Geoffery, are you sure you're alright?' Kay said, concerned, as she led Geoffery slowly into her front room. 'I would have come to the hospice, if I'd have known you wanted to see me.'

'I had a bit of a funny turn, but I'm feeling a bit better now, thanks. I needed a change of air. Is he here?' he said looking around.

'No. I'm pleased to say, he's out, at the gym,' Kay said, delighted at being able to give Geoffery some positive news.

'I won't dally. I'll come straight to the point. Kay, why did you lie to me?' said Geoffery earnestly.

'Sorry!' said Kay, taken aback. 'What do you mean?'

'About George leaving you and Tim!'

'I didn't, George abandoned us. That's the truth.'

'But, what about the reason for him leaving?' said Geoffery, probing.

'No, Geoff, leave it. It's all dead and buried. It was a long time ago.'

'Not for me, it isn't.'

'What do you mean?'

'You told me George left you because he couldn't cope with the idea of a son with no legs.'

'Yes, that's right. He couldn't.'

'Perhaps! But it's not the whole truth. Is it?'

'What are you getting at?' said Kay, fidgeting uncomfortably in her chair.

'Your divorce papers.....'

'What are you doing, digging into my personal stuff?'

'Your divorce papers say 'reason for Divorce, adultery with unknown.'

'How did you know that? Why are you prying into my life?'

'Just doing a bit of research that's all!'

'Well. Getting a divorce wasn't easy in those days. We had to invent something and I agreed to...'

'To be the fall guy?' Geoffery said, finishing off her statement.

'Yes. If you want to put it like that.'

'So, why do George's solicitors papers, suggest that George was not Tim's father. If Tim's birth certificate, says he is?'

'Where did you find that out?'

'I have my sources.'

'It was all OK. Until they were preparing for the operation, and cross matching Tim's blood type.'

'Go on,' Geoffery urged, moving to the edge of his seat.

'George said, that mine and his blood types, couldn't possibly have been the ones to create Tim's. It devastated him, us. I couldn't deny it because of what happened with ... with you and me. I knew it could be true.'

'Oh, I see,' said Geoffery, squirming.

'Geoff. We destroyed Tim's life.'

'No. That's not right. We might have been stupid but...'

Geoffery's memory flashed back to that fateful day. It was a happy day. The weather matched the radiant beauty of the lovely bride, Kay. The wedding reception was held in the old Cotswold stone rectory next to the church. The summer sun shone through the old leaded windows, reflecting off the sloping Cotswold stone window sills. Over the centuries, the stonework had become, stained, shiny, from the touch of countless hands, as people gazed out at the rolling countryside beyond. Particles of dust danced in the sun's rays, carried aloft on small thermals.

Geoffery had been drinking before the service, with some of the other guests. He had gone into the backroom alone, to regain his composure, after seeing his former lover marry his friend.

He was surprised by his heavy heart. He thought he had got over her, a long time before. But the ceremony had penetrated his protective emotional veneer.

Suddenly, the door had opened and in she came. She was looking beautiful in her white, full length, strapless wedding dress, its long train rustling majestically behind her.

She was all giggly. The champagne they had drunk at the top table, had obviously, gone to her head. Geoffery and Kay used to laugh about her inability to hold her drink. He had often taken advantage of her, due to her alcoholically subdued resistance.

'Oh,' she said, spotting him sitting in the corner. 'You made me jump. I've just come in to change out of this thing. It's so hot. What are you doing in here anyway? Why aren't you enjoying the party?'

'I thought it might be a bit cooler in here,' he lied. 'I'll just go back and let you change.'

'Before you go, can you unzip my dress,' she said innocently. 'I can't quite reach the zip at the back.'

'OK,' he said, crossing the room.

She turned away from him, lifting her long hair to expose the zip. He gingerly held the thick material at the top of the bodice; her perspiration had made the dress damp. With trembling fingers, he unhooked the small hook at the top of the dress and slowly pulled the zip down. The warmth of her body escaped as the dress gaped open. Her perfume filling his head. Small droplets of perspiration glistened on the soft down that covered the white skin of her slender back.

It had transported him back to the many occasions, when he had undressed her before.

He gazed at her long neck, the naked shoulders, and the white skin that he had kissed and caressed so many times before.

'Are you done?' she said, as the zip reached the end of its travel.

'Yes,' he muttered, his voice thick with desire.

She turned, holding the dress up to preserve her modesty. Lifting herself up on tip toe, she gave him a kiss on the nose but stayed there, looking deep into his eyes. His desire telegraphed to her. She reached up, putting her arms tightly around his neck. They kissed hungrily. He felt her pulling her body away from him, allowing the wedding dress to slide to the floor.

It had been a frantic, passionate and drunken session, which they had immediately regretted.

He had left her in tears, as the realisation of what had occurred dawned on her. Adultery on her wedding day, was not the best start to an enduring marriage. Full of remorse, he had left the rectory without going back to the reception, later claiming that he'd gone home early because he'd drunk too much.

Over the next twelve months, he had deliberately kept out of her life. Ashamed at what had happened, feeling guilty about spoiling her special day. He was therefore surprised to receive an invitation, to the Christening of Kay and George's son, Tim. He was even more surprised and uncomfortable to get a phone call a few days later from George to ask him if he would be a Godfather. George had apologised for the short notice but told him the original choice of Godfather was going to be away for work.

Tim was then, just three months old.

Geoffery was torn about whether to go or not, let alone accepting the Godfather role, but it was because of George's insistence that he finally agreed.

It was an uncomfortable event for Kay and Geoffery. This had been the first time he'd been anywhere near her since the incident at the wedding. Except for the embarrassed silence, when they were forced to stand together for the obligatory Christening photographs, they had deliberately gone out their way to avoid each other.

Having made his Godfathers promises, to help and guide Timothy spiritually, he stayed only long enough to pose for the usual photographs. Then he left, without going to the pub to 'wet the baby's head', telling George, he had a business deal to clinch.

That had been the last time that he had seen Kay and Tim, until now, over three decades later. It had been hard at first, keeping her out of his thoughts. But as he channelled all his energies into his various business ventures, memories of the times they had together faded. Eventually, having become a multi-millionaire, he moved to Monaco and a very different lifestyle.

But now the past was coming back to haunt him. Perhaps he would be doing more for Tim than he had originally intended.

He had spoilt her special day then, thirty seven years later, he wondered if he could ever make up for his misdemeanor.

The sound of Tim's key in the door, brought their discussions to a premature end.

Chapter Forty Two

The door banged noisily against the doorstop, announcing Tim was back from the 'gym.'

'Is that food on the table?' he bellowed from the hall, removing his coat.

'We have got to sort this out,' Geoffery said conspiratorially. 'Is he or isn't he my son?'

'Please Geoffery. Just leave it. It doesn't matter. It's too late to change things now. Let sleeping dogs lie,' Kay whispered.

'This is a big thing for me Kay. I need to know,' he pleaded.

'Please Geoff, please,' she replied, eyes brimming.

'I'm not sure if I can.'

'Please!'

Her pleading touched him, undermined his intent to get the truth from her today.

'OK. Just for your sake,' Geoffery lied. 'Just for you.'

However, he was determined to continue his investigations. Until he knew. Once and for all.

'Thanks,' Kay said and kissed him on the cheek.

'Oh. Is it that time?' Geoffery said loudly, glancing at his watch.

'Yes. I have to get Tim's dinner on too,' said Kay flustered. 'Or he'll be in a strop all day.'

'OK. I'll chat to him while you're getting it. My taxi is due shortly, anyway.'

'You don't need to go just yet. You're quite welcome to have some food with us.'

'No. It's OK. But thanks anyway. I'll need to get back for my afternoon rest.'

'Of course!'

'I can't smell that dinner. You'd better have it on the table,' shouted Tim shuffling into the room.

Geoffery was pleased to see that he was walking, rather than in his wheelchair.

'Oh. I see he's back,' he said, spotting Geoffery.

'Yes. Sorry Tim. Dinner's going to be a bit late. We had things to discuss.'

'You know I always have my dinner at this time,' he said belligerently.

'You'll just have to be patient today, then won't you,' said Kay, disappearing in to the kitchen.

Tim shuffled slowly over to his games console. His ambling gait, reminding Geoffery of the extent of his disability, and the difficulty of the challenge he'd set. He wondered if he had given Tim, mission impossible, after all.

'Sorry Tim, it's my fault. I kept your mother talking.'

'S'alright,' Tim said, switching on the games monitor.

'So, what do you think of the challenge I've given you?

'S'alright.'

'I gather you don't think much of it?'

'What's that stupid cow been saying?'

'Your Mother is not a stupid cow,' Geoffery remonstrated.

'What's it to you, what I call her?'

'I suggest you start being a bit more polite about her.'

'Why should I?'

'She might not always be around for you. So I suggest, that you show her some appreciation for what she does for you.'

'Hmmm.'

'Anyway, this challenge. I know you can do it,' Geoffery said encouragingly, although far from convinced in his own mind.

'What! Climb Ben Nevis? No chance,' Tim said dismissively.

'If you're determined to do it. You can succeed.'

'Yeah?' Tim said, only half listening, whilst gazing at his games console.

'Yes really. Determination. That's the way that I got my business to the point where it is today.'

'What, climbing Ben Nevis?' Tim said flippantly.

'No. Just with the desire to succeed. That's all you need.'

'Yeah, but you had all your limbs. I'm handicapped. All because of that stupid cow,' Tim said vehemently.

'Do you realise what that lady has done for you all your life?' Geoffery said angrily.

'The only thing I know is, she lost me my legs.'

'No. Septicaemia did that to you.'

'Yeah! But if she'd spotted it...'

'Earlier? I'm sure the doctors would tell you, that once you had the virus, there was nothing anybody could have done to stop the awful effects of the disease.'

'But if she'd...'

'Can you imagine the trauma? What it was like for her, watching the blood poisoning getting worse in her little baby, and not being able to do anything about it?'

'No.'

'Well. The next time you want to abuse your mother. You think about it. At least you've got your life. Use it. Enjoy it. Don't waste your time on self-pity. Get on with it.'

'Get on with it?' Do you know what it's been like growing up with no legs? I have pain where my toes should be. I can't get a woman because the thought of having sex with an amputee appals them. And you tell me to get on with my life.'

'You've got a future ahead of you, if you get off your fat ass and do something with It. Instead of feeling sorry for yourself,' said Geoffery angrily.

Have you ever heard of the three inch barrier?'

'No!'

'Well the next time you're out, see how many pavements don't have lowered sections for wheelchairs.'

'But they're addressing that now, with this equal access act.'

'Yeah, now they are. But there was no such thing as the Disability Discrimination Act when I was growing up.'

'In any case, you have prosthetic legs.'

'I can't wear them all the time.'

'Can't or won't?'

'Listen. Do you know why I like going to these American diners, such a lot...'

'No wonder you're overweight,' Geoffery thought.

'Because they kneel down, when they take your order. We have eye to eye contact. They're not looking down at me, all the bloody time. I get fed up talking to people's belly buttons.'

'Then you should use your legs more. Instead of getting your mother to manhandle that, bloody wheelchair.'

'I'm not going to listen to this crap. Who do you think you are? My father!'

Considering the previous conversation with Kay, this question rattled Geoffery.

'If I was your father, things might have been different,' Geoffery said, thoughtfully.

'Yeah well, thankfully, you're not.'

'No. Think yourself lucky.'

'I gather your cancer thing, is pretty serious. So how long do you reckon you've got?' Tim said insensitively.

Unphased by Tim's question, Geoffery said 'I don't know. But I do know that in the time I've got left, I'm going to do something with it. You've got lots of time. Don't waste the opportunity.'

'Opportunity! What bloody opportunity? You don't know anything about the problems of not having legs.'

'People have climbed Everest without legs.'

'Yeah? Well, that's all television bullshit.'

'I think you'll find it was real. One guy was fitted with carbon fibre legs from the knee down.'

'Well, that would be no good for me. Look! No knees,' Tim said, thumping his prosthetic thigh.

'The guy had crampons fitted and made it to the summit,' Geoffery continued, ignoring Tim's negativity.

'Hooray for him.'

'What I thought was a nice touch to the story, was that many of his climbing colleagues suffered from frost bitten toes, and of course he didn't.'

'Tell you what! I bet, he would have preferred to have had frozen toes rather than no legs.'

'What about that Olympic runner? How fast can he run on those blades?'

'Yeah, yeah, yeah. I've heard it all before.'

'Look. You've had a lifetime of coping without legs.'

'That's what I've been trying to tell you,' Tim said interrupting.

'Have you ever thought of helping other people, who have the same problem? What about children who also have lost limbs due to Meningitis? What about the soldiers who have recently lost limbs?'

'What?'

'What about doing something for the Meningitis Trust?'

'What? Rattling tins at a supermarket?'

'No. The Meningitis Trust do sponsored walks,' Geoffery persisted. 'It's called the 'Five valleys walk'. The route follows footpaths around Stroud. It's over 21 miles, in some of the loveliest Cotswold countryside. It would be good practice for your real challenge.'

'Just because I've lost my legs, doesn't make me some kind of bloody missionary or do-gooder.'

'Well you ought to do something, to get off your fat backside, and become less of a burden to your mother.'

'Piss off. I don't want a frigging job right. I've had enough of this crap,' Tim said, throwing down the games controller angrily. Slowly he struggled to his feet and shuffled towards the door. 'I've already told you, I'm not doing this bloody challenge.'

'That's up to you,' Geoffery said, calling his bluff. 'Just remember, the terms of my will.'

'Anyway,' said Tim, suddenly realising that his belligerent stance was likely to cost him his inheritance. 'I'm in bloody agony just walking around the gym. You should see the state of my stumps,' he said, looking pained.

'I could arrange to get you refitted with more suitable prosthetics,' Geoffery offered.

A knock on the door, announced that the Geoffery's taxi had arrived.

'Just remember what I said,' he said standing. 'You can do it. Just set your mind on the end game. It won't be easy. But then nothing worth having in life is. Kay my taxi has arrived. I'm off,' Geoffery called, making his way to the front door.

Kay came out of the kitchen and escorted him to the taxi.

'When will you tell him?' Geoffery asked.

'Soon,' Kay said. 'Soon.'

'Good girl,' said Geoffery. 'You won't regret it.'

'I already am,' she said distantly.

'You must be strong, You'll have to be firm.'

'But...'

'But nothing. He needs to change his lifestyle. He needs to become an independent man. It will be hard at the start, but I know you can do it.'

'Yes...I...OK.'

'That's my girl,' Geoffery said, giving her a kiss on the cheek and a lingering hug.

Chapter Forty Three

Kay shut the front door and closed her eyes, trying to compose her thoughts. Taking a deep breath, she joined Tim in the lounge, for what she knew would be a stormy session.

'What are you doing sniffing around him?' he demanded, as she entered.

'What do you mean?

'Getting your hair done, poshing yourself up. Don't think I haven't noticed,' Tim said cynically.

'Because I want to. It's got nothing to do with you.'

'Yes it has. If you've tried to get some of my inheritance…'

'What!'

'I know what you're up to.'

'Do you? Do you really? she said angrily. 'Then you probably know that I'm going on holiday, to Italy.'

'Italy! I don't want to go to bloody spaghetti land.'

'I don't care what you want! You're not coming.'

'What! We always go together.'

'Well. Not this time.'

'But. Who will push my chair?'

'I'm sure you'll find some way of getting around. Like, walking for a change.'

'He's put you up to this hasn't he? Ever since he came into our life, he's spoilt everything.'

'May be for you Tim. But he's made me realise, what a fool I've been all these years. From now on, you'll start doing your own things, going your own way. I'm not always going to be around, so you've got to become independent of me.'

'What?'

'I've sheltered you for too long. I thought I was doing the right thing, but now I realise what a selfish man I've brought up.'

'You owe me.'

'I owe you nothing. I've done all I could, more.'

'Yeah, well, you're my mother.'

'Yes, but not your slave. Tim, I think you should move out, and get a place of your own.'

'A place of my own! You've got to be joking. I'm disabled remember.'

'You might be less able physically, because of your legs. But there's no reason why you shouldn't have, a normal life.'

'Normal! Normal! I've got two bleeding lumps of plastic for legs. What's normal about that?'

'You've had prosthetic legs for over thirty years. That's your normality. You've just got to get on with it. I've been at your beck and call for long enough now.'

Kay ran from the room, as the tears welled up. She closed the kitchen door, and wept into a tea towel.

'I hope I've done the right thing. Poor Timmy,' she sobbed.

'It's for the best,' Geoffery's voice filled her head. 'He'll thank you for it later. It'll be the making of him and you,' he had said.

'I hope so Geoff, I really hope so.'

Chapter Forty Four

Thursday October 30th – Sunset count 60

Andy was summoned to Ann Place's office. After knocking briefly, he opened the door and said cheerily. 'Hi Ann, you wanted to see me?'

Andy was happy. He was buoyed up by his success at finding Ben, and bringing James back for Geoffery. Even more pleased, that he didn't have to make the awful trip back to London.

'Please close the door and take a seat,' she said stiffly.

'Blimey, this is a bit formal. Isn't it?' he replied, surprised.

Ann cleared her throat and looked at some papers on her desk.

'Andy. I have been informed that you have been supplying prescription drugs to non-hospice people. Drugs which we believe, you have stolen from the pharmacy here,' she added sternly, looking at him witheringly.

'What? You've got the wrong person. I would never do anything like that. You know me better than that?'

'I'm sorry, but I have no other recourse than to suspend you while the incident is being investigated.'

'Suspend me!' Andy said, in disbelief. 'Where's this come from? Who has reported me?'

'I'm sorry, I can't tell you that, for obvious reasons.'

'What! You think I might attack them?'

'I'm sorry, I can't discuss this any further. I would like you to collect your personal things and leave immediately. I will save you the embarrassment of being escorted off the premises.'

'You really are serious aren't you?' he said, trying to comprehend what she was telling him to do.

'We will contact you when our investigations are completed. At this stage we will not be contacting the police.'

'The Police! What about my Patients?' he said, overwhelmed with the turn of events.

'I have to add, that we are also concerned about your commitment to ALL your patients in your care. It would appear that you have double standards, putting extra efforts in to the care of Mr Foster to the detriment of others,' she added officiously.

'Come on Ann. You know me better than that! I treat everybody with the same level of care, as I always have.'

'Your part time working is causing administrative problems too and will also be revisited.'

'What! But we agreed that if it was causing you problems, we would review it together.'

'Can I now ask you to leave, immediately.'

'What about Mr Foster and all my other patients?'

'I have already made arrangements for their continuing care.'

Ann opened the door for a distraught Andy. Who left, as directed, going straight home.

On his way home, Andy was desperately trying to understand what he'd done which could have caused the problem. He was so totally overwhelmed by the accusation, that he couldn't think straight. He remembered how upset and totally inconsolable when, as a kid, he had been falsely accused of breaking the next door neighbours window. And even now, as an adult, he felt the same, he was absolutely devastated at being accused of something he hadn't done.

'Andy is that you?' Helen called, hearing the front door close.

'Yes,' he said, hanging up his coat.

'What are you doing home, at this time of day? Is everything alright?'

'No.' he said quietly. 'I've been suspended.'

'You've been what?' she said stunned, rushing into the hallway.

'Suspended! They've sent me home.'

'Oh Andy! What's happened?'

'Somebody has reported me for supplying drugs.'

'Supplying drugs! she repeated in astonishment. 'To whom?'

'I don't know,' he said disconsolately.

'Well have you?'

'I can't believe you even asked that,' he said, hurt. 'You know I wouldn't. Of course not,' he emphasised angrily.

'Who is saying you did?'

'They wouldn't tell me.'

'Think. Is there anybody who you've upset recently, anybody likely to bear a grudge about your nursing?'

'No, not that I can think of.' he said miserably, racking his brains.

'Did you upset anybody when the new hut was built? Think! Andy, think!'

'I wonder,' he said, suddenly thinking of his involvement with Geoffery. 'We've had a run in with the wife of one of Geoffery's godsons. I wonder if it's her?'

'Not that dreadful one you were telling me about? The one who beats her husband.'

'Yes. Come to think of it, apparently, she threatened Geoffery, after he liberated her husband the other day.'

'But, I didn't think you were with him then.'

'No, I wasn't.'

'Well, has she got any basis for her allegation?'

'No. I'm very wary about her and would never... although!' he said suddenly recalling his earlier visit with Geoffery.

'What?'

'When we visited her husband, Rupert, at home. He had just been hurt and was still in a lot of pain. He said she had taken his painkillers. So Geoffery took sympathy on him and, inspite of me telling him not to, gave Rupert one of his painkillers. I bet that's what this is all about.'

'Has she got any evidence?'

'I think we might have left the empty box there. Damn it! The packaging had the name of the hospice on it.'

'Oh Andy! What did Geoffery say?'

'I had to leave without talking to anyone,'

'Well you're going to tell him aren't you? After all it was his fault that you've been suspended.'

'Not yet. I need to think.'

'What's to think about? He lost you your job, because of something he did. I suggest you call him straight away and get this sorted.'

'Don't rush me,' he said irritably.

Chapter Forty Five

Friday October 31st – Sunset count 61

James entered the Cheltenham coffee bar sporting a large plaster on the side of his forehead. He was clean shaven and wore new clothes. He walked with a confident swagger. Gone was the shuffling alcoholic gait. But his swarthy face, his red rimmed eyes and shaking hands, bore the evidence of his harsh life on the streets. He had been invited by Geoffery, who stood slowly as he approached.

'Hello James,' he said, stretching out his hand. 'It's been a long time.'

'Geoffery. Pleased to see you old chap,' James said, trying not to show his shocked reaction, to the grey faced individual, whose bony hand he shook.

'How's the hotel?'

'Bed's a bit soft. I've had to sleep on the floor for the last few nights, and it's so stuffy in the room, in spite of sleeping with all the windows open.'

'Well, I guess after sleeping on the streets for so long, it will take you some time to get back to living in doors again. Anyway thanks for coming.'

'It doesn't look like the years have been kind to either of us, does it?' James said, studying Geoffery's sallow complexion.

'Exposure to life, eh? But I guess we had some fun, en route though. I must say it's nice to see something of the old you. Not the old tramp, that stared out at me, from the photos.'

'Photos? Oh of course, your spies.'

'That's how I tracked you down initially, and then of course Andy and Ben.'

'What I'd like to know. Was Ben and those yobs, all part of your grand scheme to get me here?' he said, touching the plaster gingerly.'

'I'm flattered that you think I am able to orchestrate such things. But I can assure you those were, totally coincidental,' Geoffery said, looking him straight in the eye.

'I'll believe you, but thousands wouldn't. I know what manipulative powers you've got, don't forget.'

'You've got too vivid an imagination.'

'Really? What about a little bit of arson to get your own way?'

'Don't know what you're talking about, to be sure.'

'Old Scout hut, New Scout hut, for instance. Ben and Andy were talking about it, on the way back from London. I recognised a similar modus operandi in some property dealings, with which you've been involved, over the years.'

'Purely coincidental, I can assure you,' he lied.

'I think Ben could do with a public declaration that he wasn't responsible for the fire, don't you? It's 'eating him up'. He's fearful that someone will convince the police, that he did it.'

'I'm sure we can get a fire report, to indicate that it was an electrical fault,' Geoffery said uncomfortably. Surprised that James had seen through his little scheme.

James felt pleased that he had been able to do this for Ben.

'You know, there's something about wearing clean clothes isn't there?' James said lightly, admiring his new jacket.

'James, I'm glad they managed to persuade you to get off the streets, and even more pleased, that we have the chance to meet again.'

'I'm intrigued that you should expound all this effort to find me, and bring me here. So, what's it all about?' he asked curiously.

'All will become clear. First let me ask you a few questions.'

'Sure, fire away. But you're not being a very good host. Do you think I could have a drink?'

'Of course. Apologies for my oversight. Americano or Cappuccino?'

'I was thinking of, something a little stronger.'

'Espresso perhaps?' Geoffery said, mischievously.

'I was thinking of something alcoholic. I need to maintain the alcohol to blood ratio.'

'I'm sorry, but this is all part of your challenge.'

'Challenge? What do you mean, challenge?'

'It's pretty obvious, that you've been down on your luck recently.'

'Yes. I think we can agree on that understatement.'

'I want to help you, sort yourself out. So you can make a fresh start.'

'What on? Buttons!'

'Don't worry about the financial side of things. I'll deal with that.'

'So long as there is an endless supply of booze available, I shall be happy.'

'You might be disappointed, with that side of the deal.'

James was clearly struggling to concentrate on the conversation. His hands were shaking, he kept subconsciously running the back of his hand over his dry lips.

'Look! About this drink, I really need something. I just want a small bottle, that's all.'

Geoffery ignored the request and carried on with his prepared approach.

'You know, your parents were great people. I owe it to them to help you now.'

'I can't really remember too much about them,' James said, irrationally running his hand through his hair.

'Pity! They were lovely people.'

'Yeah, well my guardian never spoke of them either.'

'Well that makes me feel very bad then.'

'Why?'

'I was your Godfather; I should have been there to help you.'

'That's water under the bridge. So what brings you back into my life now, after all these years?'

'Making amends.'

'For?'

'Duties that I failed to carry out.'

'Steady on old chap. This sounds like a confession. Dereliction of duty.'

'I've had people looking into your life. It's a mess, isn't it?'

'It's not gone the way I planned it. No.'

'Yacht gone. Ferrari sold. Penthouse, part of the past.'

'A temporary blip. It's the nature of things when you live my sort of lifestyle.'

'Living on the streets for over a year...is a long, temporary blip.'

'Well you know.'

'Losing Sebastian, was that the trigger?'

'Look, I'd rather not talk about him, if it's all the same to you,' said James, taken aback at the sound of Sebastian's name.

'You need to talk about it, to help you move on.'

'Are you sure there's nothing stronger in here?' James said, looking around.

'You need help, and I can give you that. But only if you want it.'

'A nice bottle of sherry would do for a start,' said James, his hands shaking.

'You need to dry out James. I can help you do that. In a clinic.'

'I don't need to dry out. Just, another bottle. That's all I need.'

'Does it help?'

'That's a stupid question. Of course it does. Just like your painkillers.'

'Sebastian wouldn't like to see you like this.'

'Sebastian is dead. Just leave it will you,' said James angrily.

Frightened that he'd drive James away, by pursuing the point, Geoffery altered tack. 'I gather that you found young Ben, in London?'

'Yes.'

'He's a nice kid isn't he?'

'I tell you what. If he'd been up there any longer, he would have been into the street life. The pimps would have had him into drugs and prostitution. There are a lot of kids like him up there. Runaways. All looking for a better life.'

'Is that what you find in the bottle, James. A better life?'

'You know his mother's an alcoholic?' James said, avoiding the question.

'Yes, he told me,' Geoffery confirmed.

'Ha, the little bugger even tried to convert me. Get me on the wagon. Incidentally the mini bar in my room is empty. Any chance of..?'

'I don't think that's wise is it?'

'A man could die of thirst,' he said plaintively.

'That's another reason why Ben ran away. Her drinking, and choice of boyfriends.'

'From one drunk to another, eh!' said James, trying to control his shaking hands.

'If you won't do it for yourself, why don't you do it for Ben? I gather you might owe him one? Probably saved your life with his first aid?'

'I think that's exaggerating it a bit. Anyway, London's not the place for him. I don't want the kid throwing his life away. Right.'

'I'm glad you said that, because I don't want you throwing your life away either. I've got a challenge for you?'

'Yes, so you said. Sounds intriguing, but I'm not interested.'

'I want you to go into a clinic, to help you to get off the booze.'

'Why should I?'

'Because you're still young, and have a life to live.'

'What's the point?'

'The point is you can take charge of your life again, and move on. It's up to you, what you do after.'

'Such as?'

'Perhaps help young runaways in London, by persuading those that will, to go back home. Or even help shelter those who won't.'

'Sorry old chap. You've got me mixed up with somebody else. I'm no bleeding evangelist.'

'No, but you could help. Look, I've done some investigations and there are a few homeless organizations that are struggling for help.'

'So?'

'Well, you know what it's like to live rough. Why don't you help to set up a homeless shelter? A bed for the night scheme. I'll obviously fund it.'

'I don't owe anyone, anything. Right now I need a drink,' James said, standing and headed for the exit.

'Damn it,' said Geoffery, hitting the table. 'Then again, nobody said it would be easy.'

Chapter Forty Six

Saturday November 1st – Sunset count 62

Geoffery's meticulous planning in setting Tim a realistic challenge included consulting various organisations who undertake the training of people who lose limbs, including a Service's Limbless Veterans organisation. Having been impressed by the incredible feats achieved by some amputees from the armed services, Geoffery decided to provide Tim with a trainer. Consequently he had recruited a former soldier, Carrie, to become Tim's trainer, in order to improve his chances of succeeding in the challenge. He insisted that Tim was not to be told about the arrangement, because of Tim's obvious dislike of him.

Geoffery had selected Carrie from a list of possible trainers, because she too, was a double amputee, who, like many Service people, kept herself incredibly fit. Born and bred in Newcastle, her Geordie accent had softened with her exposure to other dialects in the army, but she had still maintained her tough Northern values. She was the sort of person, that Geoffery reckoned would be ideal, to 'tame' the petulant Tim.

Carrie was waiting for Geoffery in the hospice day room, to give him an update of Tim's progress.

'How's it been going?' Geoffery asked. 'Hard work isn't he?'

'He's neet that bad, considerin eez problems,' Carrie said positively.

'Well, you've obviously seen something in him, that I couldn't see,' he replied surprised.

'Sure, he's unfit. But eatin the stuff he tells me he devoors, an' bein a virtual couch potato, wey, frankly, I'm neet at all surprised. Ah think I can knock him intee shape though,' Carrie said optimistically.

'It must be your influence that's doing it then. I knew I made a good choice to appoint you as his mentor. How long's it been, since he joined the gym?'

'Must be about, a couple of weeks now. But, give him credit, he does go every day.'

'That's probably because you've befriended him.'

'We get on alreet.'

'Do you think he suspects anything?'

'Neet as far as I'm aware! He thinks, I'm just somebody he's met at the gym, an we both have the same physical constraints.'

'Good. Because if he suspects I'm involved, he's most likely to give up. You might have detected, that we don't exactly see eye to eye.'

'So, if you don't get on, why bother wi him?' she asked, curious about Geoffery's motives, for continuing the strained relationship.

'It's a long story,' he said. 'Let's just say, I need to do it, for his own good.'

'Alreet, well whatever,' she conceded. 'Anyway, he's gettin sum basic level of fitness. I'm plannin to take him to Wales eventually, to give him sum real mountain experience.'

'Thanks for your persistence,' Geoffery said encouraged by her positive assessment. 'You'll of course be getting a bonus, on top of your regular trainer's wages. If you succeed.'

'That's very generous, thank you. Ah like a bit of a challenge mysel,' Carrie said, revelling in the physicality of the mission. 'We'll get him up the mountains, don't yee worry.'

Tim had also confided in Carrie, the reason he was trying to get fit, which assisted her in suggesting a training regime best suited in preparing for the challenge.

She recalled the first hint of his challenging nature, shortly after she'd latched on to him when he said 'I've been meaning to ask. Why are you called Carrie? Your gym membership form has you listed as Caroline?'

'Have yee been nosin at my stuff?'

'No, just happened to be at reception the other day and saw it.'

'Wey if yee must know, my army colleagues gave me the nickname from the Stephen King movie.'

'Carrie! Yeah I know,' he said, recalling the film from his extensive video collection.

'They said ah was a 'scary bird' wi spooky powers.'

'Why?'

'There's this army training room, that they call the 'killing house'. Wey, yee have to anticipate where targets are likely to pop oop and shoot them. Wey, consistently ah got top score,' she informed him modestly.

'Killing House! Wow, that sounds just like an Xbox game. Great.'

'Except, this game's for real, though. If you're in a real firefight, yee don't get a second life. Anyway that was a long time ago,' she said dismissively. 'In a previous life. I've moved on now.'

'So as well as a training companion, I've got my own bodyguard too, great.'

'And a trained medic too,' she added.

She had eventually persuaded him to leave the comforts of the gym and to start walking outdoors, as well.

At first, the training walks had been on relatively flat paths in the Severn Valley; but as his stamina improved Carrie planned to take him into the Forest of Dean and the hills and valleys of the nearby Cotswold Hills whose limestone escarpment dominated the countryside.

As a result of their daily training regime, Tim, although still overweight, had lost one stone but was starting to feel marginally better about tackling the challenge.

Chapter Forty Seven

Sunday November 2nd – Sunset count 63

Ben was enjoying being home. His mother had welcomed him with promises that she would give up drinking and they would do things together. All of which he hoped for, but realistically knew that neither was likely to happen. Returning from his nightmare stay in London, gave him a different perspective on his life. Irrespective of the angst that his mother caused him, he suddenly appreciated what he had by way of his friends and the pleasure he got from riding his bike. It was while he was making his way home, through an autumn cloaked park, that he saw James, sitting on a bench, clutching a bottle. 'Oh no! Not again,' he said under his breath.

Doing a dramatic back wheel skid, he pulled up in front of the bench. 'James, what are you doing?' he demanded angrily.

'Hello, my friend. My life saver! Have a drink Bengie, my boy,' James said, proffering the half empty sherry bottle.

'You know I don't drink.'

'Just a little sip, for old times' sake,' he insisted.

Under the bench Ben could see several other discarded bottles.

'No thanks. Just look at you. It didn't take you long to get back into bad habits did it?' Ben said annoyed.

'What's it to do with you, what I get up to? You're not my keeper.'

'No but you're in no fit state to stay here. You'll get arrested. They don't tolerate drunks here.'

'In which case I shall retire to my hotel,' James said, struggling to stand.

'You're in no fit condition to go back to your hotel either. Come on, you'd better come home with me.'

'I don't think I want to. Thank you very much,' James said, clearly well-oiled. 'I'm having a nice time here...and I have to say the park benches here are much nicer than those in London,' he slurred.

'Come on! On your feet,' Ben insisted.

'You know. Perhaps that's why there aren't so many drunks around here,' James said, standing unsteadily.

'Why do I always end up wet nursing adults?' Ben said quietly.

'Pardon?'

'Oh. Nothing! Come on James. Just hold on to my bike,' he instructed, grabbing James's free hand. 'Let me have that bottle. I think you you've had enough. Don't you?'

Ben threw the half empty bottle into a rubbish bin that they were passing.

'Hey, that wasn't very nice,' James said, resigned to the loss.

Ben wheeled the bike and James erratically out of the park. It was a slow and meandering trip through the back streets. Ben kept constantly remonstrating with James, to hold on to the bike. Eventually they arrived at the semidetached council house.

Propping James up, Ben dropped his bike on the grassless lawn. Opening the shabby front door, he shouted. 'Mum, I'm bringing my friend James in. Are you decent?'

Ben led James into the hallway, just as his mother was staggering out of the kitchen with a glass, half filled with some 'golden' liquid. She was obviously, also drunk.

Ben's spirits sank.

In spite of her 'problem', she prided herself on her appearance. Her first job every morning was to apply the 'warpaint. She was never seen in public with a hair out of place. And at 30, and inspite of her dependence on alcohol, she still kept her attractive, youthful looks.

'James. You must be the man that found my boy in Lunnun,' she slurred, planting a kiss on James's cheek. 'My name's Beth.'

'Hello Beth, Ben's Mum. Beth, that's a nice name,' said James, hugging her briefly.'

'Come in to the lounge and have a drink,' she said, swaying her way towards the door off the hallway. 'Pardon the mess,' she said, pointing at the dining table, still covered in the previous night's dinner plates. 'I haven't had a chance to tidy up yet.'

'Look at the pair of you! Pissed as rats,' Ben said disconsolately. 'Is it any wonder I want to get out of this shit hole?'

'It's a nice shit hole,' James said looking around.

'Please sit down,' Beth said gesturing to the large L shaped sofa. 'We don't stand on ceremony around here.'

James did as instructed. Sitting down on a well-worn soft leather sofa, whose weak springs gave way as he did so.

' This is hard looking after you two. I could do with a holiday, to get over it. Not that that's likely to happen, though,' Ben said sarcastically.

'I have taken you on holiday,' Beth riposted.

'Yeah. But you spoil it, by immediately heading straight for the bar?'

'That's what holidays are all about. Booze and sun. Isn't that right, James?'

'S'right.'

'No Mum. How about THIS son, for a change?' Ben said, pointing to himself.

'You're alright. You're a big boy now. Why. You're almost a man.'

'He's right Mrs.'

'Call me Beth.'

'He's right Beth. I know what it's like to have no childhood.'

'He's OK. He just doesn't like my men friends, that's all,' she said, tousling Ben's hair.

'No. Because they use you. They don't respect you,' Ben said, clearly ashamed by his Mother's conduct. 'My friends think you're on the game. How do you think that makes me feel?'

'Well. They're wrong aren't they? I like a bit of male company, that's all,' Beth confessed.

'So did I! until..,' said James, his eyes and thoughts distant.

'Are you gay, James?' Beth said, after a few minutes while her fogged brain grappled with the implications of James's comment.

'I had a wonderful man, as a lover. Yes.'

'Oh no! And you've been alone with my Ben,' she said, wrapping her arms around Ben's shoulders.

'Mum, he's gay. He's not a Paedo,' Ben said, pushing her, and her ignorant concern away.

'Is there a difference?' she demanded, still trying to cuddle Ben.

'Yes of course! I don't get off with kids! I don't sleep around!'

'Not like you Mum,' Ben said hurtfully, hoping his words would penetrate to her alcoholically desensitised conscience.

'I've not been in a relationship since…since…'James said, starting to cry.

'Oh dear! He's upset. Don't cry James,' Beth said. And, forgetting her previous concern, she slid along the sofa, and hugged him.

'His friend died. James found his body,' Ben informed her, coldly.

'Oh, that must have been terrible,' Beth said, patting James's back unnecessarily.

'I couldn't cope. He was everything to me,' James sobbed.

'Let me get you a drink,' Beth said, attempting to stand.

'No Mum,' Ben admonished. 'That's your answer to everything, isn't it? I'll get some coffee.'

'He doesn't understand. He's only a kid,' Beth said sympathetically. 'I find a drink helps, at times like this.'

'I loved Sebastian so much. Why did he leave me? Why?' James asked irrationally, sobbing.

'Oh don't upset yourself. You'll make me cry too,' Beth said, putting her arm around him again.

Ben returned from the kitchen with three mugs of instant coffee and set them down.

'I don't know why he left such a nice bloke like you,' Beth continued.

'Mum. He died!' Ben said patronisingly.

'Oh yes! Of course! I'm so sorry to hear about him. But I do know how you feel,' she confided.

'Do you?' James said through his tears.

'Yeah, it was like when Ben's father left me. I really loved him. He was my first lover. It broke my heart, when I found out he was already married and had kids.'

'Father left you?' said Ben surprised.

'He left, as soon as he knew I was pregnant. Perhaps I never got over it either.'

'But you always told me my Dad was dead, when I asked you about him,' Ben said reproachfully.

'I didn't want to hurt you Ben,' Beth said, suddenly realising her blunder.

'Did you try to see him, after I was born? To show me to him?' Ben demanded.

'Yes of course I did. He didn't want to see you,' she continued, adding to her insensitive revelation.

'That must be terrible for you Ben. Knowing that your father didn't want to see you,' James said, inadvertently adding to Ben's misery.

Chapter Forty Eight

Ben felt as though his head would explode at this devastating news. Deeply upset, he ran from the house in tears. Leaping on his bike, he recklessly tore off down the road.

Beth chased after him. 'Ben, Ben. Come back,' she shouted. 'I'm sorry. I'm sorry.'

But Ben was lost in his own wretchedness, and continued his headlong dash away from the source of his hurt.

As he turned the corner, Beth returned to the house. James was leaning against the door frame.

'Ooops,' he said unhelpfully.

'Oh dear,' she said. 'Now I've lost him again.'

'That wasn't very smart was it?' James said witheringly. 'Don't worry, 'I'll find him. I found him once before. But then again, he was on my territory,' he said, suddenly realising where he was. 'I guess, you'll have to help me this time, though.'

'No! He's best, left to himself,' Beth said, gently dabbing a tear from her eye, vainly trying to avoid smudging her mascara.

'I don't think that's a good idea,' James said, trying to think of a plan.

'I know my son,' she said firmly.

'I don't think you know him very well,' James said perceptively.

'What do you mean by that?'

'He loves you! He cares for you! He hates seeing you, demean yourself with these men.'

'He's never said,' she replied defensively.

'Does he have to?'

'Well, how would I know?'

'Just look into his eyes. Look into your heart. He's your child,' James said gently. 'Come on lets go.'

Beth led him through a bewildering labyrinth of alleyways. Together they staggered and swayed their way through the estate. They had been searching for thirty minutes without spotting Ben.

'I hope he's OK. Only we've had a few young people kill themselves round here,' Beth said fearfully.

'Don't think like that. I'm sure he'll be OK,' James said, sobering up at the thought.

'I've never seen him so upset like this before.'

'He's a tough kid. But sometimes, hurtful truths can breach even the toughest of veneers.'

'I wasn't thinking. What have I done?' she said, wringing her hands.

'When we find him, you'll have to make up for it, big time.'

'I know where he'll be!' she said suddenly. 'At the park! Why didn't I think of that earlier?'

As they approached the fenced off grassy area, they could see a lone figure riding up and down on the bike stunt ramps. It was Ben.

'Oh thank heaven for that,' Beth said relieved, putting her hand to her heart.

Ben ignored them, as they approached the quarter pike, and continued riding his BMX backwards and forwards with clockwork regularity.

'Ben! Look! I'm sorry I didn't tell you before,' Beth said, struggling to find the right words.

Ben continued riding, ignoring his Mother.

'Ben, your Mum is trying to apologise,' said James, trying to broker the peace.

Ben continued his metronomic riding.

'I'm sure if your Dad saw you now, he would be very proud of you,' Beth continued.

Ben stopped his bike and stared at her. 'My Dad doesn't even know I'm alive,' he said angrily. 'So why would he?' Why are adults always so self-centered?'

'Not all adults are the same,' James said, trying to find a plausible explanation.

'No. Just the ones in my life,' Ben admonished. 'Look at the pair of you! Neither of you can live, without getting courage from the inside of a bottle! So what chance do I have? Oh, what's the point?'

Ben resumed his riding.

'You're right Ben. We have been weak. Unfortunately, there are some things in life, emotional hurt, which are hard to face without...without help,' James said gently.

'Yes. But other people cope without being permanently drunk. Why can't you?'

'We're not all as strong as you. Sometimes, we need a morale prop to help us,' James added.

'So why don't you get help, and get off the booze?' Ben retorted.

'It's easier said, than done,' Beth said quietly.

'No it's not! You're not kids! You don't have people telling you what to do. You can do it yourself,' he shouted, as he still continued his bike manoeuvres.

'If only it was that simple,' said James thoughtfully.

'What's so difficult? You just make up your mind, and change things.'

'But we....,' Beth started.

'But you don't want to change do you?' Ben shouted angrily. 'That's the point. You want to carry on in the same way, and nothing will change. So don't tell me you're sorry.'

'No you're wrong,' James said quickly.

'Yeah!'

'Yes. Geoffery is going to send me to a clinic to help me, sort things out,' James was amazed to hear himself say. For up until that moment, he had no intention of accepting Geoffery's offer to enter a clinic.

'Well, I'll believe that when I see it,' Ben said sceptically.

'No I promise. Cross my heart,' James said to reinforce his, new, unexpected but, serious intent.

'What will you do now Ben?' Beth asked, apprehensive of his response.

'Probably run away again,' Ben said miserably.

'Ben. You've seen what it's like on the streets. Why would you want to go back to that?' James said, reminding him of the dreadful time he'd had in London.

'Because ...of you...because of her...I don't know!'

'You know, my life was so different before... before Sebastian died,' James reflected. 'I had pride in myself. When I put on these new clothes and met Geoffery, it felt different, almost like old times,' James confided. 'I do want to change.'

'But you went back on the bottle,' Ben reminded him.

'I know. I'm not proud of it. But then again I had never intended to give up anyway.'

'So you lied to me.'

'No. I said I hadn't intended to. That doesn't mean I won't do it now that I've said I would,' James clarified. 'I know it won't be easy, and I'm sure there will be times when I revert to the bottle, but I'll try. Right!'

Ben nodded.

'You have given me a reason to try to climb out of this…this alcoholic abyss…and perhaps we can help your Mum sort herself out too,' James continued, looking towards Beth for a reaction.

'Mum?'

'Well I…it's difficult. It's the only bit of comfort I get,' Beth muttered.

'See! I told you. She doesn't want to change.'

'No, no I do but… We haven't got any money to spend on going into these posh clinics. They're for rich people, not for the likes of me.'

'No you're wrong. They are for everybody with a problem,' James said encouragingly. 'In any case, I'm sure Geoffery would help.'

'Well I don't know.'

'As soon as she gets with those men again. She'll be back to her old ways,' Ben added knowingly.

'OK, I'll give it a try,' Beth said after some hesitation. 'I won't promise though.'

'OK, we'll do it then. Together,' James said, grabbing Beth's hand.

'Are you serious?' Ben quizzed them both, looking carefully at each one to see if they were showing any signs of deceit.

'Yes,' they said in unison.

Ben dropped his bike, ran over and hugged them both.

'Thanks. I'll help you when things get tough,' he said smiling. 'Remember now. You promised,' he reminded them. 'You won't break your promise will you?'

'So you won't be running away again then?' Beth said, hopefully, already fearful of a life without the anaesthetic comfort of alcohol or someone close to help her battle the demons.

Chapter Forty Nine

Monday November 3rd – Sunset count 64

A week after Geoffery helped him escape from the 'house of torture', Rupert returned to work still bearing some of the facial injuries that Sue had inflicted on him. He told anxious work colleagues who asked him how he got them, that he and some mates were messing around, after a night on the beer, pushing each other around on large supermarket, high sided merchandising cages. When he had a go, the thing toppled over into a pot hole and, unable to get his hands out of the mesh in time, he took the full force of the collapse on his face.

Knowing this type of behaviour was out of character, many of them were sceptical about his story. Consequently there were various rumours circulating about how he had got injured, including car crashes, being beaten up by his girlfriend's former lover. Thankfully, he thought, nobody dreamt of the real reason.

Rupert returned to his car after work that evening, relieved to be back in to a familiar workplace routine, the stress of the previous weeks at last starting to ebb away. He drove out of the car park after swiping his security card through the reader at the exit. As he joined the queue of traffic heading towards the main roundabout, he heard a noise from the back seat. Looking into the rear view mirror, he was horrified to see Sue's face staring back at him.

'Rupert. You'll really have to be more vigilant. I could have been anybody laying in wait. I could be a murderer,' she emphasised the word. His heart sank. The fear returned. 'Careful now. Mind you don't crash,' she added, as he clipped the kerb at the shock of seeing her. 'You didn't think you could escape from me did you? I have to look after you. For better for worse. Remember? You need me because you are weak and pathetic. You're not strong enough to live without me,' she shouted.

'I found that stuff you'd been feeding me for all those years. I've broken free of your chemical sedation,' he said bravely.

'Have you really? Well I think you'd better drive us home so you can resume the regime, don't you? We'll talk about your disobedience during one of our special talks.' The menace, clear in her threat.

Rupert's newly regained self-confidence, suddenly evaporating, as he recalled the horrors of her 'special talks.'

'How did you get in to the car?'

'When your boss came and got it. You forgot to tell him about the spare key. Silly boy,' she mocked. 'Where are you friends now, when you need them? Oh, don't worry, I have plans for them too,' she said malevolently. 'They'll soon find out that nobody messes with me. They'll regret the day they ever interfered in our, 'special' marriage,' she said, becoming animated.

Rupert was frantically thinking of escape, his hand moving towards the door handle. Unfortunately, she had already anticipated that possibility.

'Oh don't think you can suddenly leap out of the car. This remote central locking is great, isn't it?' His hopes died as he heard the electrical clunking of all four door locks engaging.

She grabbed his hair, yanking his head back, whispering into his ear. 'I'm going to enjoy our reunion,' she said vengefully. 'I've brought some of our special toys with me.' She let go of his hair and he heard the sound he dreaded, the ripping of Velcro.. He knew what was coming. As she tried to reach his head again, he leant forward until his chest was resting on the steering wheel.

As he desperately fought off his nemesis, the cars ahead in the queue started moving. Cars behind them, annoyed at the additional delay beeped their horns. Momentarily distracted, Rupert lifted his head and was immediately grabbed by her. She stuck her long nails into the arm which he had broken, causing him to scream in pain. 'Sit up and stop struggling,' she shouted. 'Come on, move the car forward. We don't want to upset your fellow travellers or get your colleagues concerned about your welfare, do we?' she added, easing the pressure on his arm

He sat up reluctantly and moved the car forward, as instructed.

'That's a good boy,' she said, pulling his head back, and encircling his neck with a collar.

Rupert put his fingers under the collar as she was putting it around his throat, only to be screamed at and having his hair pulled violently.

'Put your hand back on that steering wheel. It's bad driving to only have one hand on the wheel.'

He did as he was told, now totally subservient, his mind numb, his mouth dry with fear. She briefly let go of his hair and closed the Velcro strap at the back of his neck.

'Now Rupert, I think you need to be reminded of what happens to a naughty boy, when he's bad. Don't you?'

The traffic stopped again.

A jolt of electricity went through his neck, making it feel as those his brain had exploded. His eyes bulged and he let out a scream. He had a funny, familiar, tinny taste in his mouth. Involuntarily he jumped up out of the seat, stalling the car.

The electric shock dog collar used by some dog trainers had been outlawed in the canine world. But Sue had found that it met her macabre requirements very nicely.

'Right Rupert, what pain threshold setting do you think I should use now? The high voltage setting 'Very badly misbehaved dog', the medium setting 'Badly misbehaved dog' or 'the low setting Come to heel'? Not sure? Then I think this will do,' she said resetting the small controller. 'Badly misbehaved dog' it is then,' she said hitting the button again.

Rupert's reaction was the same, except this time he had bitten his lip. Blood and saliva dribbled on to his shirt front.

'Come on you naughty boy. The queue has moved on again. We don't want any road rage do we?' she said, firing the charge again and laughing manically at his reaction.

Eventually, they got on to the M5 motorway and headed north. Rupert desperately trying to think of some way to get out of the dreadful situation, which, unless he did, he knew would end in a beating.

As if she could read his thoughts, she told him to, 'Forget any ideas of escape.'

Farther up the motorway they caught up with a queue of traffic all doing less than the national speed limit of 70 mph. He correctly guessed that the motorists were uncertain whether to overtake each other, fearing they might get a speeding ticket, if, at the head, there was a Police car. Confusingly, at a distance Police cars and Highways Agency Traffic Officer vehicles looked similar.

He started overtaking the queue, until ahead he could see the familiar 4 by 4. Indeed, the procession was following a liveried vehicle, emblazoned with large yellow and blue squares and high visibility hatching on the rear. Rupert decided that, if it was a Police vehicle, this might offer him the chance for which he'd been hoping. As he got closer he could see the word 'Police' signwritten on the bumper. He felt elated.

'Steady now Rupert,' she instructed. 'We don't want you to get points on your licence do we? Now, that would be a cruel punishment,' she laughed, briefly hitting the charge button again. Recovering from the shock, he found the courage to shout. 'Don't be stupid. Do you want to kill us?'

'Just be careful,' she said.

Rupert continued slowly overtaking the queue of vehicles until he drew level with the Police Car and started matching their speed. Desperately looking across at them, hoping to attract their attention.

Sue immediately saw through his plan and warned him. 'Don't even think about it,' she said malevolently. Otherwise the next reminder will be 'Very Badly behaved'.'

Annoyed that she had guessed his intentions and in a fit of pique, a mixture of fear and foolhardiness, he decided he needed to end the situation one way or another. Pushing the accelerator down hard, he sped away from the Police Car, quickly reaching ninety miles per hour.

Chapter Fifty

'What the hell are you doing you stupid idiot? she screamed, blasting his neck with another charge. At that speed his involuntary reaction caused the car to veer across all three lanes, narrowly avoiding crashing into the central barrier.

The response from the Police Car was immediate. The blue lights came on with the two tone siren blaring. Within a short distance the patrol car had quickly caught up with them, flashing it's headlights, gesticulating for them to stop.

'You stupid bastard,' she shouted, quickly removing the dog collar from his neck and stuffing it into the seat pocket. 'You'll regret doing that.'

'No I won't,' Rupert shouted back. It's something I should have done a long time ago. Standing up to you, and your bullying. You bitch.'

'Oh, a moment of bravery, eh?. Don't worry. You might think you've won today. But never underestimate me. You'll never be able to relax. You'll never be free of me.'

'We'll see,' he said. 'You've gone too far this time.'

'I'm warning you! Don't say anything.'

He pulled the car on to the hard shoulder and shortly the passenger from the Police vehicle was at their car.

'Hello Sir, would you mind opening the door and join me in the back seat of the Patrol Car. I need to ask you some questions.'

Rupert tried to open the door which was still locked.

Sue wound down her window and moved over to the passenger side.

'It's OK officer. We have a car problem. The garage said it's a fault on the accelerator. It suddenly gives the turbo an unexpected boost. Whatever that means,' she said, feigning mechanical ignorance to give credence to her story.

'In that case, if you know that happens, you shouldn't be driving it. Sir, if you wouldn't mind I need to take some details.'

Sue unlocked the car doors with the spare key. As Rupert stepped out, he felt as though he'd won the lottery. She was going to go to jail. At last he'd beaten her. She glared at him as he walked past her, the threat obvious.

In the back of the Police Car, Rupert told the amazed Policemen that he had been kidnapped by his wife. During their journey, she had been torturing him with electric shocks. And because he was a victim of domestic violence, there was a court injunction out to prevent her seeing him.

'Well clearly, that's serious allegations you're making there. While my colleague checks out your story with control, I'll go and have words with your wife.'

The Policeman left Rupert and his colleague and went and sat in the front passenger seat of Rupert's car. He told Sue of Rupert's allegation's.

'That doesn't surprise me,' she said calmly. 'My husband suffers from a Bi-polar condition. He keeps getting episodes where he believes I am kidnapping him. It happens almost every time we go somewhere together. Sometimes happens even when we're shopping. It's most embarrassing,' she lied. 'Unfortunately we've left his medication at home.'

'I see. But he was also telling us that you have tortured him with some sort of collar around his neck.'

Sue laughed. 'Oh, that old chestnut again. He's part of a trial using electric shock therapy. When he's having an episode, and as much as I hate doing it, I have to give him an electric shock. Which is why I was sitting behind him.'

'Yes we did notice.'

'We don't normally use it while he's driving, but because we forgot his medicine. It was the only way of getting him home.'

'It's an extremely dangerous thing to do. You could have caused a serious accident. Do you not drive Madam?'

'Yes, but he needs to be doing something to keep him active. Otherwise he is liable to self-harm. That's how he got those injuries to his face. He did that to himself. If he wasn't driving, he might leap out of the car. Which is why I always take the precaution of locking us in.

The Police driver came up to the car and gestured for the other one to get out for a chat.

'There is no record of domestic violence between these two,' The driver said. 'There are no complaints lodged by neighbours or anybody else.'

'Well that seems to bear out her story. She reckons that he's suffering from some Bi-polar disorder. What about the Court injunction?'

'This time of night, there's no way of checking. Everybody has gone home from that department. What about his injuries?'

'She reckons he's self-harming.'

'OK let's have words with him again.'

The two Policemen returned back to their car.

'Right Sir. We're in a bit of a quandary. There are no reports of domestic violence on record for you or your wife.'

'But I can assure you. She did this to me,' Rupert said, pointing at his bruised face.

'Are you sure you didn't do this to yourself Sir?'

'No, of course not. What about the Court injunction? That will confirm what I'm saying.'

'I'm afraid we can't verify that either. Is there anybody you can call who will support your claims?'

'No. Umm. Let me think. Yes of course. It was my Godfather who has taken out the Court injunction on my behalf.'

'Your Godfather? Why would he do that, rather than you?' The Policeman said sceptically.

'He rescued me after she beat me up. He's got a team of lawyers that did it for him.'

'OK. Do you think we could talk to this, Godfather?' The other Policeman said patronisingly. Now starting to believe Sue's account.

'Yes, his numbers in my mobile,' he said, getting his phone out of his pocket.

Selecting Geoffery's number he pressed the call icon on the screen and listened. 'There, its ringing,' Rupert said, handing the phone over to the Policeman. After a few moments, the Policeman handed the phone back to Rupert. 'No reply,' the other said.

'Anybody else you could call?'

Before he could answer, both Policeman suddenly became intent on listening to a message on their radio earpieces. After a few moments, the Driver said. 'Look, we've got a call. There's a major RTC, Road Traffic Collision, we need to attend. We're going to give you a caution and count yourself lucky that you won't get any points. In the meantime we'll take you back to your car.'

'No. I don't want to get back in the car with her. Please believe me she's kidnapped me. I didn't do this to myself. Please I need help.'

'I'm sure you do. But it's not the help we can give you. I suggest you get back into your car and go home and take your medicine.' The Policeman unaware of the irony of what he was saying.

'Come on Sir, let me escort you back to your car. We need to be off.'

Rupert's euphoria at escaping her vanished. Depressed at the turn of events, he became morose, doubting that he would ever be able to convince them of the truth.

Arriving at their car, the Policeman suggested that Sue drove them home while Rupert sat in the front passenger seat, with the doors locked.

Sue couldn't believe her luck that they had believed her story. And smirked as the Policeman was closing the car door.

Suddenly Rupert's mobile rang. Rupert opened the phone and saw the name. It was Geoffery. His face lit up. Sue also saw the name and attempted to grab the phone from him. But he was too quick for her.

'Uncle Geoffery, thank you for calling back. Can you tell this Policeman about the Court Injunction. Sue has tried to kidnap me.'

Rupert handed the phone to the Policeman, who listened to Geoffery confirming everything Rupert had told him.

Meanwhile Sue was thinking of another ploy to escape Justice.

Chapter Fifty One

Wednesday November 5th – Sunset count 66

Kay stepped quietly into the hospice room at Geoffery's invitation to her gentle knock.

'Hello Kay,' Geoffery said, electronically raising the back rest of the bed into an upright position. 'Tell me. How did it go?' he asked keenly.

'As you'd expect! He was rude and very surprised,' she said, sitting in the bedside chair.

'But did you stick to the plan?" Geoffery asked, concerned that she'd reneged on their agreement. 'Will he move out?'

'Yes,' she said softly.

'Good girl,' he said, holding her hand affectionately.

'Oh Geoffery. I hope I've done the right thing,' Kay said, still unsure about the hard line that Geoffery had advised her to take.

'I'm sure you have. You will both look back at this moment, and see it was a turning point for you both, for the better,' Geoffery said reassuring her. 'Once he's got his own independence, he will have to cope, and then he'll appreciate how much you did for him,' he continued.

'Do you really think so?' Kay said meekly.

'I know so. Don't worry,' he said, seeking to reassure her.

'OK. If you say so,' she conceded.

Geoffery cleared his throat and looked into her eyes. 'I know you feel awkward talking about it. And I said I'd drop it. But I need to know. Why did George doubt that he was Tim's father?'

'Do we have to drag this up again? Why can't you let it go? It's all in the past,' Kay said, irritably shaking Geoffery's hand from hers.

'This is important. I need to clarify things in my own mind,' he repeated.

'Oh, very well,' Kay said crossly. 'If it's the only way that you'll promise to drop it. George had a friend who was studying to become a doctor. He borrowed some medical books from him, so he could understand more about meningitis, and the likely long term effects. You know, blood poisoning, brain damage etc.'

'It's an awful disease,' Geoffery added unnecessarily.

'He came across a chapter on combinations of parental blood types and concluded, that his and my blood type was incompatible with Tim's. That's when he decided, he wasn't Tim's father.'

'On top of everything else with little Tim, this must have been awful for you,' Geoffery said, holding her hand, again.

'Yes it was! With Tim struggling for life, the blood poisoning still progressing up his little legs and nobody knowing where it would stop...and then George deciding to start talking about blood types! We had an almighty row. The Nurses had to usher him out of the room, in the end.' Kay's eyes brimmed with tears as she recalled the memory.

'I'm sorry for raking it up,' Geoffery said, uncomfortable at upsetting her in his quest for the truth.

'He accused me of being a whore, sleeping around. I...I couldn't say anything. I just had to take it. Because of us, our....' Kay stopped short, tears rolling down her cheeks.

'Of course. I'm sorry,' Geoffery said, recalling his own guilt trip about the incident.

'Anyway,' Kay continued, gently wiping her tears with her fingers, 'he stayed until Tim was out of hospital and then he left us. Everyone was shocked that he'd gone. But nobody knew why. We both kept it quiet for the baby's sake.'

Kay 'dissolved' again as the pain of that time washed over her again. Geoffery enfolded her in his arms, kissing her hair.

'It's OK Kay,' he said, gently rocking her. 'It's OK. I'm sorry to drag it up. Please don't cry.'

'I thought this was all dead and buried, thought it was something that couldn't hurt me anymore but...'

'Ssssh, I understand. I'm sorry,' he said, his eyes filling at seeing her distress.

Geoffery plucked several tissues from the box on his bedside cabinet and gave them to her. After a few minutes, Kay regained her composure.

'I'm sorry Geoff. The last thing you want at this time, is having to cope with an hysterical woman.'

'It's my fault,' he said apologetically, 'for raising it. But, I have to tell you that I couldn't possibly be Tim's father either.'

'What? What are you saying?'

His announcement stopped her in her tracks. She sat on the edge of her chair and stared into his eyes waiting for an explanation.

'I've just had confirmation that my blood type isn't consistent with Tim's either. Moreover, prior to the start of my cancer treatment, I put some semen into a donor bank, not that it matters now, but I've just discovered that I'm infertile, and apparently, would have been all my life.'

'So if you're not Tim's father...and George isn't! What are you suggesting? That I was sleeping around?' Kay brought her hands up to her mouth in realisation of his accusation. 'I swear, you were the only two who could possibly be his father,' she said earnestly. 'You don't believe me do you?'

'Now calm down. Just listen. I'm not accusing you of anything of the sort. George got it wrong. His blood type IS consistent with being Tim's natural father.'

'What?' said Kay incredulously. 'I thought he had got it all checked out.'

'Well, if he did. Whoever did it for him. Got it wrong.'

'Are you sure?'

'Yes. I've recently spoken to two consultant hematologists and they confirm it.'

'This means....'

'This means that George is Tim's real father and I... I am just his Godfather,' Geoffery said.

'All those years of thinking that you...hiding it, wanting to tell you, so you could see your son, be his Dad, be part of his life.'

'At least the uncertainty is over,' said Geoffery, positively.

'But, do you realise the implications?'

'No!'

'I not only lost Tim his legs! But I lost him his Father as well!' she blurted.

'Now stop that,' Geoffery said firmly. 'George lost his son, himself. Not you! The disease took his legs, not your negligence. So you have no reason to feel guilty about anything.'

'But...'

'No buts! You coped extremely well in terrible circumstances. It couldn't have been easy for you as a single parent coping with all that angst,' Geoffery said compassionately. 'You should be proud of your achievements.'

'Do you think so?'

'Yes, I know so,' Geoffery said, thinking uneasily about the selfish son she had brought up. 'It's me that should take the blame for screwing up your life,' he confessed sincerely. 'A young man's lust...I'm sorry.'

Chapter Fifty Two

Saturday November 8th – Sunset count 69

After being arrested on the motorway, following her kidnapping of Rupert, Sue had been held in prison for a few days until being released on Police bail. Rupert was distraught at the news, but Geoffery was more circumspect.

Geoffery had called her to the hospice to see him, and understandably, had received a cool reception to his invitation. Eventually, she had agreed to come, but only when he appealed to her greedy nature, suggesting that there would a considerable financial benefit for her.

The door opened gently as John, Andy's replacement, led Sue into the room.

'Geoffery, are you sure you're up to this? You look very tired,' John said concerned.

'Yes, I shall be fine, don't worry about me. Sue and I have something to sort out, to clear the air.'

'I think I ought to stay,' John said, starting to close the door.

'No. I think we'll be OK, thanks.'

'Are you sure?' John said, concerned about leaving him alone with the vengeful woman.

'Yes. Don't worry,' Geoffery said calmly.

'OK. Buzz if you want anything. Don't overdo it,' John instructed, as he left.

'Please sit down,' Geoffery said, pointing Sue to a chair.

'What's this about?' said Sue suspiciously.

'I know we haven't seen eye to eye about… about things.'

'That's a bloody understatement! You come into my life and take my husband from me. Accusing me of being a husband beater.'

'I want you to help me,' Geoffery said patiently.

'Help you! I wouldn't help you, if you were drawing your last breath. You've ruined my life.'

'In which case, you'll probably enjoy what I'm going to ask you to do.'

'Go on,' said Sue, showing interest and moving to the edge of her chair.

'I want you to help me commit suicide.'

'You won't catch me like that.'

'What do you mean?' Geoffery asked. 'You hate me don't you?'

'Aiding people to commit suicide, is a criminal offence,' she said, sensing a trap.

'I have written a suicide note.'

'That makes no difference.'

'It will, in this case.'

'Why do want to die like that? she said disdainfully. 'Just look at you! The cancer will kill you soon enough.'

'The pain is just unbearable. I can't take it anymore,' said a fragile Geoffery.

'Well, you're asking the wrong person then, because I want to see you suffer, she said vengefully. Just like you've made me suffer. Taking my Rupert away from me.'

'There's money in it for you, if you do,' he added quickly.

'How much?' she asked greedily.

'I have written to my Solicitor, instructing him to pay you two hundred and fifty thousand pounds after my death.'

'Why? What possible reason would you have for doing that? It's clear you hate me,' she said suspiciously.

'Just a dying man's wishes, to apologise for messing up your life,' he lied.

'But all I need to do is just wait for nature to take its course.'

'No, I'm afraid not. If you don't help me today, I shall telephone my Solicitor and tell him, I wrote the letter while I was under the influence of drugs. And I'll ask him to destroy it.'

'Getting paid for having my revenge on you! It just sounds too good to be true,' said Sue, warming to the idea.

'That's the deal. Take it or leave it.'

'What happens if the nurse comes in?'

'Oh, he won't. He's got other patients to look after.'

'I'm not sure,' she said, trying to consider all possible ways that he could be setting her up.

'I've already written the suicide note.' Geoffery continued. 'John will discover it later this evening, when you're long gone.'

'What...what do I have to do? I'm no good with blood,' she confessed unnecessarily.

'Oh. It's nothing as barbaric as that. Suffocation is what I've chosen,' he said matter-of-factly.

'What? You mean putting a pillow over your face?'

'Oh no. The best way is a polythene bag over the head, and elastic bands around the neck.'

'Oh!'

'I will do that bit myself.'

'So what do I do?'

'Well it's human nature, that as I start to suffocate, my reaction will be to take the bag off.'

'And?'

'I just want you to hold my arms, to stop me pulling it off. That's all,' he added.

'Just hold your arms?'

'Yes. That's all. I will kill myself,' he confirmed. 'You'll be in the clear.'

'But why me?'

'I know how much you like to hurt people. And now we've taken Rupert from you. Well, I thought the least I could do, was to offer myself as a substitute.'

'You underestimate me! I'll soon have him back under my thumb, where he belongs.'

'I think you'll be in for a big shock,' Geoffery said positively.

'We'll see about that! No, of course you won't, because you'll be dead,' she laughed cruelly.

'No that's right. I won't, will I? Now if you don't mind. Let's get this thing done. Would you mind passing me the polythene bag and the elastic bands?'

'Where are they?'

'Hidden under the seat cushion. I didn't want anyone finding them and messing up my plans.'

Sue fished underneath the cushion and found what she was looking for and pulled out the small bundle.

'I'm still not sure about this,' she said, turning them over in her hands.

'I've already told you. I've had enough. I've done my suicide letter. You'll be long gone before they discover me. You want to get rid of me. So what's the problem?'

'You're right of course. You'll be doing it to yourself,' she agreed, finally convinced.

'Would you give me the bag please? Could you shake it open for me, first?'

Sue shook the bag capturing air into it and handed it to Geoffery.

'Here,' she said, giving him the bag. Her adrenalin madly pumping. It was the same erotic buzz that she got from beating that pathetic creature of a husband. But now she felt more controlled.

'Well, I think I've discharged my Godfather duties,' he said dramatically. 'My job is finally done.'

'How long do I....hold your arms?' she quizzed.

'I should think about a minute, after I stop struggling,' said Geoffery calmly, as if giving out cooking instructions.

'A minute?' said Sue, feeling her hands starting to sweat.

'About that, yes.'

'And then I leave?'

'That's it! That's all there is to it,' he said, unemotionally.

'Not a bad day's work for quarter of a million,' she said greedily.

'Goodbye then,' said Geoffery, putting the bag over his head and stretching the elastic bands around his neck.

The bag immediately started expanding and contracting with Geoffery's breathing.

Geoffery put his hands underneath the sheets and reached for the distress button. But before he could reach it, her vice like grip captured his arms and held them. The plan was going to backfire, unless he could reach the button to summon help.

He had to dislodge her grip before he lost consciousness. His lungs were already struggling, and he was getting light headed. He needed to do something urgently.

The bag was misting up, but he could see her evil eyes gazing at him, as if they were boring into his soul. She was laughing maniacally.

'Good riddance,' she said evilly.

He lifted his head and butted her on the nose. She let go momentarily and he moved his hand to get to the buzzer. In his desperation, he knocked the buzzer from underneath the covers and it fell noisily to the floor.

'Oh no you don't!' she said, clamping his arms again. 'You want to die! It will be my pleasure to help. Struggle as much as you like. You'll regret you ever messed with me. Nobody will ever know, that I put you out of your misery.'

As he lost consciousness he knew his gamble had failed. He had underestimated her strength. He was going to die after all.

Chapter Fifty Three

The white light became more intense. 'Was this heaven?' he wondered.

'Nadine!' It was the dream again. He was at the bottom of the black hole gazing up.

He felt something on his face. He couldn't breathe. Desperately he fought to get it off. His chest hurt. The dirt! Had she finally managed to bury him alive? 'Nadine, please help me.' But the thing covering his mouth stopped his words. She couldn't hear him.

'Geoffery, Geoffery'....the voice was coming from a long way off. 'Geoffery!'

He knew the voice, but couldn't remember who owned it. It wasn't Nadine. Was it the Dark Angel? Had he finally caught him?

'Geoffery. Stay with us! Come on, you can do this,' the voice pleaded.

The black hole was opening again. Oh, It would be so nice to go there and sleep.

The white light again. The pain in his chest. The sudden spasm in his body.

'He's coming back,' he heard the voice say.

Faces swam before him.

'Just take it easy,' the voice instructed.

Clamped on his nose and mouth an oxygen mask was oxygenating his lungs. He could feel the coldness of the gel on his chest underneath the electrodes. Just above him he saw the owner of the voice. Andy gave him a smile, his face flushed by the physical efforts to resuscitate Geoffery.

'You gave us a nasty scare there Geoffery. You'll be OK in a minute. Just take lots of deep breaths,' Andy instructed.

Slowly his mind cleared. He remembered. Sue, the bag and the buzzer. He could feel where the elastic bands had been holding the polythene bag, tight around his neck. It hurt to swallow. His arms hurt where she had held him down.

'You were lucky my friend. Another few seconds and you'd have been gone. Just give yourself a few minutes to recover.'

Geoffery felt as if he'd gone ten rounds in a boxing ring. Slowly his mind was clearing.

'OK? Andy said, removing the electrodes.

'Yes, I think so. Hold on! Are you supposed to be here?' Geoffery said, suddenly realising that Andy had been suspended.

'Don't worry, I've been reinstated. Thanks to you and her subsequent arrest, they now believe us. But it was nearly too late for you wasn't it?'

Andy recalled the session that he'd had earlier with Ann Place, it had been a tense affair.

'Thank you for coming,' she said stiffly. 'Please take a seat.'

'Thanks,' Andy said sitting.

'Andy, following your suspension, Mr Foster pleaded your case.'

'That's kind of him.'

'Yes, he tells me that it was him that gave the painkillers to the other person, not you.'

'Yes that was what I'd been telling you.'

'He apologies for putting your position here in jeopardy. And furthermore, he tells me that he ignored your advice about not leaving the tablets.'

'Well I did try to tell you.'

'Quite. He also informs me that there is some sort of vendetta being raised against you and him by the person who made the complaint.'

'Yes, it's the wife of one of his Godsons.'

'The police are studying the carpark CCTV recordings following the vandalism to Mr Foster's car, when somebody poured acid over the paintwork and slashed all the tyres. They seem to think it might be the same person.

'I reckon, that's a safe bet.'

I believe that that particular person has now been arrested for various reasons.'

'Yes that's correct.'

'Therefore, I have no reason to continue your suspension and would like to offer you your job back.'

'Great, thank you. I accept. When can I start?'

'Your shift starts tomorrow.'

'I will be pleased to get back to work, to get out from under Helen's feet.'

'However. May I remind you that it is a place of calm and I want you to leave your personal issues at home in future. Our primary role, as you know, is the welfare of patients in our care.'

'Yes I know, and that's what I thought I was doing.'

'You also need to sort out your values on patient commitment.'

'Come off it! That is particularly hurtful when you consider my record, especially our debate about Mr and Mrs Jones when Geoffery, umm, Mr Foster arrived. Remember?'

'Yes well, I have to tell you that as I said before, I am not happy with your heavy involvement with Mr Foster. It appears that you are giving him a disproportionate amount of attention to the detriment of other patients.'

'We agreed, before I started this part time working. I was unaware that it was causing any problems.'

'It causes some administrative difficulties. Anyway, you can resume your duties. But please take on board what I have been saying. We will review your progress in a months' time.'

Andy was brought back to the present by Geoffery holding his arm.

'Why did you...? How did you know what was going on...?'

'I was just telling John that I had been reinstated when I heard the distress buzzer sound for a split second on the nursing station. As I opened the door, there she was, the bag over your head, holding you down.'

'Thank heavens you were there. Hooray for the Cavalry.'

'She claims, you asked her to help you, commit suicide.'

'What! Why would I do that?' Geoffery said painfully, feigning innocence.

'Don't know. But she reckons, that you wrote a suicide note which would vindicate her.'

'Suicide note!' said Geoffery, continuing the deception. 'True I wrote a note. But it said that in the case of my sudden and unexpected death, she should be considered a prime suspect.'

'She also said, that you were going to give her a quarter of a million pounds, to help you escape from the terrible pain, which you were experiencing.'

'Did she now? Why would I pay somebody, especially her, to kill me? And you know how successful this latest drug is in handling the pain, when it's pumped intravenously.'

'I knew she was lying,' Andy said. 'I'm surprised that she'd didn't come up with a more plausible story though.'

'Where is she now?'

'We called the police and she's been taken into custody.'

'Thank you for doing that.'

'When you're feeling better, the police want to interview you and take a signed statement.'

'That's no problem. It will be my pleasure to help put her behind bars. Hopefully, for a long time. They'll probably want to test the polythene bag and elastic bands for fingerprints and DNA, so please make sure they're not thrown away,' said Geoffery knowingly.

'Don't worry. The police have already bagged them and taken them away,' Andy confirmed.

'Good,' said Geoffery, pleased that his plans were on track.

'I'm sure Rupert will be relieved at this turn of events,' said Andy.

'Especially as she was threatening to track him down and sort him out again. That's the problem with domestic violence. You never know when it will resurface. Still, now she has this more serious charge against her, it will be a long time before she's released,' he said satisfied. 'Rupert will be able to relax and get on with his life.'

'You know, I thought I saw a twinkle in your eye at the prospect of her incarceration.'

'Really? It's probably the drugs,' said Geoffery, satisfied with his days work.

CHAPTER FIFTY FOUR

Saturday November 22nd – Sunset count 83

'You've just got to put one foot in front of the other,' Carrie said impatiently.

'I know that. I'm not stupid,' Tim said angrily, picking himself up for the umpteenth time.

'Wey, yee can't keep stopping. The more yee stop, the harder it becomes.'

'I can't go on any further. I'm shattered already,' he said, leaning his head against the walking pole.

'Look. Just slow your pace down. Walk slowly, like this,' she said, demonstrating a slow deliberate gait to emphasise what she meant.

'This is bloody stupid. I wish I'd told him where to shove his bloody money.'

'Come on. This is doing yee good. What more can yee want? Oot in the open air, in wonderful scenery, wi the promise of getting a fortune at the end of it? Sum people would gladly be in your place,' she goaded.

'It's alright for you. You were fit in the first place, before your…um ..the bomb.'

'It was an IED, an Improvised Explosive Device. They don't call them bombs,' she corrected. 'That's how they reckon ah survived the trauma, because ah was fit.

'Well, whatever it was called, the effects were still the same,' he observed coldly.

'Anyway, you've had a lifetime to adjust to having no legs. Mine's a comparatively short time, so yee should be better on these things than me,' she said, tapping her prosthesis.

Tim admired her confidence and positive attitude to her 'little accident' as she called it.

'There are people with problems worse than mine,' she had told him. 'No point wallowin in your own self-pity. You've just got to get on wi it, and make do wi what you've got. What's done is done! Alreet, I've lost my legs, but otherwise I've got good health and all my faculties. There's no point moping over somethin yee can't change.'

'I can't be bothered, he said, sitting down heavily on a rock. 'He'll never know anyway.'

'But yee will! If yee don't put in the trainin. You'll never make the first peak let alone all three. Yee said, he already reckons you're a wimp and you'd just be confirmin it.'

'I don't care what he thinks. All I know is, I'm knackered.'

'Alreet. We'll have a short rest. But only for a few minutes,' she conceded.

'What's the point? If I can't get up a bloody Welsh hill! What chance have I got of walking up Ben Nevis for chrissake?'

'Don't forget Scafell and Snowdon,' she corrected.

'No need to rub it in. Oh it's hopeless,' he said dejectedly. His stumps were throbbing, his shirt soaked from his exertions. Tim laid back, his rucksack cushioning him against the rocks. Exhausted, he closed his eyes and listened to his pounding heart.

His face suddenly felt warmer. Then he felt her lips on his. They were soft, full, her kiss gentle. He opened his eyes in surprise. She gazed deep into his. Then she quickly pulled away.

'Come on Tim,' she said hoarsely. 'Yee can do it. Just for me.'

'Give me another kiss, and I will,' he said boldly.

'No. Yee taste all salty,' she said playfully. If yee want another, you'll have to claim it at the top of the ridge.'

'You tease,' he said, struggling to stand. 'OK. But it'll cost you more than one.'

'You'll have to catch me first,' she said, already striding up the slope.

All his aches and pains forgotten, Tim started pursuing her up the slope. He was starting to like the activity after all! It was the first indication that there could be more to their relationship, other than simply fellow hikers.

He had never had a girlfriend, and was surprised at the wonderful feeling that coursed through him as a result of a brief kiss. Determined to claim his prize, he hobbled up the rocky track after the figure disappearing into the darkness. Suddenly he had found new strength. The effects of gravity almost forgotten.

Also forgotten was their journey earlier. Tim had been apprehensive about his venture into the Welsh Hills.

Carrie had driven them in her specially adapted Peugeot 307 Estate. Tim had never learnt to drive. The limited Springfield household finances were insufficient to pay for driving lessons.

A mask of concentration etched on her face, as she negotiated the narrow high hedged country lanes. She was a highly trained army driver, fast but cautious.

As they sped around the meandering lanes that skirted the Talybont reservoir, he gazed at the mountains and forests that surrounded the large body of water, wondering how he would cope with this different terrain.

Carrie had chosen the location in the Brecon Beacons to start a tougher regime for him. The mountain terrain would give him a few additional challenges to better prepare him for the three peaks, she had told him enthusiastically.

Finally they had arrived at their start location.

'Isn't this where they do some sort of army training?' Tim said looking at the distinctive profiles of Cribyn and Pen Y Fan, outlined against the darkening sky.

'Wey aye. The SAS do a lot of exercises around here,' said Carrie, opening up the tailgate.

'They're a pretty tough lot aren't they?' Tim said, pulling on his anorack.

'Ah was part of the selection process for the Regiment a few years ago,' Carrie volunteered. 'Ah passed the physical stuff, but failed the interrogation part. So ah was returned to my regiment, Pity,' she said, 'Ah quite fancied the beret. It was my colour.'

'Typical. Trust a woman to think of fashion accessories,' he said bravely.

'Nothin wrong wi that. Yee need to feel smart in uniform. Soldiers spend a lot of time polishin boots and gettin razor sharp creases in trousers. It's all part of the discipline. Somethin yee could do wi,' she said, grabbing hold of one of the spare tyres around his waist.

'Here, careful with that. That's take away profits you're wobbling,' he replied playfully.

'Come on, get your act together,' she goaded. 'Otherwise it will be comin back time, before we've even started.'

Tim returned his gaze to the darkening skyline. 'I hope this isn't going to be too long.'

'Nay, it's a relatively short stroll. Just a circular walk around Pen y Fan, Cribyn and Fan y Big.'

'Fanny what?' Tim choked. 'You've got to be joking.'

'It's not that sort of Fanny,' she said quickly.

'I just hope I don't make a cock up of it then,' he joked.

'Ha, Ha. Very droll! It's the welsh Fan Y. It means the top of the point. Anyway,' she continued, outlining their route. 'We're going past the reservoir, up the head wall and onto the ridge before we do the peaks.'

They had only been walking an hour before his first fall.

After her kiss, it had taken them a further hour and a half, just to get up to the ridge. Barely a mile!

'At last! We're at the top. I just need to catch my breath before I claim my prize.'

'Prize! What prize was that?' she teased.

'My kiss! You promised me.'

'Oh that!' she said, barely panting from the climb. 'Now you're up here ah might change my mind.'

Unsure whether she meant it or not, Tim's face immediately telegraphed his disappointment.

'Oh Tim,' she said, 'don't be sad.' She walked over to him and gave him a kiss on the cheek.

'Ugh, you're even more salty now.'

'My lips aren't though,' he said recovering. Putting his arms around her waist, and drawing her to him, covering her mouth.

'Mmm not bad,' she said, pulling back.' Ah think we might need to work on your technique later, though.'

It was only the thought of 'later' that had kept him going, for as they progressed along the ridge it started to rain and, the night became very dark and windy.

'Can't we go back and take a short cut?'

'No. Yee need to get used to these types of conditions. We'd be very lucky if we did all three peaks, without gettin a bit of rain, and in any case,' she added, 'we can't avoid walkin in the dark.'

'I'm not so sure I'm going to like this,' Tim said fearfully.

'Don't worry. So long as we've got our waterproofs on, and we take our time, we'll be OK,' Carrie reassured him.

'If you say so,' Tim replied, unconvinced.

'When we finish, we'll sleep in the car. I've brought some sleepin bags.'

'It's getting windier. Is it safe to be up here?' Tim said, looking around nervously. A beam of light from his head torch illuminated the clouds, which 'flew' by vertically, in the up draught from the ridge.

'If it's too windy, we'll go down,' she reassured him. 'But you're talkin about gale force winds, before we consider abandonin.'

'And foggy?'

'You mean low cloud? We'll assess that based on where we are,' she shouted over the wind. 'But armed with a map and compass, that should ensure we don't walk off any cliffs, hopefully.'

'Oh. OK,' said Tim, still not convinced.

As the hike progressed, both of them had a few irritating trips and falls.

As Tim fell noisily in a heap, Carrie shouted. 'Yee must use your walkin poles more.' Tim could barely hear her, because of the noise of his anorack hood which was flapping in the increasing gusts.

'I've had enough. I want to go back!' said Tim as he, again, pushed himself up from the loose stone strewn path.

'We're over half way now. Just be more careful. There's no rush,' Carrie said, not breaking her stride.

'This is stupid. I'm wet and...'

'Miserable,' added Carrie.

As they stumbled their way along the path skirting the very edge of the ridge the rain stopped, the wind subsided and clouds lifted. Within a short time, the moon appeared and transformed the mountainside.

The moonlight lit up the crags, colouring the rocks a battleship grey. In the distance pinpricks of lights appeared from the farms nestling in the valleys. On the horizon an orange glow from Brecon reflected off the receding cloud base.

Pulling her anorak hood from her face, Carrie stopped and waited for Tim to join her.

'Isn't this lovely?' she said, scanning the view. 'We'll be able to turn our head torches off soon.'

'You can if you like,' Tim whined. 'I've had enough of tripping over.'

'Come on. You're doing really well. Just think of that nice warm sleepin bag waiting for yee down there,' Carrie encouraged.

'How much further is it?' Tim groaned.

'I'll show yee on the map,' she said, wiping the rain from the plastic front of the mapcase. 'What's the position on the GPS?' Carrie quizzed.

'Here you read it,' Tim said, removing it from under his anorak and thrusting the unit under her nose.

'You'll need to learn how to do this for yourself, sooner or later,' Carrie told him, studying the map.

'Let's forget the training tonight. You do it. I'll catch up later.'

'Yee really are a Mister Grumpy aren't you?' she said reading the GPS position. 'We are here, and the car is over there,' she said, pointing at the map.

'Hell! That's miles away. Can't we call in a helicopter to take us down? I'm knackered.'

Ignoring the protesting Tim, Carrie strode on. Eventually, they started the descent, down a narrow ravine. The water sculptured gully had been carved out over decades by outflow from the peat bog on the mountain top. A smaller stream now ran down the mountainside, underneath the loose rocks. They passed noisy waterfalls powered by the recent rain.

'Watch yourself here,' she said, carefully easing herself down the path. 'It's a bit steep, and there's lots of slippery rock.'

'Behind her, the sound of Tim slipping over again indicated her warning had been too late. A shower of stones rattled past her down the mountainside as he fought to stop himself slipping any further.

'Shit! I thought I was a goner then,' Tim said, picking himself up.

As they got to lower altitudes, the path eventually became grassy and less steep.

'At last! A tarmac road,' he said, planting his feet on the flat surface. 'Now how much further?' he demanded.

'Yee tell me,' Carrie said, thrusting the map case at Tim. 'Where do yee think we are?'

'I don't know! Just tell me which way, and let's get on with it,' Tim replied, still walking.

'We aren't goin anywhere, until yee tell me. Come on. Work it out for yourself. We've just come off the mountainside and joined a road,' she coached.

'Oh! You really are a pain!' Tim said disconsolately, switching on his head torch. Reluctantly studying the map and cross checking with the GPS, he eventually pointed a finger at a spot. 'There,' he said, 'satisfied?'

Carrie checked where he was indicating. 'Very good,' she replied. 'Ah reckon you're right, and so yee can answer your own question.'

'Yeah, OK. Another couple of miles, I suppose. But at least it's all on road, thankfully. Come on. You've got to admit it, that was hard going up there wasn't it?'

'It was challengin, aye. But yee did it! Yee should be pleased wi yourself,' she said, suddenly planting a kiss on his forehead.

'Is that all I get, after all that effort?'

'Wait and see,' she teased.

Chapter Fifty Five

They walked in silence along the two miles of winding lanes. Moonlight reflecting off the road markings, making navigation easier. Tim groaned at the few, short sharp inclines, which the meandering tarmac took through the steep sided valley.

'Just around this bend, ah reckon,' she said, 'and it's done.'

'Hallelujah,' he said, spotting the car. 'At last! I thought we'd never finish.'

Carrie slipped her rucksack off her shoulder and plunged her hand into a side pocket, 'All we need now are the keys,' she said.

A beep, a flash of the indicators and clunking from the door locks indicated that she had found them.

'Here we are. Good job done,' she said, lifting the tailgate.

Having walked without lights for the last few miles, the courtesy light temporarily blinded them.

'Hell, that's bright!' Tim said, shielding his eyes.

'See, that wasn't that bad was it?' Carrie said, busily making space in the back of the Peugeot.

As his eyes adjusted to the lighting, Tim looked at Carrie, as she dropped the rear passenger seats. Her wet tousled hair framing her face, and he realised he felt a pang of affection for this woman, who had led him through the long dark hours of the night.

'That's not what my hips and stumps are telling me,' he said, regaining his concentration. 'I'm knackered.'

'You'll be fine, when we get in the car, wi a nice hot drink inside yee. But first we need to get out of these wet clothes. I've brought a bin liner to put them in. Ah don't want water stains on my upholstery. Now ah suggest you get out of those trousers and wipe down your prosthetics.'

''I don't think I've even got energy for doing that. Come to think of it, I've never been told to drop my trousers by a lady before,' Tim said, easing off his rucksack.

'I'm sure it won't be the last time either,' she said suggestively.

She unzipped and removed her own trousers to reveal the kaleidoscope of colour that was displayed in her lower limbs; the amazing technology that replaced her own legs and enabled her to have a 'normal' life; her cold marbled thighs cushioned by white liners protecting her stumps in the orange plastic prosthetic cups; the stainless steel joints and 'shin' bone that looked odd as it disappeared into a normal brown hiking boot.

'That's one advantage in our condition,' she said, pulling her residual legs out of the prosthetic sockets.' At least yee don't have to unlace your boots. Come on, hurry up and get yours off, so we can close the tailgate. Now we've stopped I'm startin to feel chilly.'

Tim did as he was ordered, sitting on the tailgate beside her, his attention to the task half-hearted as he watched her remove her damp top. He had never been this close to a woman shedding clothes before.'

'What are you lookin at?' she said seductively

'I've never seen you in…without clothes before.'

'You've seen me at the gym,' she reminded him.

'This is different,' he said, becoming aroused.

'Stuff your trousers into that bin liner and give me your legs,' she said ignoring his stare. 'I'll put them in the front with mine. Shove up and we'll put the rucksacks in and close the tailgate,' she directed.

'You OK? I'm starting to stiffen up,' Tim said, trying to ease his aching shoulder muscles.

'So ah can see, said Carrie.' Looking at the movement in his boxers. Embarrassed, Tim put his hands over himself to hide the bulge.

'There's not enough room to swing around. Ah need to sit on you, while I put the stuff in the front,' she said, sitting on his lap, much to his restrained pleasure.'

They shared the tea that Carrie and brought in the flask, the steam, adding to the growing condensation on the inside of the car windows. Tim's cheeks glowed. He wasn't sure whether it was the heat in the car or in his loins that was generating it.

'Ah hope you like whisky,' she said, moving off his lap and getting a small flask out of her bag. 'There's nothin like a hot toddy to warm the cockles after a night exercise,' she said, pouring a generous amount of the liquor into his cup.

Tim lifted the steaming plastic cup to his lips, and coughed as the vapours from the spirit went up his nose.

'I've never had it before,' he spluttered.

'But there's a first time for everythin,' she said, looking at him suggestively over her own cup.

'Shove over,' she said, sliding close to him. 'We need to share a bit of warmth. A great walk and a lovely brew, what more could a lady want?'

Tim fought for the right words. He had never been in this situation with a woman before and didn't want to blow his chances. 'Up there, on the mountain, you said...'

'Yes?' Carrie said coquettishly.

'Umm. Oh, nothing,' Tim said awkwardly, fearful of putting his foot in it, and killing the moment.'

Just then a mobile rang making them both jump.

Chapter Fifty Six

'Is that your mobile?' he asked

'Who would be ringin me at this time in the mornin. It must be a wrong number,' she said, annoyed at the interruption to her amorous plans.

'Where is it? I'll get it for you.'

'It's in the side pocket of my rucksack.'

Tim dug into the pocket and lifted the phone out; as he passed it to Carrie he noticed the name on the screen. 'Foster Geoffery.'

'Here you are. It's a Foster Geoffery calling you. Foster Geoffery! Foster Geoffery! Is this Geoffery Foster? What's he doing ringing you in the middle of the night?'

'Well he knows we're trainin tonight.'

'Yeah. But why would you have his number in your phone?

'Safety,' Carrie said, trying to think on her feet. 'Yee should always tell somebody where you're goin in the mountains. Just in case yee have an accident.'

'Pull the other one,' Tim said doubtfully.

'Just give me the phone, will yee?' Carrie demanded, putting her hand out to receive it.

Instead, Tim pressed the green button and answered it. The voice on the other end was immediately identifiable as Geoffery. 'Carrie, Carrie is that you?'

'What's going on?' demanded Tim, handing the phone to Carrie.

'Hello Geoffery. Aye, we're alreet.'

'Is there anything wrong with Tim?' Geoffery asked, concerned.

'No, he's fine. It all went well. I'll ring you later.' Carrie ended the call.

'So what's this all about?' Tim said angrily. 'Are you on his payroll?' he asked suspiciously.

'He's asked me to help yee get fit, that's all.'

'Yeah! But why you?' Tim questioned.

'Why not me?

'There's something fishy going on here?' Tim pursued. 'I thought you were helping me because you... you know, you liked me, not because HE had employed you.' Tim pushed himself away from her.

'He is tryin to help you succeed, if yee just thought about it for a moment,' she said, shaking her head in disbelief at Tim's petulant outburst.

'I don't need anybody's help,' he said resentfully.

'Wey if you want to believe that, yee carry on by yourself. Look at yee, sulking like a fair bairn.'

'A what?'

'A little kid,' she said, translating her Geordie outburst. 'I've done what ah was employed to do. Yes employed,' she shouted in his face. 'He warned me you'd be a difficult challenge, but yee were ten times worse than ah imagined.'

'What do you mean?'

'Yee are so full of yourself and your self-deluded abilities; Ah doubt yee have any time in that selfish brain of yours to even consider somebody else and their feelings.'

'Wait, I get it. This is all part of the act isn't it? Tim said, as a thought flashed through his anger. 'To get me riled and well...his little plan isn't going to work.'

'Tim Springfield, you are so ...' Carrie stopped in mid-sentence, looked deep into his eyes and started shuffling over to him.

Tim, un-nerved by her advance backed away scared.

'What!' he managed to croak.

As he moved away from her, he found his retreat was suddenly stopped by the cold frame of the window pressing against his back. He was blocked in. There was nowhere to go. She stopped inches from him. He could feel her hot breath, her chest heaving from her anger. He winced as she raised her left arm and hooked it around his neck. Momentarily he resisted, as she pulled him towards her and then, she kissed him, hard. His arms responded and captured her firm body in a powerful embrace.

She was gentle with him in their passion. Tim had at last become a man.

Afterwards, as they lay in each other's arms, Tim asked.' Did he pay you to do that as well?

'How do yee think ah ought to answer that?' she said, pulling the sleeping bag over them.

'To be honest,' he said, propping himself on one elbow and gazing into her eyes. 'I couldn't care less, because that was something else,' he said tenderly stroking her face.

'I'm not sure whether I ought to 'chin' yee, for suggesting I'm some kind of whore or what. But ah tell you what. It's many years since ah indulged in a bit of backseat fun, and at last I've found an advantage for havin no legs. Sex in a car, is a lot less restrictin.'

'Well, if he has paid for your services, I'd like to add another charge on to his bill.' Tim said, planting his mouth on hers.

Chapter Fifty Seven

Monday November 24th – Sunset count 85

Andy opened the door a chink, and peered into Geoffery's room. Kay was standing by his side, waiting to see if it was OK to enter.

'How's he getting on?' she said quietly, as Andy assessed whether Geoffery was asleep or not.

'He's not really recovered after the incident with that awful woman,' he said quietly.

'It's OK Andy,' Geoffery said, his voice weak, his words barely distinguishable. 'I'm not asleep. Did I hear the lovely Kay's voice?'

'Hello Geoff. I won't stay if you're trying to get some sleep.'

'No. Please come in. You're like a tonic to me when you come here. Please sit down,' he instructed, pointing to the chair by his bedside.

'How are you?' she said, putting her hand around Geoffery's skeletally thin hand.

'OK, and what about you?' he asked, returning the courtesy.

'Oh I'm fine, thanks,' she said awkwardly, looking at his gaunt face. His sallow appearance making her feel sad.

'And what about that boy of yours?' Geoffery asked croakily.

'Great. You wouldn't know him. He's a different person. I've even heard him whistling.'

'So at last, he's realised he needs to get his life together. Good.'

'Yes. He's starting to lose weight as well.'

'So, I gather his preparations are going well.'

'Yes. He's getting himself fit to tackle your challenge. And moreover, he has found a lady friend,' she said happily.

'Yes, so I gather. Cupid's arrow got to him eh? Well I never!' said Geoffery knowingly. Deciding not to reveal his own, detailed knowledge of the situation.

'She's going to do the challenge with him apparently,' Kay added excitedly.

'It will be good for him to have someone to walk with,' Geoffery concurred.

'She's an amputee as well.'

'Really?' he said, continuing his deception.

'She was in the army. It was the last day of her tour. A roadside bomb apparently. She lost both legs,' Kay added dramatically.

'So they both have the same physical challenges?' Geoffery added.

'She's really taken him to task. She won't put up with any whinging. It sounds like she's a real hard task master.'

'Unlike someone else I know, then.'

'But that's different, he's my son and....'

'Yes I know. I'm only teasing.'

'Oh you!' Kay said, gently scolding him.

'So he's going to do it then! That's great news. I knew if he had some motivation, life would be different, for both of you.'

'And you Geoff?' Kay said softly, stroking his hand.

'Oh don't worry about me. I've done what I set out to do. Hopefully I've earned some brownie points. I think that I've made amends for some of my oversights. Now perhaps the man with the big book will let me in through the pearly gates after all.'

They both went quiet as they contemplated the enormity of his words. Kay squeezed Geoffery's hand trying to hold back the tears.

'Look, I've just popped in to say good…goodbye…' her words caught in her throat at the significance of saying it. For this would probably be the last time she would see him, and it might be their final goodbye. 'That is, I'd like to stay with you a bit longer. But I'm on my way to catch my flight.'

'That's OK Kay. I'm so glad you've got your life back. Don't waste it. Have a great holiday and say hello to the Pope for me.'

'Thank you. Thank you for all you've done for me, for us. I shall…'

Unable to finish what she was saying, Kay gave Geoffery a kiss on the forehead and ran quickly to the door.

'Goodbye Geoff. Thank you so much….for everything,' she said, without turning around.

Geoffery heard her sobbing as she walked away.

'Goodbye sweet Kay,' he said, tears rolling down his cheeks. 'Perhaps we'll meet again, in heaven?'

Chapter Fifty Eight

Thursday December 11th – The final Sunset

The episode with Sue continued to take a heavy toll on Geoffery's already frail health, but determined to get out for some fresh air, he asked Andy to take him for a drive into the countryside.

'You sure you're up to this?' Andy asked concerned.

'Yes. It's a shame to be inside on such a bright and sunny winter's afternoon. Besides, an injection of country air will make me feel better, I'm sure.'

'OK where would you like to go?'

'Cleeve Common.'

'Sure. Any particular reason for going there?'

'When I was a kid, I used to ride my bike up there. The views from there are fantastic and if we're lucky, we'll see the sunset over the Cotswolds.'

'OK. I'll get some medical stuff together and then we can go.'

Shortly after, Andy steered the Mercedes through the centre of Cheltenham as Geoffery studied the changing face of the Regency styled spa town, now bedecked with Christmas decorations. The streets were bustling with shoppers, many carrying bulging carrier bags and wearing seasonally stressed faces. Revellers sporting reindeer antlers and Christmas hats were staggering in and out of pubs. He noticed several noisy office parties heading back from their revellries. The girls, carrying small sprigs of mistletoe, hoping for an innocent Christmas kiss; the men carrying erotic hopes for some seasonal goodwill in the stationary cupboard.

The sound of Christmas carols filtered out from the shopping arcade, he was starting to feel better already.

As they drove out of town he recognised some of the properties he had developed. He smiled to himself, recalling the arguments he had with the controlling planning authorities about the shade of paint he had been allowed to use. No garish colours were permitted he had been told. They all had to be 'conservative' white or cream, although, occasionally he'd got away with a soft lime green.

Andy adjusted the sun visor as they drove up Aggs Hill and on to the top of the escarpment. The low sun was dazzlingly bright against the clear blue sky. It really was a beautiful day. It was the sort of day that made you feel good. Andy agreed with Geoffery's decision to go up there. The countryside was shown in its best winter finery. The sun kissed bark on the trees seemed to effuse light of their own. The winter clad bushes, standing out in stark relief against the waving limestone grasses, added to the magnificence of the scenery.

Geoffery became very quiet as they journeyed toward their destination. Out of the corner of his eye, Andy thought he could see tears in his patient's eyes.

'Not in any pain Geoffery are you? he asked, concerned that he was doing too much for the pain relief medication to control.

'No. I'm fine. I'm lost in nostalgia, that's all!'

Shortly after, they arrived at a lay-by near the giant radio masts. The ugly structures could be seen from miles away, and dominated the rolling countryside around the large grassy common.

As the powerful engine of the Merc became silent, Geoffery put his hand on Andy's and said, 'thanks for all you've done to help me fulfill my plans. I couldn't have done it without you.'

'That's OK. It certainly was something different to my normal duties, and your Godsons are interesting characters, that's for sure.'

'Yes they are, aren't they? I wonder, if I'd been closer to them throughout their lives, whether they would have turned out any differently.'

'Probably not. But you've certainly made a difference now haven't you?' Andy said, impressed at what he had crammed in to a relatively short period of time.

'I just hope it endures,' Geoffery said reflectively. 'Tim has become more independent and less selfish. Even better, he's got himself a lady friend who won't take no for an answer and won't let him get away with his petulant outbursts. I believe he is planning to move into her flat, shortly.'

'Oh really? Good for him,' said Andy, pleased to hear that the difficult Tim had at last been tamed. 'Have you heard how he's getting on with the Challenge?'

'The last status call I had from Carrie, was that, having completed Snowdon and Scafell, they were three quarters of the way up Ben Nevis. But it was snowing.'

'Oh. Does that mean they will have to abandon the attempt?' Andy said concerned.

'Hopefully not. But what Tim doesn't know, is that the local Mountain Rescue team are shadowing them, and if conditions get really bad, they will have them off the mountain in no time.'

'I thought you might have had something like that up your sleeve.'

'I promised his mother I'd look after him,' Geoffery confessed.

'That young lady has certainly got him motivated, hasn't she?'

'I'm sure the lure of the money has probably played a significant part in it too.'

'With him out of her hair, look at what you did for Kay too,' Andy added.

'Yes. The lovely Kay has become more self-confident too. She is starting to live her own life, not constantly at the beck and call of that ungrateful sod.'

'What about poor Rupert? Is he coping without that awful Sue?'

'Yes. Rupert is starting a new life free from fear, with his new lady, Joanne, down in Bristol. He's decided to sell his house. The place has horrific memories for him of her dreadful brutality. Sue is still on remand, charged with my attempted murder,' Geoffery said, with a twinkle in his eye.

'I still reckon, John should have stayed in the room with you though. Knowing what she was like. She could have succeeded in her plan and killed you. Worse still, she might have even got away scot free with this suicide idea,' Andy said, still uncomfortable about the near miss.

'I have to admit, it was a bit of a close call, 'Geoffery said, as he recalled her demonic face holding his hands down.' I have made a full statement to the Police. So if …if I'm not around for her trial, they will have the full facts for the prosecution.'

'Hopefully you will be, and you'll see her sent down too,' Andy said optimistically, knowing that it was unlikely.

'I've got you to thank, for getting James sorted,' Geoffery said, changing the subject.

'I can't tell you how much I hated those trips to London,' Andy confessed.

'I do appreciate that. The big city is not everyone's 'cup of tea'. At least James is now trying to dry out at the clinic, and hopefully my legacy should help him get his life back together too.'

'Isn't there a danger that he will just spend it all on booze and go back to his old lifestyle?' Andy asked, aware of the long and difficult road alcoholics have to take to permanently kick the habit.

'I'm sure there will be times when he struggles to stay on the wagon. But I have put some pretty tight restrictions on the terms of his legacy. And I'm hopeful that the clinic will be keeping a careful eye on him, after he leaves, to make sure he doesn't stray. I think my generous donation to the Clinic should also help them to be proactive.'

'If he remains around here, then I'm sure Ben will also make sure he stays on the straight and narrow too,' Andy added.

'It was a good suggestion of yours to pay for Beth to go into the same clinic as James. Hopefully, with Ben's nagging, they'll both keep on the wagon.'

'Pardon my curiosity, but did I see Ben with a new bike the other day?' Andy asked tentatively.

'It was an early Christmas present. I think he earned it, don't you?'

'Just as long as he keeps off the pavement,' Andy added.

'He's quite a bright kid. I'm sure he's learnt his lesson. Especially after all he's been through, what with the hut fire and everything.'

'I'm glad you commissioned a fire investigation report, which vindicated him. He was really wound up about that. Strange, that they should find that faulty socket, which apparently overheated.'

'Why was that?'

'I don't recall, when we cleared the site, that we had that type of socket fitted in the hut.'

'Oh? Geoffery said hesitantly. 'You…umm…You said it was a former builders hut. You never know what temporary bodges they do in their own huts, until something goes wrong. I should know. I used to do them,' he said unconvincingly.

'Anyway. I'm quite pleased with how things have turned out for all of them,' he said, quickly changing the subject.

Just then Geoffery's mobile rang. He looked at the Caller's ID on the small LCD display and saw the name 'Carrie'. Answering it quickly, he put the phone to his ear. Initially all he could hear was wind noise and then a very excited Tim.

'Right Godfather, Mr Geoffery 'effing' Foster. Where's my money? I've done it! I'm here, in the snow, on top of BEN NEVIS,' he shouted jubilantly above the wind noise. 'I'm 'effing' knackered, but we did it. Give us a hug girl.' Geoffery heard him say to Carrie.

'Congratulations to you both,' Geoffery said beaming. 'See I told you that you could do it. …and no frostbitten toes either? Take care coming down. Give my love to Carrie.'

Sitting next to Geoffery, Andy could hear the conversation and punched the air with joy at the news.

'He's done it then,' he said. 'Well! Well! Well! Just goes to show what you can do, if you have the right motivation.'

Geoffery switched off the phone. He was pleased that his planning and persistence had finally given the slothful Tim a sense of worth and achievement.

'Although, I think we can say, that without Carrie he would still be glued to his Xbox or whatever it was he used to play on.' Geoffery said smiling.

'Yes, you're probably right,' Andy agreed.

'That reminds me.' Geoffery said, foraging in the briefcase at his feet. 'While we're feeling pleased with ourselves. Here are the wages that I promised you when you negotiated your terms of engagement,' he said, handing Andy an envelope. 'Happy Christmas. I've signed this car over to you as well. You'll find the log book in there too.'

'I don't know what to say! Except, thank you very much,' Andy said, taking the envelope. 'When we first met I wasn't sure that you had a…I hope you don't mind me saying…a conscience. But the last few months have shown me a different side to your character. Your thoughtfulness and persistence in helping your Godsons and their families, in spite of your health challenges, has convinced me that you are a very caring person after all.'

'I had a very good mentor, didn't I?' Geoffery said weakly, as if the effort of reminiscing about the last few months had drained all his energy.

'You sure you're OK?' Andy said concerned. 'Do you want me to give you anything?'

'No, it's OK, thanks. It certainly has been a busy time. I'm feeling a bit tired that's all,' Geoffery said quietly. 'I'll just rest my eyes for a bit.'

'It sure has,' Andy agreed. 'Did you want to go back to the hospice?'

'No, I'm quite happy here thanks.'

'OK I'll wander off and stretch my legs, while you have a doze. I won't be long,' Andy said, getting out of the car. 'Are you sure you're going to be OK? Are you warm enough?' he asked concerned for him.

'Yes fine. I feel wonderful. Better than I have for a long time,' came the unconvincing reply.

Andy closed the door gently. Pulling his coat collar up and hunching his shoulders against the cold winter wind, as he moved away from the car. The tyre rutted ground was as hard as iron. Andy had been told that in certain windy conditions, the wind came directly from Siberia, as there was no other high ground in between here and there. The icy wind, that chilled Andy's face, convinced him that there might be some element of truth in the rumour.

Here and there, where the winter sun had not penetrated, white patches of Jack Frost's handiwork still lingered in the hollows. He wandered up to the edge of the common looking at the skeletal trees and bushes that made up the small nature reserve. The sun was dipping below the horizon turning the sky multicoloured, oranges, yellows, golds. The soft heavenly colours making the winter landscape like a surreal painting, creating bizarre patterns on the rare limestone grassland. Across the other side of the windswept, grass covered common, he could see the gently rolling hills which would normally be speckled with cotton wool dots of grazing sheep.

'It had been a strange few months,' he reflected. 'Hopefully, the initiatives that Geoffery had put in place, would improve his Godsons lives.'

He thrust his hands deep into his pockets and felt the envelope that Geoffery had given him. 'Wow, how lucky was he? A new car and a cheque.' He felt almost greedy opening the letter to see the contents.

Turning his back against the chill wind, he opened it excitedly. Inside he found a brief note, and clipped to it there were two cheques with the Car Registration Certificate. The first cheque was made out to him, it was for Two hundred and fifty thousand pounds, a quarter of a million pounds. Andy couldn't believe the amount. He had to do a double take, but the figures read the same. Beneath it, another cheque fluttered in the breeze. It was made out to the Scout Troop for Twenty Thousand pounds. 'What's this for, I wonder?' He turned back to read the note.

Dear Andy,

No words that I can conjure up will ever convey my deep gratitude for what you have done for me over the last few months. You have helped me fulfill an impossible dream. To achieve something special in the closing phase of my life. My Godsons and their families have a lot to thank you for also. Happy Christmas and Thank you.

Your good friend Geoffery

P.S. I hope the cheque for you and your family doesn't upset your high principals about wealth. The cheque for the Scouts is to be invested for the young people and ongoing maintenance of the Foster Lodge.

A noise suddenly cut through the stillness and broke into Andy's thoughts. 'Ha, Ha, Ha, Haha.' It was the sound of the 'woody wood pecker' ring tone on his mobile.

He had to continually tell astonished bystanders, that it was his daughter's choice, not his.

'Good afternoon. Yes this is he. Sorry, what did you say?' he said shielding the mobile from the piercing wind. 'Oh that's great, I'll let him know straight away.'

Andy ran quickly back to the car, pocketing his mobile. His breath, a vapour trail of his exertions.

'Geoffery! Geoffery,' Andy said, gently pulling open the driver's door.

Geoffery's head was leaning against the passenger window. Against his chest was a picture. It was a picture in a frame. A picture of a smiling woman in a silver picture frame, which was twisted and dented.

Andy leant into the car and put his hand on Geoffery's shoulder shaking him gently.

'Geoffery. There's a lady at the clinic, waiting to see you. I think her name is Nadine. She's flown in from Monaco....Geoffery!'

There was no response. Andy knelt into driver's seat and quickly searched for a pulse in the thin neck. There was none. Geoffery was gone.

'Oh Geoffery,' he said quietly at the still figure. His eyes brimming with tears. 'I'm sorry. She was just too late, wasn't she?' Uncharacteristically, he found himself weeping. 'What was the George Elliot thing you used to say? *It's never too late to be who you might have been*. Goodbye my friend. You succeeded in your own challenge. You were a great Godfather after all.'

The Sun had finally set for Geoffery Foster.